D1588235

WITHDRAWN
FROM
STOCK

SPECIAL MESSAGE TO READERS

This book is published under the auspices of

THE ULVERSCROFT FOUNDATION

(registered charity No. 264873 UK)

Established in 1972 to provide funds for research, diagnosis and treatment of eye diseases. Examples of contributions made are: —

A Children's Assessment Unit at Moorfield's Hospital, London.

•

Twin operating theatres at the Western Ophthalmic Hospital, London.

•

A Chair of Ophthalmology at the Royal Australian College of Ophthalmologists.

•

The Ulverscroft Children's Eye Unit at the Great Ormond Street Hospital For Sick Children, London.

You can help further the work of the Foundation by making a donation or leaving a legacy. Every contribution, no matter how small, is received with gratitude. Please write for details to:

**THE ULVERSCROFT FOUNDATION,
The Green, Bradgate Road, Anstey,
Leicester LE7 7FU, England.
Telephone: (0116) 236 4325**

**In Australia write to:
THE ULVERSCROFT FOUNDATION,
c/o The Royal Australian College of
Ophthalmologists,
27, Commonwealth Street, Sydney,
N.S.W. 2010.**

Laura Matthews has written eighteen Regency romances, as well as ten contemporary novels, and she's an active member of her regional Jane Austen Society. Ms. Matthews and her architect husband, Paul, live and work in San Francisco. Her favorite pursuits are swimming, traveling, and searching for research materials in old bookstores. She may be reached via e-mail at nef@belgravehouse.com.

A FINE GENTLEMAN

Lady Caroline Carruthers was enjoying her visit to the Hartville home. But one thing made life at the estate complicated — Lady Hartville was intent on convincing her son, Richard, that Caroline would be a perfect wife for him. Lord Hartville kept his distance from his mother's schemes, which was fine with Caroline, who had no intention of marrying such an obstinate, infuriating man! Then a surprise arrived on the doorstep — and, suddenly, Lady Hartville's plans didn't seem so far-fetched at all . . .

LAURA MATTHEWS

A FINE GENTLEMAN

Complete and Unabridged

ULVERSCROFT
Leicester

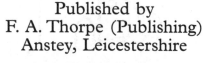

First published in 1999
in the United States of America

First Large Print Edition
published 2001
by arrangement with
Signet
a division of
Penguin Putnam Inc.
New York

The moral right of the author has been asserted

Copyright © 1999 by Elizabeth Rotter
All rights reserved

British Library CIP Data

Matthews, Laura
A fine gentleman.—Large print ed.—
Ulverscroft large print series: romance
1. Love stories
2. Large type books
I. Title
813.5'4 [F]

ISBN 0–7089–4393–4

Published by
F. A. Thorpe (Publishing)
Anstey, Leicestershire

Set by Words & Graphics Ltd.
Anstey, Leicestershire
Printed and bound in Great Britain by
T. J. International Ltd., Padstow, Cornwall

This book is printed on acid-free paper

Leabharlann
Chontae na Mí

1

Hartville Valley, 1817

Viscount Hartville could not have been away from the stables for more than an hour. He had galloped his black stallion past the home farm to the far end of the spring green valley, and then turned directly back toward his estate. Being at Berwick Hall these days had become particularly irritating, and the ride was necessary to release some of his pent-up energy.

If his mother became any more obvious in her intention that he marry Caroline Carruthers, Hartville was going to eject her — his own mother! — from the estate. Not that Miss Carruthers was ineligible to be his viscountess, or even that she was an antidote — far from it. But she was too angelic and too insipid for his tastes.

When Lady Hartville had invited a distant relation to stay, Hartville had surmised there was some plot in the making. His mother had a genius for schemes and stratagems. In the main, they were useful plans — how to circumvent a visit from the vicar or entice a pastry chef away from a neighbor — nothing to cause him a moment's disquiet. His mother had not so much as hinted that she wished him to marry, prior to this latest start. Hartville had always assumed she preferred being the female in charge of the domestic side of the estate.

His mother could have invited her cousin, a fifty-year-old matron of no discernible talent or conversation, to provide her with the companionship that she protested Hartville failed to supply her, what with his penchant for wandering off to London or the Continent. But no, a miss of four-and-twenty had arrived, just two weeks past, and Lady Hartville showed every sign of keeping the girl permanently — at Hartville's expense. Not wishing to embarrass the quiet, angelic Caroline Carruthers, Hartville merely avoided her whenever possible. He refused to exhibit the smallest sign of interest, fearful that it would be interpreted as an indication that he planned to make her an offer.

As the viscount drew Warrior into a trot, he could see that something out of the ordinary was taking place near the stables. The grooms and coachman were gathered around a small child of four or five. Hartville could not tell if the child was a boy or girl, there were so many people in the way. The group turned as one at the sound of his horse's hoofbeats. John Coachman stepped forward, drawing the child with him.

'This here is Viscount Hartville,' he said forcefully, glaring at the viscount in a most extraordinary way. 'You tell him what you done told us.'

The child raised wondrously blue eyes — not unlike Hartville's own — and said, 'Papa!'

★ ★ ★

'Mother,' Hartville said firmly. 'I am not the child's father. I assure you I've never set eyes on her before in my life.'

Lady Hartville, an imposing woman of forty-eight years, remained unmoved. 'You may never have seen her before, Hartville. That doesn't mean you aren't her papa.'

Hartville's blue eyes hardened. 'I'm not aware of any by-blows, Mother, and I promise you that any woman who conceived my child would not be remiss in informing me and insisting on my support — which I would naturally give.'

'Oh, naturally,' she said, and sighed. Her feet were propped up on a stool, and a woolen rug covered her legs, obviously one of the kind attentions of the ubiquitous Miss

Carruthers. But Lady Hartville was not disposed to allow these comforts to lull her into a false sense of contentment. 'You've sown your wild oats with remarkably little consequence, Richard. It's time you settled down.'

'So you've informed me.' Hartville wondered where the virtuous Miss Carruthers had got to. She was ordinarily to be found seated near his mama, needlework in lap, patiently and elegantly knitting some fringe or other. Since her arrival he would have sworn she'd produced more finery than his mother's modiste in the village. In fact, he sometimes wondered if Miss Carruthers had aspirations to replace that worthy woman, should she fail to fulfill his mother's ambition for her.

'What do you intend to do about the child?' his mother asked.

'John Coachman said she was left by a man who wouldn't give his name. He was wearing a farm laborer's clothing, but he was no one John had ever seen before. When John asked if he was the girl's father, he denied it. He also denied knowing where the mother was.'

'Why didn't they detain him?'

'How, Mother? By force? The two came by horse. Apparently he placed the child on the ground, said she belonged here, and rode off.'

Hartville tapped his riding crop impatiently against the side of his boot. 'Perhaps if I had been there, I could have induced him to be a bit more forthcoming. But I was not there, and my loyal retainers seem to have all taken the man at his word, damn their hides.'

'Well, she can't stay here,' Lady Hartville protested. 'She'll have to go to the orphanage in Grassmere.'

Which was exactly what Hartville had decided himself. Having his mother voice the option, however, tended to set up his back. And yet, what other alternative was there? She couldn't very well stay on the estate. Sometimes the illegitimate child of a member of the gentry was raised by a rural family in the vicinity, but in those situations the precise circumstances of birth and parentage were known and subtly acknowledged. With this little one . . .

'What's her name?' Lady Hartville asked.

Hartville shrugged. 'She wouldn't say.'

At that moment the door to the salon, which had — unbeknownst to him — been partially open, swung wide and a vision of blond elegance appeared there. His many-times-removed cousin Caroline Carruthers stood hand in hand with a clean, blond, curly-haired child who could surely not be the urchin he'd seen in the stableyard.

'This is Wilhelmina,' Miss Carruthers said.

And the child looked adoringly up at her and said, 'Mama?'

At this Lady Hartville laughed merrily. The viscount ground his teeth. 'Just why are you willing to believe I'm the child's father, but find it absurd that Miss Carruthers could possibly be her mother?' he demanded.

'Oh, Hartville, do mind your manners,' his esteemed parent snapped. 'A woman cannot miss the fact of her parentage; a man most assuredly can.' She beckoned toward the two females in the doorway. 'Come, let me see the child. She told you her name?'

Caroline Carruthers, keeping a tight grip on the girl's fingers, drew her closer to the older woman. The child kept her eyes lowered, as though she were either shy or intimidated by her surroundings, and followed meekly along with her 'mama.' Hartville could distinguish no similarity between Miss Carruthers and the girl, with the exception of the blond hair, and even that was of a different type.

The child had the kind of white-blond hair that was almost guaranteed to make her look like an angel. In the stable yard her head had been partially covered with a knit scarf, and her hair had not been particularly clean. They had learned that she had ridden with the man, whom she called JoJo, for several days.

'Yes, she told me her name,' Miss Carruthers agreed, with a rather odd look in Hartville's direction. 'She pronounces it more like Wilmina, but agreed that it was Wilhelmina when I suggested it. She's been called Willy.'

'Not around here she won't be,' Lady Hartville proclaimed. 'Come, let me see you, child.'

Wilhelmina hesitated until Miss Carruthers pushed her gently forward. There was something forbidding about his mother, Hartville thought. Even when he was a child he hadn't trusted that she meant him well when she got that particular frown on her face. Her bristling eyebrows drew together, her eyelids narrowed, and she studied one with an intensity that couldn't help but alarm. Just now she was remarking on Wilhelmina's eyes.

'They're the very shade of blue of yours, Hartville.'

'No, they aren't,' he protested, though he wasn't quite sure that was true. 'Besides, they're very like Miss Carruthers's as well.'

Miss Carruthers's lips curved in a demure smile. 'You're teasing, cousin. My eyes are more gray than blue.'

Hartville did not appear to agree with her.

He had studied her eyes one morning in the conservatory when she was bent over a long-leafed philodendron, concerned about the mildew she had found there. Her eyes were decidedly blue, though with a pearly cast that might have convinced someone that they were gray if they were not paying close attention. 'The child does not have my eyes,' he said.

Lady Hartville had concluded her examination of the girl, having taken in the shapely head, the steady blue eyes, the rounded cheeks, the still chubby hands, the feet clad incongruously in a pair of aging slippers.

'How old do you take her for?' she asked Miss Carruthers.

'She says she's four, milady,' that young woman answered. She cocked her head, considering. 'She's a deal shorter than your cook's five-year-old son, to be sure, but that might be just her small stature. Mrs. Bluestone thought perhaps she was approaching five. She had just bathed Wilhelmina and was searching about for a change of clothing when I happened upon them on the nursery floor.'

Now, what was Miss Carruthers doing on the nursery floor? Hartville wondered. She must have heard of the child's presence and gone in search of her, which showed a great deal more curiosity than Hartville would have expected in the woman. Mrs. Bluestone, the housekeeper, was an old hand at dealing with any crisis that arose. Hartville himself had relegated the child to her keeping until a decision could be made as to her disposition.

'Mrs. Bluestone found this old dress in one of the trunks, but she was unable to find a pair of shoes that fit,' Miss Carruthers explained. 'I thought perhaps I could drive into the village this afternoon and purchase an appropriate pair for her.'

Hartville balked at this. 'You don't want to go getting attached to the child, Miss Carruthers. She'll have to be taken to an orphanage straight away. Allow Mrs. Bluestone to care for her until then.'

'An orphanage?' His mother's visitor looked genuinely distressed. 'But, my lord, that would be most unkind. Have you not heard of the conditions in orphanages?' She turned to Lady Hartville for support. 'Oh, ma'am, I don't think it's right that Lord Hartville's child should be placed in an orphanage!'

'She's not my child!' he objected, attempting to keep his temper. 'I've never seen her before in my life.'

'That hardly signifies,' Lady Hartville opined. She turned her rather fierce gaze on the child and asked, 'Have you ever seen my son before?'

Wilhelmina's eyes moved from one person to the other in the room, uncertain. 'Him?' she asked, pointing at Hartville.

'That's right,' Miss Carruthers said gently, stepping forward to stand beside the child and encircle her shoulders encouragingly. 'Have you seen him before?'

Wilhelmina shook her head. 'But he's the Fine Man,' she explained.

Lady Hartville leaned forward. 'The Fine Man. Hmm. How do you know that?'

'Well, ma'am, JoJo told me my papa was a Fine Man. He told me I would see him here. And this man is very fine, is he not?'

Hartville didn't know whether to laugh or cry. The child at least knew quality when she saw it! 'And your mama?' he asked. 'Is she a Fine Lady?'

Tears welled up in the girl's eyes. 'She was sick when I was born, they said. I think she died. She never came to see me.'

'Then where did you live? Who did you live with?' Hartville questioned, in a voice determined enough to earn him a rebuking glance from Miss Carruthers.

'With JoJo and Molly. But Molly says as there's too many kids and too little money, I was to go live with my papa.'

Hartville snorted. 'How did they know who your papa was?'

Wilhelmina looked helplessly at Miss Carruthers. 'It's all right,' the young woman soothed her. 'Don't worry about that. Do you know where you lived?'

The child shook her head.

'Was it a big city? Or a village with just a few houses?' Miss Carruthers prompted.

'Just our house.' The thought seemed to make her sad. 'There are cows and pigs and chickens.'

Miss Carruthers smiled at her, giving her a hug. 'Very good. You lived on a farm. Did you ever go into town for shoes or clothes?'

Wilhelmina nodded. 'There's market day. We took animals and lettuces to sell. And if JoJo had some extra shillings we got shoes from a cart.'

'You must know the name of the town,' Hartville insisted, his frustration obvious. Didn't even four-year-olds know such a simple thing? But Miss Carruthers was once again frowning at him, and he backed off. 'Well, perhaps it will come to you.'

Lady Hartville had observed these proceedings in silence. 'She was probably put out to nurse with this woman Molly and never reclaimed. Perhaps for a while money came for her care. When that stopped, and they had so many children of their own . . . ' She paused, a frown creasing her brow. 'There must be some reason they believed Hartville to be her father. They wouldn't have just picked his name from a hat.'

Hartville had a sudden inspiration. 'But perhaps they picked it from a newspaper. Last week my name was in all the papers for introducing legislation in the House of Lords. They must have seen it there!' he said triumphantly.

Miss Carruthers shook her head. 'It's very unlikely, my lord, that JoJo and Molly can read.'

Realizing that she was probably right, Hartville did not disagree with her. He turned, instead, to the child and said, 'Wilhelmina, I know I must seem like a Fine Man to you, but I'm afraid I'm not your papa.'

From the corner of his eye he could see both his mother and Miss Carruthers draw to attention at this. He refused to let them push him into doing something he knew very well was not his responsibility. However, he tempered what he had been about to say to the girl. 'You may stay here for a while. Mrs. Bluestone is a nice woman, isn't she?'

Wilhelmina nodded, but moved to take Miss Carruthers's hand. 'I like her better,' she said shyly, looking up at her presenter.

Hartville sighed. 'Well, it's not really a matter of whom you like better,' he explained.

To his surprise, his mother interrupted him. 'Oh, don't browbeat her, Hartville.'

'Browbeat her? Of all the exaggerations! Be so good as to tell me how you feel arrangements should fall out, Mama. I thought you wanted her sent to an orphanage.'

'That was before I saw her,' her ladyship admitted. 'She bears a certain resemblance to you, Hartville.'

'Only her eyes!' he protested. 'And by your own reasoning, I would have to have been the man who sent money to support her. I assure you I am not! You have my permission to question Wilson about that if you wish. I am not the child's father.'

Lady Hartville regarded him in silence for a moment. Her hair, brown liberally dashed with white, had thinned considerably in the last few years. Her fingers now unconsciously moved to touch the limp and meager strands above her forehead, something she did when she was greatly distressed. No other sign of agitation was manifest, but Hartville knew his mother. She was on the point of making an important decision.

At length she said, 'I believe you, Hartville, about the money.'

Her son flushed. It seemed impossibly wrong to have her decree such a thing in front of the near stranger Caroline Carruthers. But there was worse to come.

'And yet, I feel it is possible that you are in some fashion involved in this matter.' She held up a hand to still his protestations. 'No, no, you need not tell me again that you aren't the child's father. I tell you that you cannot possibly know whether you are or not. Let's not bicker about that. You've told Wilhelmina that she may stay here for a while, and I agree with that decision. My concern is in what capacity you intend to entertain her. I think — don't you, Caroline? — that Wilhelmina is likely rather gently born.'

Not only did this astonish Hartville, but his mother's request of their visitor that she accede in this opinion very nearly caused him apoplexy. Miss Carruthers, however, did not hesitate to respond.

'Exactly so!' she exclaimed, her cheeks a becoming pink. 'Yes, that was precisely my impression, Lady Hartville. There is just something . . . '

'Indeed,' Hartville drawled. 'She cleans up well.'

2

The viscount had more pressing matters to deal with than the arrival of Wilhelmina. In addition to broken drainage tiles and lightning damage to one of the cottages, there was this new demand for financial assistance from a Yorkshire Carruthers. Wayne Davis, his estate manager, could carry through with the repairs once Hartville had established what he wanted done, and Joseph Wilson, his man of business, could dispense the necessary blunt once Hartville determined if the newest demand against his purse was legitimate. But determining the necessity would be a task Hartville himself had to perform.

There were branches of the Carruthers family throughout the kingdom (one of which had no doubt produced Caroline Carruthers herself) which were without fail impoverished families perpetually threatened with ruin. Hartville's own family, the Winslows, were in fact a minor branch of the Carruthers's family tree. It was fortunate for Hartville that his great-grandfather had been of particular assistance to the king some years previously, for a title and estate were bestowed on him in gratitude. Through the ensuing decades the Winslows had tended their fields, seen to their livestock, and generally, through good management and upright living, seen their estate prosper.

The various Carruthers branches of the family, while far more numerous than the Winslows, had not managed to achieve any monetary success that Hartville could discover. Weekly the post brought him requests, couched in the most desperate terms, to meet the needs of some new member of the family with whom he was not even familiar. This letter from Yorkshire, however, was not the typical request. Hartville thought it more in the nature of a demand, or perhaps a threat.

Frances Carruthers wrote that he had been taken up by the law and was being accused of stealing merchandise from a hostler in his neighborhood. This was all a dreadful misunderstanding, of course, but the good name of the family was at stake. Frances had apparently bragged that he was cousin to a viscount who would set matters to rights. And, Frances noted, he would have to have five hundred pounds in order to do so.

Hartville despaired of learning the truth of such incidents.

On the one hand, his forebears had established a policy of generosity, which he respected. So he was not in the habit of ignoring those family members who found themselves in need. On the other hand, every family had its ne'er-do-wells, and one could not continue to support them forever, or the well would run dry. Occasionally Hartville sent Wilson to discover the truth of such situations, but Wilson could not be spared for every demand that arrived on the silver salver at Berwick Hall. Nor could five hundred pounds be expended on one havey-cavey settlement, when Hartville could offer sub-stantial support to five families for such a sum.

Perhaps because he was resisting the decision to travel to Yorkshire, Hartville agreed to accompany Miss Carruthers and the child to the village of Crowell, where they would purchase a pair of shoes for Wil-helmina. 'And perhaps a few clothes that do not look so old-fashioned,' his mother had suggested.

What the devil the townfolk of Crowell were going to make of his arriving in town with a charming young woman to buy clothes for a little girl, Hartville could not imagine. He knew his mother would have a sharp rejoinder if he voiced this thought, so he kept his musings to himself. However, when the three of them were arranged rather tightly on

17

the seat of his curricle, he posed the thought, with only a trace of irony, to Miss Carruthers.

'We shall say that Wilhelmina is an orphan sent to live with Lady Hartville,' Miss Carruthers answered immediately. 'I think we need not elaborate on that.'

'Oh, certainly not,' he agreed, flicking her a look of pure disgruntlement. 'They will not at all wonder who she is, or why Lady Hartville should take an orphan in.'

'Of course they will wonder,' Miss Carruthers admitted, smiling down at the child, who wiggled happily on the seat. Wilhelmina had mentioned that the 'cart' was oh, so much more comfortable than riding with JoJo on his horse. 'And you may be sure that your stable lads will have managed to mention the circumstances of her arrival to a sister or a mother, or even the good Reverend Lockhart. But, you know, Lord Hartville, that is only to be expected. You will always be a matter for discussion in the village — what you do, where you go, how you behave.'

'And most especially, whether the child is mine.' He ground is teeth. 'I suppose you feel it would be quite unnecessary to issue any denial.'

'Oh, quite,' she agreed, and Hartville thought perhaps he detected the smallest twitch at the corners of her lips. If so, it was gone before he could be sure. Miss Carruthers continued, 'They would not believe you, you know. So you might as well not provoke their interest further by making hearty protestations.'

'I'm not in the habit of making hearty protestations,' he complained, feeling indeed hard put upon. He supposed it would end up that he'd have to provide the child with a dowry, in a score of years or so. He sighed. The child looked up at him and smiled. She had a slightly lopsided smile. Quite fetching it was, if truth were known. Hartville sighed again, and smiled back at her. 'You're going to be the devil of a nuisance,' he muttered.

Miss Carruthers disagreed. 'I doubt that, my lord. See what an obedient child she is. And so appreciative of everything she's received.'

Which included, he now noted with narrowed eyes, a locket of sorts. Or had she had that on her arrival? He gestured toward it with his head, since his hands were occupied with the reins. 'Where did she come by the locket?'

'She was wearing it when she arrived. Mrs. Bluestone had removed it to bathe her and only remembered to restore it a few minutes ago.'

'Is there anything in it?'

Miss Carruthers nodded. 'A miniature of a woman. Clearly dressed in the fashion of a gentlewoman.'

Hartville's eyes moved heavenward. 'Why am I not surprised?' he asked himself. 'Does she have blue eyes?'

'It's impossible to tell, my lord, in so small a picture.'

'Is there anything else distinctive about the locket which you haven't mentioned? Such as her mother's name engraved upon it?'

'Your sarcasm is unnecessary, sir. There are indeed initials.'

Hartville brightened. 'Yes? What are they?'

'MM.'

'Nothing more?'

'No, nothing.'

'Hmmm.' Hartville kept his eyes on the hard-packed road surface before him, but allowed himself to muse aloud. 'Perhaps her mother's initials. Upside down, they would be WW, which could be for her own name. Wilhelmina, do you know JoJo's surname?'

The child shrugged her shoulders.

Hartville kept a firm grip on the reins as he expertly guided his horse around the stand of poplars onto the main street of the village. There were half a dozen trim, freshly whitewashed shops on either side of the road. Two shop-keepers, an elderly woman with white hair and a young lad dressed in a smock, were conversing on the wooden walk in front of their buildings. Hartville drew his horse to a stop near them and the lad hurried forward to stand at the horse's head. Mrs. Biggins, he could see, was already eyeing his companions with curiosity.

Hartville jumped down from the curricle and came around to hand Miss Carruthers down first. He liked the way she allowed him to take a solid grip on her hands to give her purchase for her drop to the ground. Too many women were skittish about even such a courteous act, as though a gentleman were about to pull her straight down onto his chest. Miss Carruthers merely nodded her thanks, the feather on her hat waving daintily with the slight movement. Hartville turned from her to Wilhelmina, who had slid her little body over to the edge of the seat, her blue eyes sparkling, her shoulders wriggling with excitement.

Since she was so small, Hartville reached up to grasp her around the waist and lift her down to the ground. He was startled by how little she weighed, a regular feather pillow. They'd have to put a little meat on her bones, he thought. When he saw Miss Carruthers reach out for the girl's hand, he did likewise. Mrs. Biggins raised her brows.

21

Hartville tipped his hat to her. 'Good day, ma'am. This is Miss Wilhelmina, who's come to stay at the estate. We're hoping to find her a pair of shoes.'

Mrs. Biggins beamed on them, tucking a wisp of hair under her cap. 'Well, my lord, you've come to the right place. I believe there may be something she can wear in the shop, but if not, we'll measure her foot and Martin can make her up anything she wants in a day or two.'

Miss Carruthers lifted her skirts to climb onto the wooden walkway and fall in beside Mrs. Biggins as the two of them discussed various leathers. Hartville was accustomed to having his bootmaker specially make his Hessians and top boots, but he had not thought one went to so much effort for a four-year-old foot. Still, what did he know? Miss Carruthers appeared to be discussing the subject knowledgeably with Mrs. Biggins. How did she come to know so much about four-year-olds and their shoes?

When Hartville discovered, to his chagrin, that the women weren't the least interested in his opinions on the topic of clothing a child, he abandoned Wilhelmina there with her champions, saying, 'Please place all the charges on Lady Hartville's account, Mrs. Biggins, as she requested.'

Mrs. Biggins dropped him a curtsey and said, 'As you wish, my lord.'

And Hartville made a hasty exit.

★   ★   ★

Caroline hid the small grin his escape caused her and returned her attention to Wilhelmina. The child needed a little room to grow in her clothes, certainly, as she was young and decidedly not as well nourished as she might have been. 'We'll need several muslin frocks,' she said to Mrs. Biggins as she ran her fingers over a roll of figured sprig. 'Or natural-colored nankeen. Something that will wear well. And perhaps one white muslin with a strip of lace for better occasions.'

'I have just the thing,' Mrs. Biggins assured her, trotting toward the back of the shop.

Though she'd only been to the village twice during her stay, Caroline felt comfortable there, especially with Mrs. Biggins's guidance. While Wilhelmina played with a hoop she'd found under one of the counters, Caroline wandered over to the table carelessly heaped with ribbons and feathers and gewgaws which the local ladies would certainly use as decoration on their hats and dresses. Caroline's own dress, an older one of palest yellow, could have benefited from a rouleau of roses along the sleeves. She was intent on determining which of the flowered pieces she most preferred — the roses or the peonies — when Mrs. Biggins returned, and she hastily dropped the satiny fabrics.

Holding up a pink frock to Wilhelmina, Mrs. Biggins cocked her head to one side. 'No,' she judged from her years of experience, 'I don't believe this will suit her. Her cheeks haven't much color, have they?' she asked kindly, giving Wilhelmina a slight pat on one of them. 'I believe our little friend may need to spend more time outdoors in the fresh air.'

'Indeed she may,' Caroline agreed, coming forward to take the dress. She rubbed the muslin between her fingers, feeling its fineness. 'But this is the right quality for her good dress. If you will sell me a few yards of the everyday muslin, I could make up two frocks in no time.'

Mrs. Biggins frowned. 'I'm sure her ladyship never meant for you to do the sewing, miss. Come, I'll show you what I have ready-made here in the back.'

Caroline followed her past tables piled with rolls of fabric, a chair placed at the end on which the older customers such as Lady Hartville could rest while goods were brought for her inspection. Beyond was a cabinet with every imaginable pomade and perfume, and shelves with a variety of shoes, half boots and top boots. In a bin were pairs of gloves, with which the shop appeared to be especially endowed, and then came stands with ladies' hats. Finally they arrived at a rack displaying children's dresses, high-waisted gowns of printed cotton with sashes tied in bows. Wilhelmina actually gasped at the sight of such finery, her eyes blinking with astonishment.

Her companion laughed. 'Mrs. Biggins has more than enough for us to choose from, hasn't she? What do you think of the blue one with the eyelet smocking for a good dress, my dear?'

Wilhelmina said that she'd never seen anything so pretty. 'Even Cassie hasn't a better one for church,' she whispered.

'Is Cassie one of Molly's children?' Caroline asked, before she remembered Mrs. Biggins's waiting ears.

'No. She lives at the manor.' Wilhelmina reached out to touch the smocking with a small, hesitant finger. 'I'm afraid I'd get it dirty,' she sighed.

Caroline hugged her. 'Don't worry about that, my dear,' she said. 'We want you to do Lady Hartville proud when you take tea with her, don't we?'

Wilhelmina nodded uncertainly.

If Mrs. Biggins found anything unusual in this interaction, she allowed no hint of her surprise to show in her face. Caroline decided they would take the frock, and have another two made up in the sturdier material the shopkeeper set before her. 'The green will do nicely, and the beige.' Caroline looked about her at the stacks of children's items — socks and shoes and nightdresses. It mightn't do to buy so much at once, but Wilhelmina had come with nothing but the clothes on her back and needed everything. So, despite Mrs. Biggins's obvious interest, Caroline systematically worked her way through the shop, consulting Wilhelmina on preferences, but acquiring the whole of a wardrobe all the same.

When Hartville returned, Caroline could see his astonishment at the pile of parcels they'd accumulated. Mrs. Biggins had insisted on wrapping the dresses separately in rough brown paper and tying them with string, so that they would not get wrinkled. Hartville's gaze wandered to the new shoes the child wore. 'I didn't realize new shoes came with so many attachments,' he grumbled. 'Or perhaps you've done some shopping for yourself, Miss Carruthers.'

'No, not a thing for me,' she said with forced cheeriness.

Wilhelmina poked her head around one of the counters and held up the rouleau of roses Caroline had looked at earlier. 'She liked this one. It would look pretty on her dress, wouldn't it?'

Caroline flushed at the girl's words. Hartville regarded her curiously. 'Then why not purchase it, ma'am? I've never been shopping with a lady who didn't chose a few trinkets to ornament her day dresses or perk up an older hat.'

'This is not my shopping trip,' Caroline said firmly, taking the rouleau from Wilhelmina and returning it to its spot on the table. 'We have accumulated quite enough for one day.'

Hartville shrugged and grabbed a handful of parcels. 'We'll be on our way then, Mrs. Biggins. Thank you so much for your assistance.'

'Thank you, my lord,' the older woman murmured, dropping him another curtsey. 'It's been a pleasure to serve the young lady.'

Caroline and Wilhelmina smiled at each other, picked up the remaining parcels and swept through the door Hartville held for them. The black curricle with its yellow wheels and black-and-gold insignia on the doors stood directly outside the shop. Hartville, with exaggerated care, deposited each of the parcels (of which there were seven) in the space behind the seat before handing the woman and the child up into the carriage.

Caroline assumed from his long-suffering air that the viscount was not pleased with the extent of her shopping. Had he expected the child to run about barefoot in one frock for the extent of her stay? Though he would not likely see the contents of the packages, he could hardly have objected to the handker-chiefs and aprons and bedgowns which Caroline had found it prudent to purchase.

Caroline sighed. Well, Lady Hartville could easily afford the purchases, and she would understand the necessity for them. The viscount obviously did not know the first thing about children, and Caroline had no intention of enlightening him.

★ ★ ★

Hartville, hearing her sigh, decided that Miss Carruthers was a great deal less angelic than she appeared. Despite the charming face and pretty manners, she could not resist spending his mother's money with a very free hand. As he gave his horse the office to start, he glanced at her briefly. Though she could be all sweetness and light around the house and

28

in the presence of his mother, she'd certainly taken a firm stand with regard to outfitting the child. There had been none of the meek 'Yes, ma'am,' and 'No, ma'am' that he'd heard over the past two weeks. In the shop she'd made it clear that his assistance was not needed. Which had allowed her full sway in purchasing anything she wished for the girl.

The curricle swept past the remaining shops and the stand of poplars and out onto the country road. Spring had touched everything by now — the leaves, the grasses, even a few flowering weeds. The road stretched straight for half a mile before the entrance to the estate, and Hartville was in the habit of springing his horse in an attempt to break his own speed record. Spartan, who knew his master's habits well, had to actually be reined in a bit to keep his pace at a reasonable level. As it was, the child murmured with excitement.

And sneezed, a great gusting burst of wet air, which startled Hartville, and apparently Miss Carruthers as well. 'Oh, my dear,' the good lady said. 'Have you taken a chill?'

'No, ma'am,' Wilhelmina assured her in a stuffy voice.

A quick glance informed Hartville that her eyes looked puffy, and he felt a flash of alarm.

'What is it?' he asked, a little abruptly. 'Is she going to be sick?'

'In your fine carriage? She wouldn't dare,' Miss Carruthers retorted in a voice so amused that Hartville felt himself rebuked. And for what? Had he not merely expressed his concern for the child?

Wilhelmina sneezed again, this time covering her mouth with the handkerchief Miss Carruthers had handed her. 'It's the weeds,' Wilhelmina explained. 'Molly said the weeds make me sneeze.'

'Poor dear.' Miss Carruthers patted the child's head comfortingly. 'I've known it to happen to many an acquaintance at this time of year. We'll see if Mrs. Bluestone has any posset for the spring megrims.'

Wonderful, Hartville was thinking. Now we learn that the child has to be cossetted as well as clothed. He very much feared he would rue this day when the child appeared on his doorstep, for he had the distinct feeling that Wilhelmina was not destined to end up in an orphanage.

3

When Hartville halted the curricle near the front steps to the Hall, Caroline felt a great sense of relief. Being in Hartville's company was something of a burden, especially in the present circumstances. Possibly Caroline would have felt as encroached upon as he obviously did, had she been in his situation, but she doubted it. After all, there was a child here to be concerned about. This was not a matter of some overlooked estate improvement, or of deciding on the purchase of new hayricks. This was a living, breathing human being.

The Berwick Hall butler, Bluestone, had come down the entry stairs to hand Caroline and the child down from the curricle. Wilhelmina's eyes widened at Bluestone's stately bearing and his booming voice. She hid her head in Caroline's gown and had to be coaxed to step forward. Just as the two of them were beginning to ascend the stairs, Hartville called, 'Miss Carruthers, I wonder if I might see the locket for a moment.'

'Certainly, my lord,' she assured him, but without pausing in her climb. 'I shall bring it

31

down with me to supper, if that is all right with you, Wilhelmina.'

'He won't keep it, will he?' the child whispered.

'No, he won't keep it. He would just like to see the picture in it and the initials. You'll have it back by the time you awaken in the morning.'

'Then I s'pose it would be all right. He mustn't lose it.' Wilhelmina, looking anxious, stroked the golden metal with her small fingers. 'It's all I have, you see.'

Caroline's heart ached for the girl. 'Yes, I see. Lord Hartville will be very careful with your locket.' She glanced back at Hartville, who wore a long-suffering expression, and added, 'I shall make certain that he is.'

Wilhelmina tucked her hand into Caroline's, saying, 'Thank you.'

Bluestone followed the two of them up the stairs with his arms full of their parcels.

*   *   *

Dinner was served at early country hours at Berwick Hall. Caroline had become accustomed in the past two weeks to changing into one or the other of her two best gowns for the meal. The family met first in the drawing room, where Lady Hartville never failed to tell Caroline how attractive she looked, and Hartville never said any more than was strictly necessary about anything. Not that he was surly, precisely, Caroline admitted to herself. But he seemed impatient with domestic conversation, and his mother insisted that he not dominate their mealtime talk with 'boring' matters of state.

When Caroline descended the stairs to the drawing room, she carried the promised locket in her reticule, but she was determined not to let it out of her sight. Wilhelmina had handed it over reluctantly, and glanced unhappily back over her shoulder before she followed Mrs. Bluestone away to dinner.

Caroline smoothed the lace sheer which was layered over the blue mull of her gown as a footman held the drawing room door for her. She was thinking that the rouleau of roses she'd seen that afternoon would have been particularly fine on this dress, which she had now worn on eight occasions at Berwick Hall. Hartville must be heartily sick of the sight of it. Caroline would have liked to purchase a few yards of fabric for herself while she was in Crowell, but the expense would have put a sizeable dent in the small cache of funds she had managed to scrape together to bring with her on her trip.

Lady Hartville had not yet arrived in the

drawing room, which was a little unusual. Caroline had, on each previous occasion, found her already seated in her favorite chair when her guest arrived. Hartville was there, however, his shoulders propped casually against the mantel. His shoulders fit so well into the black coat he wore that Caroline thought his valet must have had something of a struggle getting him into it. Hartville straightened, and bowed. 'Miss Carruthers,' he acknowledged. 'I wonder if you have brought the locket with you.'

'Of course.' Caroline opened her reticule and drew out the small object. Its chain caught on the clasp and she carefully disengaged it before dropping it into Hartville's waiting hand.

For some time he studied the initials, holding the locket first in one direction and then upside down. 'Hmmm,' was all he said. Then, with a practiced flick — Caroline had watched him take snuff — he opened the locket to examine the miniature. After a moment he lifted his gaze to hers and said, 'She looks something like you.'

'Yes, I suppose she does,' Caroline agreed, holding her hand out for the locket.

But Hartville was not ready to return it. Moving closer to the wall sconce, he studied the woman's face for some time. 'You're right,' he said slowly. 'She's obviously gentry. The clothes, the way she's wearing her hair, even the fact that the miniature was made. To say nothing of the locket itself, which is of good quality, I would guess.'

Caroline nodded, and once again extended her hand.

'I'm not going to lose it,' he said, grudgingly returning it to her.

'It's very important to the child.'

Hartville sighed. 'Yes, I could see that. Did you ask her when she'd gotten it?'

'No. She seemed to indicate that she'd always had it.' Caroline moved toward the fireplace, skirting the viscount. Though the day had been mild, the evening was rapidly chilling. A fire burned on the grate, and she extended her hands toward it for warmth. 'I'm surprised Lady Hartville isn't down yet,' she remarked, glancing toward the door.

At that moment Bluestone opened the door, but it was not to admit the viscount's mother. 'Her ladyship asks you to excuse her, Miss Carruthers, Lord Hartville. She's feeling a trifle indisposed.'

Caroline immediately withdrew her hands from the warmth of the fire and turned. 'I'm so sorry. Shall I go to her?'

Bluestone regarded her with approval. 'I think not, miss. Her ladyship's dresser said she wished to get some rest. She urged you and his lordship to dine without her. And dinner is served.'

Hartville, who generally took his mother into the dining room, offered his arm to Caroline. 'Shall we?'

'Of course.' Caroline slipped her reticule under one arm and placed the fingers of her other hand on Hartville's arm. He had exquisite manners, especially when his mother was present. Her brother, Jeremy, had a far more relaxed attitude toward the niceties of society, but he could exhibit polish when he chose. *En famille* he tended to be just the tiniest bit careless, expecting his sister to accept him as he was, even if that happened to be a bit less than perfectly dressed or smoothly mannered. More than once he had dined in his riding clothes, laughing at her chagrin. 'Now, Caro,' he would chide, 'we ain't at Carlton House.'

The mahogany table in the dining room was large enough to seat a dozen people with room to spare. During Caroline's stay, Hartville had sat at the head of the table, with one of the ladies on either side of him. Tonight Lady Hartville's place setting had been removed. Hartville held Caroline's chair for her, as he usually did for his mother.

Caroline watched as he seated himself, the

light from the candles in the chandelier softening the hard planes of his face. He was not precisely a handsome man, though he had even features and a regularity of smooth skin over aristocratic bones. His chin had too prominent and stubborn a set to it. His eyes were disquietingly sharp. And his genteel manners seemed at variance both with the restrained energy and cool remoteness that he projected. There was none of the fun-loving ease of her brother, Jeremy, and Caroline missed that ready comfort she had with her sibling.

Hartville had, for the most part, kept to himself during her stay. That was partly Lady Hartville's fault for having taken the odd notion into her head, only a few days into Caroline's stay, that the two of them would suit. It was probably ill-advised for any parent to indicate to her offspring a preference for a particular party. In this case it had been positively disastrous. The viscount had balked from the first hint, finding unending duties which kept him out of Caroline's vicinity. And, unfortunately, out of his mother's as well, for Caroline was frequently with her.

Caroline was well aware that Hartville did not relish dining alone with her.

When he didn't offer any conversation, she took it upon herself to do so. Unlike his mother, she was not averse to discussing the politics of the day. And she had some decided opinions about the legislation he had himself introduced into the House of Lords.

'My brother tells me that your bill would make it easier for an unscrupulous man to run a county workhouse,' she remarked as she helped herself to the mutton Bluestone offered her.

'Does he?' Hartville waved aside the boiled salsify and regarded her with a sharper gaze. 'What makes him think so?'

'Apparently there would not be any effort made to verify a man's statements about himself and his probity. Jeremy knows of such a case in Sussex, where the workhouse is run by a veritable monster with a record of terrible conditions in a previous workhouse he administered. Your bill apparently does not protect a county from being duped in such a way.'

A muscle in Hartville's jaw twitched. 'It is a county's responsibility to assure themselves that anyone they hire is of an acceptable reputation.'

'Perhaps, but they are not required, under your bill, to do so.'

Hartville set down his knife and fork, his eyes narrowed, and demanded, 'What happened to the meek little milk and water miss who has been staying here for the past two weeks? She does not seem to be in evidence now.'

Caroline laughed with genuine amusement. 'Did you like her better, Lord Hartville? I was only trying to adjust to your mother's expectations. It's not my natural disposition to be altogether accommodating.'

'So I see,' he murmured.

'But I can do it if you prefer,' she added, giving him something of a roguish grin. 'I am perfectly capable of discussing the weather ad infinitum, or discoursing on items of apparel in the latest mode, or even, should you approve, considering the finer points of the various pieces of horse-flesh in your stables. You must choose the subject. I'll not be at a loss for totally useless comments and unwise preferences, I promise you.'

'I don't wish you to be accommodating for the sake of it,' he declared, picking up his fork again. 'And what could you possibly know about the finer points of my horses?'

'Precisely.' Caroline ducked her head, giving herself an altogether meeker appearance. She allowed the passion to die out of her voice and the fire to be extinguished in her eyes. When she raised her head, only slightly, her face had become bland, her very bearing less confident. 'The black one that you call Warrior is very pretty, is he not?' she asked in a hesitant voice. 'And so strong. One of the grooms told me he could gallop for an hour with scarcely breathing hard.'

Hartville regarded her with a frown. 'I particularly dislike having the wool pulled over my eyes by my relatives. My mother invited you here in good faith. You should have served her properly by not trying to ingratiate yourself with her.'

Caroline snorted. 'My duty as a visiting relative, sir, was to behave with gratitude to your mother for her kindness. I am accustomed to the ways of society. Your mama would not have been over pleased to have a presumptuous young woman appear on her doorstep. However, I have shown her that I'm not lacking in sense, nor am I unfamiliar with making decisions on important issues.'

'Such as the child.'

'Yes, such as the child. If your mama had insisted on Wilhelmina being sent to an orphanage, I would have attempted to change her mind. If she, and you, had persisted, I believe I would simply have taken her with me to my home.'

Hartville's brows rose. 'My understanding was that you haven't much of a home, Miss Carruthers.'

Her cheeks flushed at this plain speaking. 'Enough of one to assure that the child wouldn't be consigned to a life of poverty and hard labor.'

'That's not inevitably the fate of a child in an orphanage, surely. A perfectly decent family might have adopted her. Might still,' he added with emphasis, 'adopt her.'

He had her at a stand. Caroline should welcome the thought of a family adopting the girl. After all, she herself would not be at Berwick Hall forever. Lady Hartville was past the age of truly welcoming a child of four into her family. Hartville apparently had no interest in children. At Berwick Hall Wilhelmina would be raised by the servants as neither fish nor fowl, in all likelihood.

And yet Caroline felt, unaccountably, the strongest aversion to Wilhelmina being brought up by strangers. Was that because she thought the girl was Hartville's love child? And what business was that of hers?

Confused, and more than a little irritated, she applied herself to her meal. Let Hartville choose another topic of conversation if he wished the meal not to proceed in silence.

Hartville had dismissed the servants, and now applied himself to his cutlets and stewed tomatoes. Seldom did it fall to Hartville to provide the conversation at

41

Berwick. Generally it was Lady Hartville who entertained her companions with chat of the neighbors, or the parish doings, or news arrived in letters from her London friends.

His mother had assured Caroline that Hartville was quite an accomplished raconteur, amongst his set in London. At home he seemed to prefer to be entertained rather than to exert himself to amuse his companions. Or perhaps he merely felt so uncomfortable in Caroline's company that he could not dredge up the enthusiasm to find a topic which would suit her tastes. Every subject must seem fraught with some difficulty — politics, family, estate business. There was always the weather, Caroline thought with amusement.

'Do you ride?' Hartville finally asked.

'Yes.'

'I don't believe you've ridden since you came to Berwick.'

'No.'

'Should you like to?'

Caroline paused in lifting her fork and eyed him curiously. 'Why do you ask?'

'Because I'd be pleased to mount you on one of my hacks, if you've a mind.'

'Would I have to ride with a groom?'

He frowned. 'I'd be happy to accompany

you. You don't know your way around the neighborhood.'

'I'm sure you're far too busy to ride out with me. And I don't at all like being burdened with a groom. It seems so much like being in the schoolroom, having someone tag along to make sure you behave yourself and don't do mischief to the poor beast.'

Hartville sighed impatiently. 'So what you're saying is that you don't wish to ride.'

'No, that's not what I'm saying.' She lifted her shoulders in a slight shrug. 'But I'll be perfectly satisfied, as I have been for the past two weeks, to remain indoors with your mama, or to walk in the shrubbery with her. And I can explore the immediate vicinity on foot, when time allows.'

'Surely you have as much time as you please. My mother didn't invite you here to be her personal companion, Miss Carruthers.'

'Then why did she invite me?'

'Damned if I know,' he muttered.

'Ah, but I think it's quite obvious,' she said. 'It appears that your mother has some intention of your marrying me.'

4

The viscount stared at her, unbelieving. It was not, Caroline realized, that he didn't believe his mother was trying to be a matchmaker, but that a woman of purportedly gentle upbringing would bring up such a subject with him.

'There's not the least need for you to worry,' she assured him, dabbing daintily at her mouth. 'Or to try to avoid me so constantly. I haven't the slightest intention of marrying you, even were you interested, which I perfectly understand that you are not.'

'I beg your pardon!' he exclaimed, color infusing his cheeks. 'I'm sure you have misapprehended my mother's intent, Miss Carruthers. Why, she was not even acquainted with you until your arrival.'

'Come, come, Lord Hartville. Let's not beat about the bush. For some reason which I do not indeed comprehend, your mother has decided that it is time for you to marry, and that I should be the lucky woman with whom you spend your life.'

Caroline laughed a little at his absurd

expression. 'Yes, this is plain speaking, something I am sure you are not accustomed to at your own table. But it is a subject best laid to rest between us, is it not?'

'It is a subject best not discussed at all,' he pronounced grimly.

'Very well.' Caroline folded her hands in her lap and adopted a most docile mien. A servant arrived to remove the second course covers. 'Should I ask your mama if I might take over the management of the household while she's indisposed?'

Hartville glared at her. 'I'm sure there's no need, cousin. I dare say it is but a very temporary disability.'

'No doubt.'

Caroline exclaimed with delight at the lemon cream that was then offered to her. 'How lovely. Yes, I do believe I'll have some. Is this one of your favorites, too, Lord Hartville?'

'I'm partial to it,' he admitted.

'I'll remember that,' she replied, her eyes sparkling. 'And the cutlets. I could tell you were especially fond of them. Your chef makes a fine soubise sauce.'

She thought perhaps he growled, but she could not be absolutely sure.

The lemon cream was tart and delicious. She allowed her tongue to savor its richness.

Caroline was not accustomed to such extensive variety nor to such treats in her meals. Since her brother cared little for food, it was one of the places where she could economize. He never invited company to dine with them, except, of course, for Giles Markingham. Caroline pushed aside the thought of Giles. It was her habit to dwell on him only when she was alone.

When she looked up from her plate, she found Hartville regarding her with curiosity and she felt a blush steal into her cheeks. He could not possibly have guessed what she was thinking. And yet, suddenly a knowing smile stretched his mouth.

'What's this, cousin?' he challenged. 'Surely *I*'ve said nothing to put you to the blush.'

Caroline had no idea how to answer the viscount. Sparring with him was not as easy as it had seemed at first. He kept turning the tables on her. And the unholy light in his eyes at the moment very strongly suggested that he suspected her of some impropriety.

'I was thinking,' she said, most untruthfully, 'about Wilhelmina and what will need to be done to see she is taken care of properly. I suppose you have given Mrs. Bluestone permission to engage a nursery maid.'

'Well, you suppose wrong, cousin,' Hartville said, completely diverted from his skirmish, as Caroline had hoped he would be. 'There's no saying that Wilhelmina will be here long.'

'No matter how long she's at Berwick Hall, she will need someone to be in charge of her.' Caroline cocked her head at him. 'Or had you wished me to act nursery maid, sir?'

'Certainly not!' Hartville would no doubt have said more had the servants not been present. 'You're here on a visit, cousin. It is not my intention, or my mother's, to see you fagged with onerous duties. Did Mrs. Bluestone have someone in mind?'

'As it happens, Gladys has a sister at home who is particularly good with children.'

'I see. So it's already settled, is it?'

'Of course not. Mrs. Bluestone is awaiting word from you or Lady Hartville. And your mama, I fear, is too indisposed to see to the matter directly.'

'Oh, very well,' Hartville said with poor grace. 'I'll see that Gladys's sister is brought in to take care of the child. But only for the time being, mind. I'll make every effort to find her own family, or, failing that, to find a proper family to adopt her.'

'Yes, my lord,' Caroline said meekly.

Hartville shook his head, but more with amusement this time than annoyance. 'You really are a complete hand, Cousin Caroline.

Do you always get precisely what you wish?'

'Not always,' she admitted. 'I have not, for instance, been offered a chance to drive those bays of yours.'

'Nor will you!'

'Ah,' was all she said.

'You won't, you know. They're prime bits o'blood and no amateur is going to cozzen me into allowing her to rip up their mouths.'

'Of course not.' Caroline set her serviette down beside her place and said, 'I'll leave you to your port, Lord Hartville.'

For a moment it seemed as though he would stay her, but the moment passed. He rose and drew back her chair, saying, 'If you will be in the parlor, I'll join you presently.'

'Thank you, sir, but I fear it's been a tiring day, and I have every intention of seeking my room now. Perhaps I'll see you on the morrow,' she said with a mock wistfulness.

'I'm sure you shall.'

His eyes met hers in something of a duel, but as she turned and walked from the room, Caroline was not at all certain who had won their engagement.

★   ★   ★

Hartville stayed to take a glass of port. It was a time that he especially liked, when he was alone in the dining room. In summer the view out over the lawns to the home woods was almost enchanting. Now, because it was spring, dusk was turning to dark and he could see little but reflections in the windows.

The candles in the chandelier twinkled in the glass, but cast their light only a short distance. His own features were not at all clear in the reflection. He might have been his own father, for all the clarity the glass provided. He was about the same height, had the same brown hair, though his father's had grayed considerably before his death the previous year.

Hartville was finding it difficult to step into his father's shoes. The old viscount had been content his entire life to remain on the estate, to see to his tenants and manage estate affairs. His had not been the restless spirit that Hartville's was. Hartville lifted his glass and took a healthy sip, thinking how he would prefer to be in London, drinking with his companions, looking forward to an evening of sophisticated entertainment.

But instead he was in the Lake District with nothing to look forward to but an early night in bed. His cousin Caroline might at least have stayed up to play the pianoforte for him, or joined him in a game of chess. Hartville rather thought it likely she would be a challenging opponent at the chess table. There was something about the way her mind worked . . .

He set his glass down without finishing the port, tugged his shirt cuffs down and rose from the table. Things had really come to a bad pass, he thought, when he regretted not being able to play chess with a woman who probably didn't even know *how* to play chess. And one, moreover, who seemed intent on believing him the father of a child he'd never laid eyes on in his life. To say nothing of her being so lost to all sense of propriety as to declare to his face that she wasn't interested in marrying him. As if he wanted to marry *her*.

Really, he decided as he made his way across the rose-patterned carpet, his mother had a lot to answer for. Too bad she wasn't feeling well enough for him to express his displeasure. Not that she took him seriously when he did. Lady Hartville persisted in believing that her son merely experienced the crotchets from time to time, nothing to be regarded. In fact, she persisted in believing that he was basically cut from the same cloth as his father — an upright man of sober habits with an earnest desire to be a country squire.

Little she knew.

* ★ *

Caroline rose early and took sustenance in the breakfast parlor before his lordship had made an appearance. The first thing she did after her meal was check on Lady Hartville's health. My lady's dresser, Griffin, informed her that though Lady Hartville intended to stay in her room for the time being, she was feeling better and was in need of nothing.

'She would take it as a kindness, however,' the austere Griffin stated, 'if you would speak with Mrs. Bluestone about today's meals and about the Young Person.'

'With the greatest pleasure,' Caroline assured her. She had no confidence in Hartville's remembering to instruct that Gladys's sister be brought to care for Wilhelmina, but found, on being ushered into Mrs. Bluestone's corner office that this task has already been accomplished.

'Gladys was that happy to bring Meg here,' Mrs. Bluestone confided. 'Good, honest, hard-working girls, they are. Meg has helped out on many occasions, and I'm that glad to have her here again.'

Caroline had seated herself in the comfortable chair opposite Mrs. Bluestone's desk. In most of the households where she'd stayed, and there had been several, the housekeeper had occupied a suite of rooms — sitting and bedroom — where she conducted her tasks. Here her working space was an office close to that of the butler, perhaps because the two were a married couple. Caroline liked the professional look of Mrs. Bluestone's space — the desk and the records cabinet. Mrs. Bluestone could probably lay her hands on the receipt for any household purchase over the eighteen years of her tenancy in the post.

'I'm a little concerned about Lady Hartville,' Caroline confessed. 'She doesn't seem the sort of woman who would take to her chamber willingly.'

'That she isn't!' agreed Mrs. Bluestone. But her face became troubled and one hand unconsciously stroked the arm of her chair. 'It's two months now that she's had some trouble. Not that she'd let his lordship know! Passes it off as a mere nothing, with him. And with everyone else who will buy such a packet of nonsense.'

The older woman looked a little stricken at having told tales to a veritable stranger, and Caroline smiled encouragingly. 'If I could be of help, take some of the burden off her . . .'

Mrs. Bluestone nodded sharply. 'As I was thinking. It will last two or three days. Always does. She won't have any fuss made.'

'But hasn't she seen a doctor?'

'Doesn't hold much truck with them, and that's the truth.' Mrs. Bluestone tapped impatiently on the chair arm. 'Not as you could blame her, miss. The local fellow, a Mr. Draper, does nothing but bleed anyone as is sick. Hasn't the least notion what's wrong with my lady.'

'I see.' Caroline frowned as she looked out the window over the kitchen garden. 'Don't you think perhaps if his lordship realized the extent of the problem that he'd bring someone in from London?'

'He might. But she won't have it, miss. Says there's nothing much wrong and she'll be fit as can be in no time.'

But Lady Hartville brought me here, Caroline was thinking. A month ago the younger woman had received a very cordial but also rather firm letter urging Caroline to visit. Rather suspicious timing for a woman who thought there was nothing much wrong with her — and who had spent the previous two weeks trying to make a match between her son and Caroline.

When she left the housekeeper, Caroline headed directly to the 'schoolroom,' to which Mrs. Bluestone had directed her. The housekeeper had reminisced about her early days at Berwick Hall, when Hartville himself had been but a boy. 'Used to get into every

53

kind of mischief,' she'd said, smiling broadly. 'Never a bad lad, you understand. Just always filled with jumping beans.'

Since no one had used the schoolroom for years, there were two maids dusting and putting things to rights. Caroline watched in amusement as one squealed when she opened a desktop to find a snake — wooden, of course, but very lifelike.

'Oh, may I keep it?' Wilhelmina breathed reverently.

'I'm sure no one would mind, if you don't leave it lying about to frighten the maids,' Caroline stipulated.

Behind her a voice said, 'Ha! Every little thing frightens the maids.' Hartville relented and waved the two shrinking girls on with their work. 'I had a spider collection that used to send them into fits.'

'Spiders.' Caroline shuddered. 'Why would you collect spiders?'

While Hartville mused on this, Wilhelmina said, 'Perhaps the Fine Man wanted to send the maids into fits. Timmy used to try to scare us girls.'

Hartville raised his brows in mock offense. Caroline laughed and said, 'Perhaps he did, sweetheart. Boys are like that, aren't they?'

'Yes, but I miss Timmy and Sally and Anne and Bitty,' Wilhelmina admitted, her little shoulders drooping. 'They were my friends. We played hunt the slipper and whoop and hide together. I don't think I'll ever see them again.'

'Well, I shall help you make new friends,' Caroline assured her. With a questioning look, she turned to Hartville, who shrugged.

'There are certain to be other children around,' he said, sounding vague. 'Mrs. Hedges's son must be about her age. Where's the nursery maid we sent for?'

'Gladys's sister? She's gone down to bring up Wilhelmina's breakfast, I believe.'

A young woman came hurrying along the corridor, a tray in her hands, the ties of her apron flying behind her. She made a quick curtsey in Hartville's direction, but didn't hesitate to enter the schoolroom and set her burden down on a table.

'I'm Meg, ma'am,' she said to Caroline. 'Come to care for the child.'

She looked a healthy young thing, robust and pink cheeked with a few freckles sprinkled on her face. 'I'm so glad you could come,' Caroline replied. 'Between the two of us I'm sure we'll keep Wilhelmina so busy that she won't be too lonesome.'

Hartville interjected smoothly, 'Meg had best get settled in on her own, Cousin

Caroline. I have other plans for you this morning.'

'You do?' Caroline couldn't keep the surprise from her voice. 'Does your mother need my help?'

'In a manner of speaking. She'd appreciate your exercising her mare. The poor beast hasn't been ridden in ages by anyone but a stable lad.' He cocked his head and smiled at her. 'And you wouldn't have to take a groom along — if you rode out with me.'

5

Hartville wasn't at all sure why he'd asked his cousin to ride with him. He certainly hadn't intended to. His resolve to spend as little time as possible with the woman had not changed, especially since she seemed to be as aware as he was of his mother's scheme. Though Miss Carruthers had protested that she wasn't interested in marrying him, Hartville found this a little difficult to believe. Knowing her impoverished circumstances, he could imagine no better reason for her coming to Berwick Hall.

And she'd brought a fetching riding habit with her, he noted as she descended the staircase into the hall. Blue enhanced her eyes, and contrasted nicely with her fair hair. As she came closer, he could discern that it wasn't a new riding habit. There was some sign of a skillful repair at the shoulder, and the skirts were slightly dulled from washing. He learned, too, that she was uncomfortable with his close scrutiny.

'No, it is not new, Lord Hartville. It's many years since I've ridden regularly, and therefore had any need of a habit. I only brought it because your mother specifically indicated that I ought.'

'It's charming,' Hartville said, using that voice he was so accustomed to employing in London. Flattery was everything with the female of the species. Even his mother was not immune to it.

His cousin ignored this remark, with a look that told him perfectly clearly that she disapproved of his attempt at light flirtation. Well, he would have said nothing at all if she hadn't tried to chide him for staring at her. Which he most certainly wouldn't have done if the riding gown hadn't been just the tiniest bit snug over her chest.

'Tell me about the horse I'm to ride,' she suggested diplomatically as she followed him across the hall to the door leading outside. 'I trust she's a gentle nag.'

'Holly? Indeed, yes. Though my mama used to be a bruising rider, she's become more sedate of later years.' Hartville frowned as he pushed open the door and held it for his cousin. 'But Mama hasn't ridden much since I've been home. That's not like her. Perhaps it's because you've not wanted to ride out with her.'

His companion lifted the skirts of her habit to clear the stairs, and Hartville caught a glimpse of a very shapely ankle. 'She hasn't suggested that we ride, cousin. Which surprised me, after her particularly asking that I bring a habit.'

Hartville thought it was likely Cousin Caroline had somehow communicated her disinterest in riding to her hostess. Otherwise how to explain his mother's absence from the stables? He tapped his riding crop thoughtfully against his top boot as he strode along, forgetting to slacken his pace for his companion in her skirts. The possibility was beginning to dawn on Hartville that there was more to his mother's illness than met the eye.

One of the stable lads already stood waiting with Holly, and a second lad was coming out of the stables with Warrior. Hartville watched Caroline as she approached the horses, to look out for any sign of fear or distrust, but she seemed perfectly at her ease. Warrior was always a bundle of nervous energy before he'd been ridden a mile or two, but Holly waited patiently, her ears pricked toward Caroline. For all her gentleness, Holly was actually a spirited little mare. Hartville had seen her more than once leave most of the field behind at a hunt.

'She'll jump anything you put her to,' he told Caroline as he came up beside her. He was surprised to see that Caroline brought a bite of apple for the horse, and Holly eagerly munched it from his cousin's palm.

'Are we going to be doing much jumping today?' Caroline asked with alarm.

'Not if you don't wish to.'

'It's been years since I've ridden, Lord Hartville. I hate to sound like such a poor-spirited soul, but you'll have to allow me the opportunity to reacquaint myself with being in the saddle.'

Hartville could not imagine a life without riding. What in heavens name did you do with yourself? But then, she was a woman, and women did very different things with their lives, didn't they? 'I have no wish to rush you,' he assured her.

The stable lad holding Holly had set a block for Caroline to stand on. Hartville moved closer to her, asking, 'Do you remember how to mount?'

'Yes, but even with the block I think I'll need your help,' she admitted as she pushed her skirts back.

Hartville made a foothold for her, and expertly tossed her up onto the sidesaddle. Caroline swung easily into place and smiled down at him a little ruefully. 'I'd forgotten how far one was from the ground.'

'Holly won't toss you, but she will try to keep up with Warrior.' Hartville took the stallion's reins from the groom and gracefully mounted. Warrior danced with eagerness, but Hartville kept him tightly reined in. His horse was not accustomed to such restraint and shook his head energetically. 'Not yet, old lad,' Hartville warned him. 'Behave yourself.'

And he led the way from the stable yard at such a sedate pace that the stable lads grinned at each other before returning to their duties.

★ ★ ★

Caroline had missed riding, and she had especially missed the association with horses. She'd never owned a horse, but had been spared an older gelding at her aunt's when a group went riding. As she had mentioned to Hartville, the only times she'd ridden alone, she'd had a groom to accompany her. Her aunt was a stickler for propriety, and had not, in fact, really approved of Caroline riding even *with* the groom in attendance. 'There's something not quite ladylike about riding,' Aunt Matilda had said more than once.

As with so many of her aunt's oddities, Caroline had attempted to accommodate the ancient lady. But she was drawn to the horses themselves — those big, powerful, warm-blooded creatures that would nuzzle your palm with their satin noses or nudge you with

61

their heads. Though Caroline had not managed to spend much time with them, she had regretted leaving them behind altogether when she and her brother moved to London to set up an establishment of their own.

In town her brother didn't keep a horse, though he often threatened to purchase some touted animal that a friend was selling. They both knew that stabling a horse would be an unnecessary expense which they could ill afford. Besides, Jeremy had taken to the craze of the day for driving all sorts of carriages. A carriage, of course, was out of the question. But Jeremy had friends who encouraged his interest. Caroline suspected it was Jeremy's being a top sawyer which made it possible for him to drive his friends' curricles and high perch phaetons. He had even on occasion allowed her to take the reins — an exciting if rather demanding proposition.

As she rode behind Hartville, she reached down to stroke Holly's neck, murmuring words of affection so blatant that her host turned in his saddle to stare at her. 'Well,' she said, a blush stealing up her neck, 'I want her to know that I think she's splendid.'

Hartville shook his head with rueful amusement. 'She'll go along just as well without.'

'Don't you ever encourage your horse?'

'Only when I want something extra from him.'

'That's the problem with most people,' Caroline mused. 'They think there's no need to show their appreciation for the normal things, the everyday things. It would never occur to them to acknowledge Mrs. Biggins's expertise on even the smallest matter in her shop, which no doubt saves them endless time and energy. They take her for granted.'

'Well, of course we do,' he retorted. 'It's her shop. It's to her advantage to know precisely what she has and to convince us to buy it.'

Caroline could see there was no sense in arguing with him. Probably he was even right, given that any shopkeeper would be delighted to have a viscount's patronage. But she knew from experience how much it meant to receive a kind word. When you were expected to manage a household — to plan the menus and maintain the linens and oversee the silver polishing, and a thousand other duties — and in exchange you were given a roof over your head and food on the table, a word of thanks did not come amiss. Her Aunt Matilda had not been one to offer such a word, but occasionally a guest or visitor had shown appreciation for her thoughtfulness, and it had meant a great deal.

Lost in her thoughts, Caroline did not

notice when Hartville set his horse to a canter. Holly's surge forward was the first warning she had. One hand tightened on the reins, while the other grabbed a fistful of Holly's mane. This was *not* how she'd intended to treat her poor mount.

The horse's pace was frightening. Caroline feared she would be unable to keep her seat. The trees to her left seemed to be whizzing past at a terrific speed. Ahead, unaware of her plight, Hartville was urging Warrior on to a gallop.

Caroline's heart beat frantically in her throat. In her panic she had allowed Holly her head, and the mare was striving valiantly to keep up with the black stallion. Caroline was *not* going to be able to maintain her seat on the sidesaddle.

She was too alarmed to call out. Her body rocked wildly forward and back as her horse raced down the dirt road, its hooves pounding out a beat as raucous as her heart's. It was several minutes before Caroline realized she had fallen into the rhythm of Holly's gallop, that she was not going to topple off her mount after all.

Hartville and Warrior were a fair distance ahead of them, but Holly surged down the road like a feisty contender. Caroline marveled at the smoothness of her gait and the power of her stride. This was a far cry from the sedate walk or trot she'd experienced as a younger woman at Aunt Matilda's. This was exhilarating, Caroline decided, as her heartbeat calmed to a more normal pace. This she would not mind doing again — if she were given sufficient warning.

After ten minutes Hartville drew Warrior in to a canter, and then a trot, until Holly caught up with them. He smiled across at Caroline. 'That's what Holly needs, a chance to stretch her legs. She's not had it for too long.'

'Really? You'd never know.' Caroline could feel the color high in her cheeks. She was not going to tell him that the ride had frightened the devil out of her. Which perhaps would not have happened had she been more honest about the extent of her riding experience when he queried her.

Only after a moment did she realize that Hartville was staring at her chest, again. Really, he was too annoying. Yes, her riding habit was a little snug over her bosom, but there was little she could do about that. He made a half gesture with one of his gauntleted hands. Caroline frowned sternly at him.

'Your button . . . ' he said.

Caroline glanced down at the jacket of her habit and found that not one, but two of the buttons had come undone, exposing her undergarment to his view. No doubt her exertion to remain seated on her horse had stressed the buttons beyond their ability to cope.

Caroline automatically clasped the front of her jacket closed with one hand. However, with her gloves on, she found she could not possibly push those tiny buttons through their tiny holes. The color in her cheeks rose higher.

'Here, hand me the reins and your gloves,' he advised.

Seated sidesaddle, she was directly facing him. Caroline had never felt the least bit missish, but this was an awkward situation indeed. Hartville moved Warrior closer and held out his hand for the reins. Unwillingly, she gave them to him. And then she had to let go of her jacket in order to remove her gloves.

A gentleman would have averted his head, wouldn't he? Of course, then he would not have been aware when she attempted to hand the gloves across to him. Still, Caroline felt certain Hartville could have found some way to manage both feats if he'd tried.

With the gloves disposed of, Caroline restored first one and then the other of the buttons. Despite the close attention this called for, she continually glared across at

Hartville to make sure his gaze was on her face and not her chest. He was the picture of propriety and concern, *now*, gallantly avoiding any glance below her neck. When she had finished, he handed across her gloves, which she quickly worked over her fingers.

'Ready?' he asked.

Caroline nodded, her color still high.

Hartville handed across Holly's reins. 'What do you say we jump a few fences?' he asked, an unholy gleam dancing in his eyes.

'Go soak your impertinent head,' she advised, and gave Holly's side a nudge with her heel.

6

Before he left for Yorkshire to sort out the difficulties of Frances Carruthers, who was apparently in need of five hundred pounds to set matters right with an ostler, Hartville stopped by his mother's room to see for himself how she went on. She was not, as he had feared, in her bed, but seated in the pretty little alcove off her bedchamber which overlooked the topiary garden.

Her color was not wonderful. Hartville thought perhaps the hideous puce shade of her dressing gown might be contributing to her pallor.

'How are you feeling, Mother?' he asked as he drew up a chair.

Lady Hartville laid down the volume she was perusing and regarded him with amusement. 'I'm perfectly all right, Hartville. Were you worried?'

He told himself not to be distracted by her geniality. His mother had a talent for making one overlook the obvious if she wished it overlooked. 'Your color isn't good,' he remarked.

'And no wonder,' she retorted. 'I've been

feeling dyspeptic for the past two days, but there's little amiss with me now.'

'You're eating well again?'

'You know Griffin. She will have me on an invalid's diet for longer than is necessary. I humor her.'

Since Lady Hartville was not in reality given to humoring anyone, her son included, Hartville doubted this. On the side table were the remains of a meager meal — toast and tea from the looks of it. 'This isn't the first time you've suffered such an attack, is it?' he demanded.

'My dear boy, everyone is subject to an attack of dyspepsia from time to time. Surely you've experienced it yourself.'

'Not that I'm aware of. Don't try to cozen me, Mama. If there's some physical indisposition that you're concerned about, I wish you'd acknowledge it to me. Perhaps this is a matter for that local fellow. What's his name — Dragon?'

'Draper. And he's no better than a horse doctor,' her ladyship said with disgust. 'Last time he was here he could think of nothing better to do than bleed me. Everyone knows that's his one method for killing or curing his patients. I won't have him.'

Hartville regarded her with narrowed eyes. 'But you've had him in previously. Which tells me that you took this illness seriously.'

'That was six months ago!'

'And you're suffering the problem again, I take it. Perhaps you've had it a time or two in between?'

'More than a time or two,' said a voice behind him.

Hartville turned to find Griffin standing in the doorway, her arms folded tightly against her chest. 'I urged her ladyship to tell you about it, my lord.'

Lady Hartville scowled at her dresser. 'Thank you, Griffin. That will be all. I'm perfectly capable of telling my son what I think he needs to know about my health.'

Griffin did not argue with her mistress, nor did she appear unduly intimidated by Lady Hartville's cold tone. She bowed her head slightly, picked up the tray of breakfast remains and left the room.

When she had gone, Hartville regarded his mother with mild puzzlement. 'But why haven't you told me, Mama? Do you suspect that something is seriously wrong? Please tell me if you do. I can send for a man from London. There are some very talented fellows there.'

His mother merely shrugged. 'Have a doctor come all the way from London? Ridiculous. I'm sure there's no need of it.'

'Well, I'm not.'

'Look at me, Hartville. Do I appear at death's door? Not a bit of it. I've experienced dyspepsia off and on for months. It's probably something I eat, though I have yet to discover what it may be.'

Though this sounded reasonable, Hartville didn't doubt there was more to the matter. 'Why did you send for Miss Carruthers?' he asked abruptly.

'Because Emma Parcivel wrote that she thought Miss Carruthers was about to get herself into a very bad situation.'

Hartville's brows flew up. 'In what way?'

'Oh, it is none of your business,' his mother said, waving aside his curiosity. 'Rest assured her coming here has put the matter to rest.'

This was scarcely enough to satisfy Hartville. 'Really, Mama, you are too exasperating. From the moment that young woman arrived here, you've tried to make a match between us. And now you tell me that the innocent Miss Carruthers was embroiled in some alarming situation before she left her home. Pray, how do you reconcile those two things?'

'I did not say she was embroiled, Hartville. I said she was about to embroil herself. There's a vast difference.'

'Well, I don't see it,' he retorted. 'Why

71

would you wish to pair me off with a young woman who had no better sense than to get herself into trouble?'

His mother regarded him with studied patience. 'Did you think I would choose a woman for you who would bore you to tears, Hartville? Did you think I wouldn't know you needed a woman with spirit?'

'Frankly, Mama,' he drawled, 'it never occurred to me that you would attempt to choose a bride for me at all!'

Lady Hartville sighed. 'And so I shouldn't have, if you'd made the least effort to choose one for yourself. You're nine-and-twenty, my dear fellow. When were you planning to set up your nursery?'

Hartville picked up one of her hands and pressed it. 'You cannot rush these things, Mama. It would make no sense for me to fly off and marry some suitably endowed young woman only to find later that her chatter drove me to the brink of insanity, or her want of sense made me take her in dislike.'

'No one wishes you to act precipitously, Hartville.'

'I'm so glad to hear it.' He restored her hand to her lap and smiled engagingly. 'I know you want what's best for me, Mama. But I'm afraid you're mistaken in Miss Carruthers's appeal for me. All you are doing is raising the girl's hopes when there is no chance of our marrying. You must have seen that nothing sparked between the two of us.'

'Humph. I don't see how it could have, with you avoiding her like the plague.' Lady Hartville stroked the book on her lap and looked thoughtful. 'But she didn't seem to take to you, either,' she admitted. 'Pity. I took an instant liking to her myself. You won't mind if I urge her to stay on for some time, will you?'

'Not at all, if that's what you'd like.'

'Yes, that's what I'd like.'

'It's settled, then.' Hartville rose and stood looking down at her. He was still uncertain as to just how ill she was, and whether he should do anything about it. 'I'd planned to drive into Yorkshire for a day or two, but perhaps I'll stay here.'

'Not on my account! I promise you I have quite enough people hanging about trying to cosset me. You should take care of whatever business calls, Hartville.'

Though he hesitated, he thought she was probably better taken care of by her various minions than by himself. And he did want to put this matter of Frances Carruthers's 'five hundred pound misunderstanding' behind him. 'Very well. I shouldn't be more than three days.'

'I'm sure we can manage quite well for three days without you, Hartville,' she replied, accepting the kiss he bestowed on her cheek.

'I daresay you can.'

★ ★ ★

When Caroline returned to her room, a generous and well-furnished apartment, she tossed her riding gloves on the bed and frowned at herself in the cheval glass. The riding habit was decidedly too snug across her bosom. But the possibility of the two buttons popping open had certainly not occurred to her when she was dressing.

Curious, she released the two buttons as she stood in front of the glass. To her surprise, and chagrin, the view which had been available to Hartville had not been entirely, as she had supposed, of her undergarments. A small but significant amount of flesh was visible. Caroline felt the color rise to her face again. Really, it was most embarrassing.

With impatient fingers she released the rest of the buttons on the jacket and stripped it off, as though removing the offending item could make her discomfiture vanish. Instead she was confronted by her reflection in the

74

glass, and what she saw merely aggravated her dismay. Rather than the thin, austere body that she longed to possess, Caroline was burdened with a body that looked 'ripe for the picking,' as she had once overheard a young man say. True, he was not a gentleman, but she very much feared he was not the only one who viewed her that way.

Even Jeremy had remarked once, in his teasing way, that it was too bad she hadn't been born into the right class to be a stage actress. 'For you look the part, and could have made our fortune,' he'd lamented. Caroline had told him not to be so foolish, but his words had hurt her. It was not her fault, was it, that her body was fuller and curvier than that of other women.

What was her responsibility, she knew, was to see that she dressed in an unexceptionable fashion, and that she paid no attention to those odd messages that her lush body occasionally delivered to her. Until, of course, she found herself married. Then, she fervently hoped, it would not be so wrong to acknowledge the very strange and *urgent* sensations that plagued her.

Caroline stepped out of the riding skirt and laid it carefully on the bed. Well, she wouldn't ride again, but there was no reason to mistreat her riding habit just because of her frustration. Perhaps she could use the material to make a pretty dress for Wilhelmina. Heaven knew there was enough yardage in the skirt alone to fashion more than one.

At the thought of the little girl, Caroline frowned. A woman had given birth to a baby some five years ago and had perhaps never held her or whispered to her or run her hands over the baby's smooth skin. How sad! Caroline thought it entirely possible that Wilhelmina's mother had indeed died, either at the child's birth or shortly thereafter. But what had become of the father who placed her with a rural family? Surely the cost of his child's upkeep would have been minimal. Caroline could scarcely imagine such indifference.

As she returned the riding habit to the wardrobe, she once again remembered its two popped buttons and the look on Hartville's face. Heat suffused her body and she gave herself a mental shake. Goodness knew she had more important things to concern herself with than whether the viscount had caught a glimpse of her skin. Caroline had no doubt that Hartville had seen a woman's flesh more than once in his life. And touched it, too, probably.

Which was no more her concern than

where he was headed, she thought as she caught a glimpse of him riding off on Warrior.

★　★　★

Amelia Winslow, Lady Hartville, was eight-and-forty years of age. Had she been asked, she would have declared herself ready and willing to live to some grand old age in her eighties. Not that she had seen her mother do so, or her father. But it was her mother's health that was most on Lady Hartville's mind each time she became ill, for her mother had suffered what seemed to Lady Hartville a very similar illness, and it had been the death of her.

My lady was not ready to accept that she might be sticking her spoon in the wall anytime soon, but she had to consider the possibility. And the last thing she wanted to do was die and leave Hartville without a bride and prospective family.

Bringing Miss Carruthers to Berwick Hall had been a long shot, of course, but even for her son Lady Hartville was not willing to brave the rigors of a London stay. In addition to her having no fondness for the metropolis, Hartville would have been seriously annoyed with her if she had attempted to push young ladies in his path when he was enjoying the

77

more sophisticated pastimes of London.

Not that he wasn't annoyed with her for bringing Miss Carruthers to the country. No doubt that had made it easier for him to depart for Yorkshire two days before. But Lady Hartville would have summoned Miss Carruthers to her in any case. The dowager had always had a soft spot for a young woman in trouble.

Caroline's request for an interview shortly after Hartville's departure did not discompose her ladyship one whit. Though she intended to keep to her room during Hartville's absence, Lady Hartville was feeling quite well enough to sustain a visit from her young visitor. When Griffin showed Caroline into the dowager's sitting room, Lady Hartville smiled kindly at her and waved aside the young woman's concerns about her health.

'I'm feeling well enough, just not in such spirits as to let Griffin dress me and fuss about me for an eternity.' She patted the red velvet seat of the chair beside her chaise. 'Come, tell me what has put that worried frown upon your face.'

'Oh, no, it is not worry, really,' Caroline protested as she took her seat. She produced a letter from the pocket of her gown and again the frown appeared between her brows.

'This note is from my brother, who finds himself in the area on his way to Grassmere with a friend. I should like to see him, of course, but I would not dream of inviting him here when you are ill. Would you mind if I were to meet him in Crowell for the afternoon?'

'Not invite him here! Whyever not? As if my being the tiniest bit indisposed should keep you from seeing your brother.'

'But I *would* see him, ma'am, if I went into Crowell.'

'Nonsense. If Hartville had not left for a few days, I would urge you to have your brother stay with us, but he and his friend must certainly come to dine.' Lady Hartville gave Caroline's hand a comforting pat. 'Now let us have no argument, my dear. I shall join you this evening if at all possible, but if not, you are perfectly capable of entertaining two young men by yourself.'

'You are very kind,' Carolyn said.

'Your brother's friend, is he someone you know?'

'Oh, yes, I've met him in London many times. Giles Markingham. He is a particular friend of Jeremy's.'

'Well, I should like to meet them both. Now, tell me how the child goes on,' Lady Hartville suggested.

When Caroline had left, Lady Hartville rose from her chaise and walked into her bedchamber. Emma Parcivel's letter was still in the drawer of her bedside table, and the dowager moved now to retrieve it. Emma had been Lady Hartville's link to London for many years, since the dowager no longer traveled to the city. Her friend had an eye for the delightful details of metropolitan life, and an ear for any *on dits* that would be of interest to someone so far away.

And Emma had an uncanny ability to sort out the complicated and far-flung members of the Winslow and Carruthers families. She had taken it upon herself to keep Lady Hartville apprised of the doings of any such relations upon whom her attention happened to fall. She was, in fact, the reason Lady Hartville had sent to London for Caroline.

Now the dowager spread the closely crossed sheets on the table and refreshed herself on the particulars of Caroline's situation:

Caroline Carruthers is an accomplished and attractive woman, probably in her twenty-fourth or -fifth year. Her brother, Jeremy, is perhaps two or three years younger. He is one of those scamps who get away with everything because he's good-looking and has a witty tongue. But I hear that he has debts, and no means of rescuing himself from them save gambling.

Here is the problem, my dear Amelia. He has a friend, Giles Markingham, who has plenty of blunt but who is what you and I would call a bounder. I have personally watched him, over the course of several seasons, pay court to one young lady after another, only to disappear from town when it might have been supposed that he was about to make an offer. This young man has his eye on the sister, and I very much fear she has formed an attachment to him as well.

You know how it is for a woman who does not go about much in society; it is all too easy for her to succumb to the blandishments of a well-heeled, presentable fellow. The brother sees no harm in the association. In fact, I think he encourages it, inasmuch as Markingham might prove generous in a settlement.

If I had it in my power, I would remove the young woman from such a dangerous situation, but I do not. I trust, my dear friend, that you will see fit to do what is in your power.

★   ★   ★

Lady Hartville folded the sheets and returned them to the drawer. Suddenly she wished most heartily that Hartville was not away from home. Though she had felt it necessary to welcome Caroline's brother and his friend to Berwick Hall for a meal, at least there was no need to invite them to stay, owing to her mediocre health.

But Lady Hartville did not like this turn of events. Not one bit.

7

Caroline had mixed emotions about the arrival of her brother and his friend. Though there were probably no two people she would prefer to see, their coming now, so soon after her own appearance at Berwick Hall, felt a bit awkward, and something of an intrusion. True, they would put up at the Duck and Hare, but Caroline, knowing that Jeremy's pockets were never plump, suspected he hoped the two of them would be encouraged to stay at the Hall.

With Hartville away and his mother not feeling well, that simply could not happen. But Caroline feared that Lady Hartville would exert herself to join them for dinner, an effort which might be unwise, given the dowager's current state of health. No, it was not a propitious time for Jeremy to descend upon them.

And yet Caroline could not regret the opportunity to see her brother and his friend Mr. Markingham.

After she sent a note off to the inn, Caroline hastened to her room to make sure that her most flattering gown was pressed.

Not that Markingham hadn't seen it before, or her brother dozens of times, but there was a world of difference between dining in their tight accommodations in London and the elegance of the Berwick Hall dining chamber. That spacious room, with all its crystal and silver, its liveried footmen and unending covered dishes, made one feel just the tiniest bit more glamorous oneself.

Of course, Markingham was accustomed to such genteel living. Jeremy, who had visited his friend's estate on several occasions, not infrequently commented on the luxuries available there. It would do no harm for Markingham to see Caroline in surroundings of a certain opulence, rather than the rather meagerly furnished flat in St. John's Wood.

As Caroline brushed her hair until it gleamed, she allowed herself to savor the memory of the last time she had seen Mr. Markingham. This had been some weeks before Lady Hartville's invitation, as Markingham had been in the country on family business when she departed. On leaving for his estate, Markingham had said, looking directly into her eyes, 'I shall look forward to seeing you upon my return, Miss Carruthers.' Caroline wondered what Markingham had thought when he returned to town to find that she had journeyed as far away as Cumberland!

Perhaps that was the reason for this surprise visit, she thought, feeling a blush color her cheeks. Surely not, she scolded herself. To come so far from London just to see her was not at all a likely thing for Giles Markingham to do. Why, he was invited everywhere in London, and had a dozen engagements each week.

Jeremy was given to wistfully commenting on the balls and routs that Markingham attended, but the level of society that Markingham could afford was way beyond Jeremy's means. Since he was not much in the petticoat line, Jeremy contented himself with being on the fringes — taking in the sporting events and racketing about with the set which spent more time in the stables than in drawing rooms.

Caroline's heart beat a little faster as she dressed, taking the greatest care with her appearance. She wished now that she had spent one of her few shillings on the rouleau of roses she'd seen at Mrs. Biggins's store. Her dress looked inordinately plain to her today, though the rich blue did complement her eyes. She would never in a thousand years have allowed Griffin to come to her, as Lady Hartville had offered. But Caroline did just wonder what the dresser could have done with her hair that might have made her look more like the ladies Markingham met with in town.

She consoled herself with the thought that Markingham had once remarked, 'They are all too pampered and polished, those chits making their come-out. Give me a woman with honest, natural beauty any day.' And he had looked at her in such a way that she'd been unable to meet his gaze.

Outside she heard the sounds of a carriage drawing into the courtyard in front of the Hall. *Heavens*, they were here already! With a last glance in the mirror, she turned around and hurried from her room.

* * *

Lady Hartville was already seated in the drawing room when Caroline breathlessly rushed into the room. Her ladyship looked up at her young charge with a mild expression of surprise. 'My dear, there is no need for such haste. Our guests have not as yet arrived.'

'No, but I heard a carriage in the courtyard,' Caroline admitted, 'and I wished to be here to introduce you to my brother and his friend.'

Lady Hartville studied the young woman,

with her heightened color and her careful toilette. Oh, yes, there was certainly something afoot here. Her ladyship did not consider it likely that a young woman would dress with such care for a brother she had seen scarce two weeks ago.

'Are you feeling well, my lady?' Caroline asked, stooping to pick up a handkerchief that Lady Hartville had dropped. 'I wouldn't have you experience a setback for all the world.'

'I'm perfectly comfortable,' her ladyship replied, and indeed she felt rather better than she'd expected. Having a vast amount of curiosity and an inherent desire to meddle in the affairs of others, she felt certain an interesting evening was in the offing.

There were the sounds of arrival in the echoing front hall and in short order the butler opened the door to announce: 'Mr. Jeremy Carruthers, Mr. Giles Markingham, my lady.'

Two of the most presentable young gentlemen Lady Hartville had seen in years walked into her drawing room. The younger, a tall, slender man with the same wheat blond hair as his sister, moved forward first and made a graceful bow. 'Lady Hartville,' he said, a twinkle in his eyes, 'I'm charmed to meet you at last. Caro has written the most intriguing things about you.'

'Has she now?' Lady Hartville asked, instantly if warily captivated by his brashness. 'I shouldn't have thought enough time has passed since her arrival for a letter to reach London already.'

'I've had two,' he assured her, and turned to his sister. 'Caro, you look magnificent. This country air does wonders for you!'

'As though I were knocked all to pieces in London,' she protested. But she moved forward to embrace him. 'How wonderful it is to see you, Jeremy. I had not thought it possible you would find yourself so far from home.'

Lady Hartville also would have liked to hear how her brother explained his presence in the Lake District, but the other gentleman, who had hung back while his companion introduced himself, now came forward and made his own bow. Here was a different kettle of fish altogether, her ladyship realized. There was nothing frivolous or lightweight about the man who stood before her. He was tall, even taller than Jeremy Carruthers, and more broadly and powerfully built. His darkness, too, contrasted with his companion's fairness.

Giles Markingham had thick black hair and heavy black brows. His eyes were a piercing green that appeared to see the world about him clearly. Where Carruthers had offered a playful deference, Markingham, though polite to a point, presented himself quite naturally as a person of consequence.

'Lady Hartville, it gives me a great deal of pleasure to make your acquaintance,' he said gravely. 'I do hope we are not imposing on your hospitality. My young friend was difficult to restrain in his eagerness to see his sister.'

Very becoming manners, Lady Hartville decided grudgingly — and a very attractive man. She was all graciousness in assuring him that the two of them were welcome. 'For my son is away from home, and Miss Carruthers and I have been very quiet these last two days,' she explained.

She cast a surreptitious glance at her young charge, and found that Caroline was patiently awaiting her turn to greet Mr. Markingham. Only by the heightened color in her cheeks could Lady Hartville discern that the young woman had a particular interest in him. There was a decided tension in the air as Markingham turned toward Caroline Carruthers.

'Miss Carruthers,' he said, in a voice grown suspiciously husky. 'How enchanting to see you in a setting worthy of your person. Jeremy's lodgings hardly do you credit.'

Caroline stepped slightly forward and offered him her hand, smiling and saying, 'They are my lodgings as well, Mr. Markingham, and I wish you will not disparage them.'

Though Lady Hartville could not see that he held her hand any longer than was proper, she suspected that he introduced a slight pressure, as Caroline's eyes dipped in modest confusion. As he had with her brother, Markingham made a striking figure alongside Caroline's angelic fairness.

Naturally, Lady Hartville preferred the couple that her son and Caroline made, but she was not blind to the appeal of these opposites. And their very familiarity, restrained as it was in the circumstances, held a certain promise which piqued her ladyship's interest.

'How was it that you and Mr. Carruthers met, Mr. Markingham?' she asked, to draw his attention from Caroline.

Markingham looked the slightest bit taken aback. Lady Hartville, if she were prone to being fanciful, might have taken his brief pause for wariness. But he glanced over at his young protégé with amusement and said, 'I believe it was at the racetrack, was it not, Jeremy?'

'Well, yes! But you mustn't think I frequent the races any more than the next fellow, Lady

Hartville,' he protested. 'Friend of mine took me to Epsom Downs, oh, years ago. Fellow I met in school, Tommy Multon. He knew Markingham, by George! Said he raised some of the finest race horses in the area.'

'So your acquaintance is of very long standing,' the dowager pressed.

'As to that, I hadn't seen Markingham for years when we ran into each other in town last year, eh, Giles?'

'Yes, when you were newly sprung on the metropolis,' his friend agreed. 'Ready to get up to every possible mischief.'

'And Mr. Markingham has helped keep a check on Jeremy's naturally high spirits,' Caroline interjected. 'I hate to think what might have become of him if he'd had no older friend to guide him.'

'Guide me! Well, of all the inane things to say!' Jeremy exclaimed. 'As if I were still in leading strings. Pay no heed to Caro, Lady Hartville. She's listened to our Aunt Matilda too long. And that good lady would have had me up at Oxford studying to be a cleric if you will.'

The foolishness of this idea struck Lady Hartville forcibly. 'I'm sure your sister never entertained such an ambition for you.'

'No, indeed I did not,' Caroline agreed heartily.

'I fear Jeremy was never destined for the clergy,' Mr. Markingham said with a laugh. His lightly mocking tone hinted that his knowledge of that young man suggested far otherwise. Caroline regarded him questioningly, but Lady Hartville thought it prudent to change the course of the conversation.

'How do you find the Hare and Duck?' she asked.

★　★　★

When they went in to dinner, Markingham demonstrated his ability to entertain with amusing anecdotes. Compared to his smooth, sophisticated style, Jeremy Carruthers appeared both young and inexperienced, but delightfully roguish as well. All in all, Lady Hartville was hard pressed to keep in mind her friend Emma's strictures on the two men, and wondered if perhaps her friend had been unnecessarily hard on them.

Over the rhubarb tart, Jeremy leaned toward his sister and said, 'Just before we left town I ran into your friend Miss Salston, Caro. She begged me to inform you that she has set the date for her ball and refuses to consider the possibility that you will not be in town to attend.'

His sister cocked her head at him and

asked, 'And what excuse did she offer, pray, for not having written and informed me herself?'

'She is far, far too busy to take pen in hand,' Jeremy mimicked, using a high female voice. 'Shopping and being measured for gowns takes up every spare hour. Why, she has hardly even been to Hyde Park to see her vast acquaintance in the light of day.'

'Poor love,' Caroline opined. 'What date has she chosen for her ball?'

'May seventh.'

Though it was more than a month away, Lady Hartville immediately interposed, 'Oh, I hope you shall not have left us by then, my dear. I was so counting on a long visit.'

'I daresay you will be bored with me long before May,' Caroline said with a slight laugh. 'But I doubt that I should attend in any case.'

'And why not?' demanded her brother.

'She moves in entirely different circles than we do, Jeremy. I should feel dreadfully out of place.'

'Nonsense. Markingham and I shall attend, shan't we, Giles?'

The older man's lips curved ruefully. 'We had certainly discussed the possibility. But if you are not to attend, Miss Carruthers . . .'

Lady Hartville thought it was a look of chagrin that passed swiftly across the young woman's face. But it was gone so quickly, she could not be sure. Caroline adopted a tone of finality when she said, 'I don't wish to think about it so far in advance. What I should so much like to hear is whether you were successful in finding the perfect match for Mr. Markingham's bay.'

8

When the gentlemen stayed behind to sample Lord Hartville's port, Caroline accompanied Lady Hartville to the drawing room. Though Caroline thought her hostess appeared a trifle fatigued, Lady Hartville protested that she was perfectly fine. She patted the spot beside her on the green velvet sofa, and Caroline complied by seating herself there.

'Your brother is a charming rascal,' Lady Hartville said with approval. 'Very entertaining with his scandalous tales of opera singers and the doings of the *ton*. Do you suppose he knows Hartville?'

Caroline shook her head. 'I don't believe they've ever met, ma'am, else Jeremy would have mentioned it when I received your kind invitation.'

'Hmm. I suppose not.' Lady Hartville regarded her with a keen eye. 'And Mr. Markingham is a frequent visitor to your lodgings in London, I imagine.'

'Yes, he often comes to take Jeremy up in his carriage, or to dine with us. He maintains a small establishment in the city, where Jeremy is allowed to run tame.'

Caroline found herself waiting for Lady Hartville's opinion of Markingham. The older woman, if occasionally too critical and frequently curious, did have a very sharp mind and a keen understanding of character. The guarded look on her ladyship's face puzzled Caroline, and alarmed her just the tiniest bit.

'Obviously an astute man,' Lady Hartville decreed with a mildness Caroline could have wished were more enthusiastic. 'He spoke of an estate in Surrey, was it?'

'Yes, somewhere in the vicinity of Epsom. Jeremy has been there several times. Mr. Markingham breeds horses for racing.'

'It is sometimes difficult for a young man of limited means to find himself in the company of an older man so much more plump in the pocket,' Lady Hartville mused.

Caroline felt the truth of this observation, though she wondered at her hostess's bringing the subject up so baldly. Jeremy was indeed a young man of very limited means, and he was frequently run ragged in his attempts to keep up with Markingham's circle. She had spoken to him about it on numerous occasions, only to be reassured that Markingham was the most generous of fellows and scarcely allowed Jeremy to pay for anything.

'Yes, it is difficult,' she agreed. 'A disparity in resources will always cause an imbalance in a friendship. The same problem exists between my friend Miss Salston and myself. But it is easier for me to resist the pleasures of the *ton* than it is for Jeremy.'

'Why do you suppose that is?' Lady Hartville queried, her eyes bright with curiosity.

Fortunately for Caroline, who had no wish to delve into the answer to that question, her brother and Giles Markingham joined the ladies at that point. Jeremy was insistent that Caroline play for them on the fine pianoforte which resided in the corner of the room. Though she had played for Lady Hartville and her son a few times, she had never sung. Her brother was astonished.

'You haven't sung for her ladyship?' he asked, frowning as fiercely as he was capable of doing. 'They haven't heard your voice? Caro, you are too exasperating.'

'There is nothing particularly wondrous about my voice, Jeremy,' Caroline demurred. 'You may be partial to it yourself, but . . . '

'Nothing particularly wondrous! What a gudgeon you are! There isn't a finer voice in England, and let me tell you I consider myself something of a judge.' He turned to his friend and demanded, 'Am I not, Markingham?'

His companion's countenance was all seriousness when he nodded, but the gleam of amusement in his eyes was not missed by either Caroline or Lady Hartville. Perhaps all Jeremy's tales of opera singers were not merely repeated gossip, but first hand observation, his sister thought. Knowing his love of music, she could readily picture him in the infamous Green Room at Covent Garden, though she rather hoped Markingham was not his companion on such occasions.

'Well, I am,' Jeremy maintained, using his forefinger to loosen the cravat which must have seemed suddenly a little tight. 'Come,' he admonished his sister. 'Show me what music her ladyship has, and I'll sing with you.'

He sorted rapidly through the sheaf of songs Caroline handed him, selecting one and placing it on the stand for her to play. 'We've done this one since we were children,' he remarked. 'I think perhaps our singing was the only reason Aunt Matilda took us in, don't you, Caro?'

Caroline could not believe that her brother was advancing such a theory right here in front of Lady Hartville and Giles Markingham. Never once in the dozen or so years since they were taken into Aunt Matilda's

98

home had he suggested such a thing. That they had literally sung for their supper at their aunt's house had always been an embarrassing realization for Caroline.

'Aunt Matilda was uncommonly fond of our singing,' she admitted as she seated herself at the pianoforte. 'Which was fortunate for us, because she did not hesitate to provide us with quite a good singing master. You wouldn't know half what you know today, Jeremy, if she hadn't.'

'Possibly not,' he said grudgingly, but bent and whispered in her ear so that only she could hear, 'The old nipcheese!'

Instead of scolding him, Caroline let her fingers play over the keys, picking out the chords that would open the song he'd chosen. And then the two of them were singing with that remarkable harmony that only siblings are able to create. Their voices soared and merged and dove and winged about the room like a pair of skylarks.

Having sung together all their lives, they knew precisely when to give full range to a line, and when to whisper it like a secret. Caroline came alive while singing in a way that she could not in any other occupation. She gloried in the music, absorbed the richness of its rhythm and gave voice to the joy she experienced when she sang.

As the last clear notes died from the room, Lady Hartville remained sitting forward in her chair, stunned. 'I had no idea,' she breathed.

'Remarkable, aren't they?' Markingham commented, with something of a proprietary air.

Caroline tried to ignore Lady Hartville's obvious astonishment and approbation. A well brought-up young woman did not bask in the glow of others' admiration. Jeremy had never felt himself under any such restriction, however, and he grinned at his hostess. 'We're good, ain't we? But I can't hold a candle to Caro for performing alone. Show her, Caro.'

His sister lifted her eyes heavenward. 'There never was anyone like Jeremy for putting me to the blush,' she said, allowing her fingers to run over the keys, teasing out the first notes of a ballad. She knew her brother well enough to know that he wasn't going to leave off until she did as he bid. With an apologetic smile at Lady Hartville, Caroline accompanied herself as she sang a breathtakingly beautiful version of 'Lord Lovell.'

There were tears in her ladyship's eyes when the song ended. Caroline had found that sometimes a particular song elicited a very emotional response from her listeners, so

100

such exhibits failed to alarm her. Jeremy, however, was dismayed.

'Whatever is the matter?' he beseeched the dowager, pulling a handkerchief from his pocket and pressing it into her hands. 'Are you all right? Has she sung the wrong song? She never meant to, you know.'

'No, no. It was perfect.' The dowager dabbed at the corner of her eye. 'I was reminded of the day I met my husband. His sister sang that song — only not nearly so well as Miss Carruthers.'

Jeremy shrugged. 'Well, if that's all . . . Here, Giles, pick something a little livelier and you sing with Caro. Mind, he doesn't have the voice I do, Lady Hartville, but he sounds pretty good with m'sister.'

'Anyone would sound good with your sister,' Markingham assured him, but he rose and moved to stand beside Caroline at the pianoforte.

It was not the first time they had sung together. Caroline treasured the occasions on which her brother's friend had joined her in song. There was something almost intimate about the blending of their voices, and always when Markingham sang with her he engaged her with his eyes.

Caroline found it difficult not to read too much into his gaze. As in a country dance, one's partner could gaze soulfully into one's eyes without being thought a hopeless rattle. But flirtation was not something that came easily to Caroline. She realized that other young women took such locked glances for granted, and made little more of them than they would have a profuse compliment on their charming smiles or glorious locks.

Not having spent much time in society, Caroline could not so easily dismiss a man's penetrating look, especially if that man was the darkly handsome Giles Markingham. And when the song they sang was one of love and longing, she could almost believe she saw those emotions in his eyes, as she certainly heard them in his expressive voice.

Thou art my life, my love, my heart,
The very eyes of me,
And hast command of every part,
To live and die for thee.

Foolish of her to take his musical expressions so to heart, but there it was.

Lady Hartville was regarding her closely when the song concluded. Though her hostess expressed her appreciation of the duet, she did not seem as enthusiastic as when Caroline sang alone or with her brother. The difference in her attitude was subtle, however, and Caroline could not be sure that she was not misreading the older woman.

'That's quite enough for one evening,' Caroline said as she rose from the bench and set aside the music. 'Jeremy and I have learned that even an appreciative audience tires rather quickly at a private gathering, have we not, dearest brother?'

'Indeed, though I think her ladyship would not have found one more song amiss, Caro.' Jeremy's eyes sparkled with mischief. 'However, this way folks beg us to come another day. As I'm sure your ladyship has been contemplating.'

Lady Hartville shook her head at his impudent playfulness. 'How long were you planning to be in the neighborhood, Mr.Carruthers?'

'Just another day, and I'd hoped to spend some time with Caro before we join the houseparty at Grassmere. Thought I could take her for a drive tomorrow, don't you know, if the weather is fine.'

Caroline hadn't the heart to protest this plan, and Lady Hartville appeared not at all averse to it. She turned to Mr. Markingham and said, 'Indeed, I hope you and Mr. Carruthers will join us for dinner tomorrow evening.'

'That's very kind of you, ma'am,' he said. His gaze traveled to Caroline as he added, 'We must certainly be on the road first thing the morning after, but it would be a pleasure to join you again tomorrow.'

Jeremy interjected his intention of arriving to take his sister driving the next morning. 'For Giles never minds my handling the ribbons and you really must see this pair, Caroline. They're slap up to the nines, I promise you.'

'I haven't a doubt of it.' But Caroline could see that Lady Hartville's energy was flagging in spite of how much she'd enjoyed the evening. 'Be off now, before Lady Hartville hears any more of your nonsense and changes her mind,' she advised.

Though Jeremy might have dismissed this suggestion, Markingham instantly arose and made his bows to the ladies. Caroline was grateful for his exquisite manners, and the deftness with which he moved her brother toward the door. She rewarded him with a grateful smile. He offered a quizzical tilt of his head, which made her pulses quicken. And then they were gone.

Caroline took Lady Hartville's arm and walked with her up the grand staircase toward her ladyship's suite of rooms in the main wing of the manor house. 'I trust you don't mind Jeremy's foolishness,' she said. 'He's accustomed to charming the ladies he encounters in London and thinks everyone will be as delighted with his patent nonsense.'

'I daresay I should be a bit more discriminating,' her ladyship replied with a sidewise glance at her companion, 'but I must admit to enjoying his gossip and tall tales and impudence. It can't be good for him to get away with it all the time, though.'

Caroline, suddenly serious, nodded her head in understanding. 'Exactly. That's why I think Mr. Markingham is a particularly good influence on Jeremy. He won't let Jeremy get away with any wild starts, or behave in a way that is beyond the line. A frown from him makes Jeremy reconsider and apologize for any indiscretion.'

'Does it? How very interesting.' They had arrived at her ladyship's door, and she placed her hand on Caroline's arm in a confiding way. 'Sometimes we place more confidence than we ought in other people. We come to depend on them when we should depend on ourselves.'

'I'm not sure I take your meaning, ma'am.'

'No, well, your brother must learn to be his own guide in such matters. He must develop his own sense of what is pleasing and what is not.'

'Did he say something to offend you, my lady?' Caroline asked anxiously.

'No, no.' Lady Hartville patted her companion's cheek. 'Just have a caution, my dear,' she said, and slipped into her room without allowing Caroline a chance to respond.

★   ★   ★

Caroline did not sleep well. Though she told herself it was because the night was chilly and the fire on her hearth fitful, she knew it had more to do with the way her mind restlessly grappled with several disturbing questions. Lady Hartville's words refused to be muffled by Caroline's attempts at stuffing the goosedown pillow over her ears. Were they a serious warning, or a mere passing comment? Did they apply to Jeremy, or to herself?

When midnight had passed and Caroline was still unable to wrest sleep from her bed, she sat up and leaned back against the headboard. The four poster had pale blue hangings that merely covered the head area of the bed. From where she sat, she could see out the window into tree tops, though there was very little moonlight to illuminate more than stark branches against the sky.

Caroline hugged herself as a chill shook her

body. She had just decided to climb out of bed and put more wood on the fire when she was surprised by a sound from overhead. The dull thump, like something heavy dropping, seemed to happen directly above her.

Running her mind over the layout of the house, she determined that the room above her must be the nursery, where Wilhelmina would be sleeping. Caroline realized that in the excitement of her brother and his friend coming to visit, she had not visited her young charge the previous evening. How very remiss of her!

And now, it seemed possible that the child had fallen out of bed. Certainly something had happened to make such a thump, and whatever it was, it needed investigating. She pulled a robe about her shoulders and slid her feet into cold slippers. The candle she'd brought up to bed with her was sitting on the bedside table, but in the darkness she was unable to locate the flint with which to light it. There were no glowing embers on the hearth to accomplish her purpose either. With a shrug of annoyance, Caroline abandoned the candle and crossed to her door.

Silence reigned once again in the house. The servants were long since abed, no doubt. Caroline opened her door into a dark corridor and felt a tremor of trepidation. She was not entirely familiar with the attic floor of the manor, and a light would have been most appreciated. But the thought of Wilhelmina in some distress made Caroline close her door behind her and step quickly along the hall to where she knew another door led to the staircase above.

Her eyes were growing accustomed to the heavy shadows as she turned the corner and felt along the wall for the door. To her surprise it was not closed as she'd assumed it would be, and a frisson snaked down her back.

Nonsense, she told herself bracingly. There is not a thing to fear in this perfectly ordinary house. If the door is open, it merely means that someone forgot to close it. Probably Meg, who is not familiar with the routines here at Berwick.

Caroline listened for a moment at the foot of the stairs, but could hear nothing from above her. Finally, with determination, she set foot on the first carpeted step. It gave a deep protest, startling her and making her pause for a moment. Still, there was no sound from above, so she quickly climbed to the top, trying to ignore the loud squeals made by her passage.

Why had she never noticed how noisy these stairs were?

9

At the head of the stairs was a high window, but even with her eyes accustomed to the dark Caroline was not able to see anything outside the black square. The corridors here were narrow, heading to her right and left. The nursery was likely to be the first door down to her right. Caroline placed one hand against the wall to judge its distance away from her. The wall felt rough and cold, but she eased her fingers along it as she progressed toward the door.

Because Mrs. Bluestone had been the one to discuss Meg's duties with her, Caroline did not know if the nursery maid would be sharing a room with Wilhelmina. Perhaps she slept in the room across the hall. Caroline's fingers encountered the door frame, and then discovered that this door, too, was open.

'Wilhelmina,' she whispered, so as not to frighten the child. 'Are you there?'

'Yes,' said a small voice. 'Who is it?'

'It's Miss Carruthers. I thought I heard a noise come from your room. Are you all right?'

'Yes,' said the small voice again, but this time it quavered.

Caroline stepped into the room. Her eyes were able to pick out the white bed linens, and she moved in that direction. 'Is Meg with you?'

'She went to the kitchen to get me some hot milk.'

'Ah.' That explained a good deal, Caroline thought. 'Were you unable to sleep?'

'I had bad dreams,' Wilhelmina admitted. 'I was scared.'

'Poor love.' Caroline knew she'd reached the bed when she stubbed her toe against it. 'May I sit down?'

'Yes, ma'am.'

Caroline carefully seated herself beside the little girl. 'You know that bad dreams are just in your head, don't you? That they're not real?'

'Molly said they can't hurt you.' There was a long pause. 'But why are they there?'

'I'm not sure,' Caroline admitted. She felt Wilhelmina's hand slip into hers and she gave it a squeeze. 'Were you worried about something?'

Again there was a long pause. 'The Fine Man doesn't like me.'

'Oh, Wilhelmina, that's not true! Lord Hartville hasn't had a chance to get to know you yet.'

'But he's angry with me.'

'No, he's not angry with you. He's upset because JoJo thought he was your father, and he doesn't believe he is.'

'Wouldn't he know?'

Caroline knew this was getting too complicated for a five-year-old. It was too complicated for *her*. She sighed. 'Not necessarily, my dear. But he intends to see that you're well taken care of.'

'Will he keep me here?'

'I don't know.' Caroline shifted on the bed so she could look directly into Wilhelmina's eyes. 'But no matter what he decides, he'll make certain that you have a good place to live.'

'Could I stay with you?'

Since Caroline had no good answer for this question, it was fortunate that suddenly they heard the sounds of Meg climbing the stairs. A flicker of candlelight made its way into the room as the nursery maid moved toward them. Caroline was reminded that she didn't know what had caused the noise she'd heard.

'Did you fall out of bed, Wilhelmina?'

The child shook her head.

'Did something fall on the floor in your room?'

'I don't know. I think I fell asleep after Meg left, and something wakened me.'

'Perhaps Meg will know what it was,' Caroline said, and turned toward the door in time to see the candlelight flicker and die.

Or had the candle been blown out?

'Meg?' Caroline called, a little nervously.

There was no response from the hall. The footsteps had stopped. *Someone* was outside the room. Caroline felt her heartbeat speed up. What was this all about?

'Meg?' she said again, louder. Behind her she could feel Wilhelmina shrink down under the covers.

And then the footsteps in the hall retreated. Caroline could hear them move toward the stairs, and then down the squeaking steps with no hesitation, despite the darkness. She jumped up and hurried from the room, but all was black outside. Rushing to the head of the stairs, she could see the slight difference in light as the door below swung closed.

Though Caroline felt she should pursue this intruder — something she did not at all wish to do — her first concern was to reassure Wilhelmina. She found the child hunkered down, her head completely covered. 'Everything is all right, Wilhelmina. Whoever it was has gone.'

From under the blankets a small voice asked, 'Who was it?'

'Well, I suppose it was one of the servants,'

Caroline suggested, improvising wildly. 'Someone new here, who came up the wrong stairs, and then realized she'd got the wrong place.'

'But why didn't she answer?'

'Perhaps because she was shy. Or thought she'd be scolded for being in the wrong part of the house.'

'But where is Meg?'

A good question, Caroline realized. Where was the nursery maid? Possibly still in the kitchen getting Wilhelmina's warm milk. Caroline decided she was going to have to go and find out. But she couldn't very well leave Wilhelmina here alone when something strange was going on, could she?

'Here's what we'll do,' she said. 'You come with me to my room and stay there while I find out what's keeping Meg. My room is on the floor below and you'll be safe there.'

Wilhelmina's head came slowly out from under the covers. 'I could come with you to the kitchen,' the child said bravely.

'Oh, I don't think that's necessary.' Caroline riffled the girl's tousled blond hair, and then ran her hand along the bedside table until she found a flint and a candle. When she had finally produced a flame, she added, 'No need for both of us to wander about the place in the middle of the night. Here, let's put

113

your robe and slippers on, so you'll be warm.'

Wilhelmina allowed herself to be wrapped up and guided down to the floor below. She was obviously overwhelmed by the grandeur of Caroline's room. Her eyes grew even larger when Caroline assured her that she might lie down in Caroline's four poster bed with its draped canopy of pale blue material. 'You won't mind?' she breathed.

'Not at all.' Caroline lifted the slight child into her bed and smiled down at her. 'Do you think you'll feel safe here? Do you want me to leave the door open?'

'Yes, please.'

'Fine. I'll be back as soon as I can.'

Wilhelmina nodded with a small measure of confidence. Caroline looked around the room to see if she could find something that would interest a five-year-old. On her dresser was a handcarved box of inexpensive jewelry, most of which she'd been given by her brother and her aunt over the years. 'You might like to look at these,' she suggested, holding up a locket to demonstrate what she had in mind.

'Oh, that's like mine,' Wilhelmina said. She tugged the chain out from under her night dress for Caroline to see. 'I wear it all the time.'

Caroline had an odd feeling, staring at the

child's locket. But she said nothing, merely bringing her box across and setting it on the coverlet beside Wilhelmina. 'You can try on anything you wish. I'll be back as soon as I can.'

Instantly distracted, the girl dipped into the box and was examining a ring when Caroline hurriedly left to discover what had become of Meg.

As she moved down the corridor, her candle throwing wild shadows on the walls, Caroline thought she could hear something from the floor below. A thumping, a muffled voice, but quite a distance away. She was not feeling especially brave. Whatever was going on here, she wished Lord Hartville were home to see that it was taken care of. Trust a man to be off somewhere when he was needed at home!

The noises she was hearing did not seem to grow appreciably louder as she glided down the massive staircase leading to the front hall. Only when she arrived at the checkerboard of black and white tile did Caroline realize that Meg would have taken the servants' staircase which led down to the service areas on the ground floor. There was no candle left burning in the hall, as she and Jeremy had a habit of doing in their small flat in London. Everything was black beyond the range of her candlelight — black and distressingly unfamiliar at this hour of the night.

For all Caroline could tell, there might be someone waiting in those deep shadows, or hidden behind the closed doors off the hall. There had certainly been someone on the nursery floor who did not belong there. But, she reminded herself, if that person had meant to do her or Wilhelmina harm, it would have happened up there in the attics where it was least likely the noise would penetrate to the living quarters of either Lady Hartville or the servants.

She mentally girded her loins and turned toward the back of the hall. Meg *had* to be down here somewhere, and it was most likely she was in the kitchen. Caroline pushed her way through the green baize door and hastened past the storage rooms and offices to the kitchen at the very back of the building. Now the noises were becoming more distinct — and what they sounded like was someone pounding on a door and calling out.

The door to the main room of the kitchen was closed. As she approached, Caroline could smell burned milk. The pounding echoed down the hall from the solid oak panels. A muffled voice, angry, and probably frightened, kept calling words that had become clear now: 'Let me out! Let me out!'

Since Caroline could think of no reason on earth for the door to be locked, she was puzzled by this cry. And yet, when she tried the handle, the door did not open. The handle turned as though it would, but nothing happened. On the other side came renewed pounding.

'Is that you, Meg?' she called.

There was an abrupt silence, and then a tentative reply. 'Yes, it's me. Who's that?'

'It's Miss Carruthers. I don't seem to be able to open the door from this side, either.'

'I don't think it's locked, Miss. I didn't hear a key turn in the door.'

Caroline held her candle closer to the door, and could not even find a keyhole. So she lowered the candle to floor level and saw that a wedge had been shoved under the door, effectively blocking it from opening. When she kicked at the wedge from the side, it didn't budge. 'Hold on. A wedge is in so tightly that I'll need to find something to get it out.'

She tried three of the storage rooms before she found a drawerful of tools. Both the hammer and the mallet seemed to offer possibilities and she carried them back with her. But the wedge was so close to the wall, she couldn't get much purchase to knock it out of the way. Perhaps the best solution was to waken one of the footmen, but she was loathe to do that in the middle of the night. Somehow it seemed wise to keep this whole situation from becoming a rumor throughout the household.

So, with encouraging words to Meg, she began a slow, steady hammering at the wedge. Gradually, it seemed to loosen, and finally it popped out from under the door. Caroline drew the door open and Meg practically fell into her arms. The kitchen was in complete darkness.

'You poor dear,' Caroline said, giving the young woman a bracing hug. 'Whatever happened?'

Meg took several deep breaths, trying to steady her nerves, Caroline thought. 'Well, miss, I'm not quite sure. The little one had bad dreams, and I came down to get her some warm milk to help her sleep. I've been at the Hall before, you see, and I knew where the milk was and a saucepan to warm it up. Cook always leaves a fire going in one of the ovens so it's easier to start in the morning.'

Meg led her to the stove, where a scorched saucepan with all the milk boiled away rested on a burner. 'Cook is not going to be happy about that,' she said, grabbing a towel and removing the pan to the sink. 'But you see, miss, when I was waiting for the milk to warm, my candle went out. I'd left it there,' she said, pointing to a cabinet where only a cup now rested. 'I can see that it's not there now, but I promise you that is where I put it. When it went out, I walked in the dark over here, but it was gone.'

Her cheeks were flushed and her eyes determined, as though she expected Caroline to insist that this wasn't possible. Instead, Caroline nodded. 'I see. And then what happened?'

'Mmm. Well, I felt around on the counter for a long time, but there was no sign of it. Not knowing where there would be any candles, I started to open drawers and dig in bins, but I didn't find anything. So I decided to go into the hall, since no one was up, and find a candle and flint there. That was when I found the door wouldn't budge.'

'And you didn't hear anyone who might have blown out your candle and taken it away, or pushed the wedge under the door?'

Meg eyed her companion skeptically. 'But who would do such a thing, ma'am?'

'I don't know, but there must have been someone, Meg. Candles do not walk off by themselves, and wedges don't stick themselves under doors.'

'No, miss. What are we to do?'

'I'll get Bluestone and explain the situation. He and the footmen really should make a complete search of the house to see if there's any sign of an intruder.'

Caroline shook her head with frustration. 'They won't believe us, you know. They'll think we're imagining things — missing candles, wedges under doors, things that go bump in the night. Which reminds me, Meg. Before you came downstairs, did you hear something fall onto the floor with a thump?'

'Not as I recall, miss. Wilhelmina cried out in her sleep and told me she'd had a bad dream. I thought some warm milk might help her, so I came down.'

'Did you leave her in the dark?'

Meg looked instantly indignant. ''Course not! I lit both candles and put one on the dresser before I left so she wouldn't be afraid.'

'The room was dark when I got there,' Caroline explained. 'The candle might have blown out, of course. But there's something else. After I'd been sitting with her a while there were footsteps on the stairs. Someone carrying a candle came down the hall, but then suddenly the candle-light was gone and the footsteps retreated down the stairs.'

'Mercy! You didn't leave the poor child there alone?'

'No, she's in my room. Why don't you stay with her now, and I'll talk with Bluestone?'

'Very well, miss.'

Caroline set in motion a search of the house which, as she had predicted, none of the footmen took particularly seriously. Bluestone himself was skeptical, but Mrs. Bluestone had listened to Caroline with a worried frown on her brow. When they were alone in the housekeeper's room, Mrs. Bluestone said, 'I suppose it might be one of the servants up to some mischief. Playing a prank on Meg, perhaps. But it don't sound like any of ours, you see. They're a good lot, even the young ones.'

'I know.' Caroline drew her dressing gown more closely about her. 'Do you think I should wake Lady Hartville?'

The housekeeper nodded. 'Much as I don't like to have to. But, mark my words, she'll fret if she's left out. I do wish Lord Hartville weren't off gallivanting.'

For the first time since she'd awakened, Caroline chuckled. 'Is that what he's doing? Off gallivanting?'

Mrs. Bluestone shook her head at Caroline's teasing. ''Twere an expression, Miss Carruthers. Like as not he's gone to bail out another relative. It happens all the time.'

'Does it? I had no idea.' Caroline tucked

her cold hands in the pockets of her dressing gown and turned to leave. 'I'll speak with Lady Hartville. No doubt Bluestone will report to her if they find anything amiss. Or even if they don't.'

What the search party found was inconclusive. Caroline and Lady Hartville received Bluestone's report in Lady Hartville's sitting room: A window had been open in the dining room, but that might have been an oversight of the footman locking up. There had been a candle found on the floor down the hall from the kitchen. The wedge that had stuck the kitchen door tight was one frequently used to hold it open. The latter two things, Bluestone intimated, could have occurred if Meg had been careless in handling her candle or pushing the door open in her panic.

Lady Hartville didn't comment beyond saying, 'Thank you, Bluestone. Have everyone keep a keen eye out for anything missing or out of the ordinary in the morning, won't you? And please, have Mr. Davis send off for Hartville at daybreak.'

'Yes, my lady.'

When Bluestone had bowed and retreated, Lady Hartville turned to her companion. 'Nothing quite like this has ever happened here before. In fact, the last few days seem to have been filled with unusual occurrences.

First a child is deposited on our doorstep, then I have another episode of illness. And now we have an intruder in the house. What do you make of it, my dear?'

'I hardly know what to make of it, ma'am. Do you think Lord Hartville could be back by tomorrow night? I must confess I'd feel a deal safer with him in the Hall.'

'Well, if he isn't, perhaps your brother and Mr. Markingham could stay here with us.'

10

Lord Hartville actually encountered the groom who had been sent with the message when he was halfway back to Berwick Hall. His business concluded, if only slightly satisfactorily, he was determined to make it back home by midafternoon at the latest. When he saw Thomas cantering one of the Berwick Hall horses, the first thing he'd thought was, Oh, my God. Mother.

'Is her ladyship ill?' he demanded as Thomas drew in his horse and reached inside his coat for the message.

'No, sir. Leastways, that ain't what everyone's in a stew about,' the groom said darkly.

Hartville frowned. 'What *are* they in a stew about?'

'I reckon Bluestone has 'splained it, sir. Probably all a big hoax.'

The folded note was proffered and accepted. Hartville scanned its contents and his frown deepened. 'Do you know this girl Meg?'

Thomas nodded. 'A solid one, sir. Gladys's sister. Not one to be making up things. But that don't mean someone else ain't humbug-ging the lot of us.'

Hartville fingered the sheet of paper, considering the possibilities. 'Well, Miss Carruthers is hardly likely to be party to that kind of nonsense. Do we have any new people at the Hall?'

'There's a stable boy, but he were in the stable all night. I'd swear to that. And what would he be doin' in the Hall?'

'What would *anyone* be doing there?' Hartville asked as he tucked the note into his pocket. The fact that Bluestone was wont to dismiss the incident did not weigh so heavily with him as the fact that his mother had instructed that he be sent for. Or that Miss Carruthers had been a participant in the events and swore to their accuracy. Cousin Caroline was no one's fool.

Hartville had found himself thinking of his young relative during the long hours of riding on his mission to investigate Francis Carruthers's claims on his purse. When he had discovered that Francis's problem could be settled with a fifty pound payment to the ostler at the inn, Hartville had imagined the pungent things Caroline might have had to say about the ramshackle Francis.

But Hartville had not forgotten that Caroline herself had come to Berwick Hall under some sort of cloud. He was determined to find out what mischief she'd been up to, with or without his mother's help.

'Then there was the two gentlemen,' Thomas offered.

Lost in his thoughts, Hartville took a moment to realize that Thomas was still considering new people at the hall. He stared at the groom. 'What two gentlemen?'

'Them as came to dinner last night. Toffs they was. One of 'em Miss Carruthers's brother, so they said. But they left afore ten, and all the ruckus happened after midnight.'

Hartville decided he'd been rash to leave Berwick when he had. 'Thanks for bringing the message, Thomas. Stay and have a wet one and a meal at the Goose and Sage. We won't look for you at Berwick until this evening.'

And with that he tossed a coin which the groom neatly caught, and urged Warrior forward into a canter.

★ ★ ★

The light of day had brought a little peace of mind to Caroline. Yes, she still believed that what she'd seen and heard had in fact happened, but she also thought its having happened in the dark in the middle of the

126

night might have added to the menace she'd felt. Perhaps after all there was some innocent explanation — some servant bent on a lark which had got out of hand, or even someone who had been too embarrassed to come forward when an explanation was needed.

Meg and Wilhelmina were once more on the nursery floor, with a footman checking up on them regularly. A sensible girl, Meg accepted that at least during the day nothing untoward was likely to happen. Wilhelmina, promised the treat of going down to the home farm to see the animals, seemed to have forgotten all about the incidents of the previous night.

Lady Hartville maintained her room, though she swore to Caroline that she was not feeling any the worse for the night's upsets. Caroline executed the duties she'd taken on in her ladyship's absence, ordering the meals and consulting with Mrs. Bluestone about plans for the upcoming wash day. But her ear was tuned for the arrival of her brother and his friend, and she was not disappointed.

The two young men made their appearance soon after Caroline had dined alone on a light nuncheon in the breakfast parlor. Instead of waiting for them to come into the Hall, she hurried down the side stairs and met them as

127

they drew into the stable yard.

It was Jeremy who had the reins in hand, with Markingham seated beside him. The pair of bays was matched for more than color and size. Caroline could see that their strides were precisely the same as well. They were a real treat for the eye, complementing Markingham's deep burgundy carriage with its black wheels.

Jeremy brought the horses to a swift halt, grinning at his sister as he did so. 'There never were such sweet goers!' he exclaimed. 'Even you could handle them.'

Caroline looked indignant. '*Even* me? You know I'm not half as cow-handed as your friend Benjamin.'

'Well, he don't bear hearing about,' Jeremy agreed as he jumped down from the carriage and handed the reins to a groom. 'That last stretch was a good place to show Giles the maneuver I learned from Harrison last week. And *he's* a member of the Four Horse Club.'

Markingham had descended by this time and approached Caroline with his usual look of amused tolerance for Jeremy. 'Your brother has certainly become quite the whip, Miss Carruthers. He drives to an inch, as he proved by only barely scraping that tree you pass coming out of town.'

'Not a bit of it,' Jeremy protested. 'He'd have you thinking I scraped his precious carriage. At most the wheel just barely rubbed the tree trunk. Who would have thought they'd leave a tree right at the turn that way?'

'It was there yesterday,' Markingham commented, but with no rancor. 'And how are you today, Miss Carruthers? And Lady Hartville?'

'Her ladyship is fine, I think, but maintains her room. There was a bit of excitement here last night, however.'

She proceeded to enlighten them about the night's intruder, but Jeremy was inclined to pooh-pooh the story. 'Just one of the servants, I'd wager a quid.' Markingham expressed more concern, but seemed satisfied that no one had been harmed. They accepted her invitation to take tea, and followed her into the hall. Caroline had arranged to have them served some of cook's best cakes. Her brother was most appreciative, assuring her he had had nothing finer in the last twelvemonth at least.

'When's his lordship due back?' he asked as he helped himself to one more confection.

'He was supposed to return tomorrow, but Lady Hartville has sent for him.'

Markingham's brows rose. 'She takes the night's events seriously, then.'

'Oh, yes. You see, we're all a little

concerned about Wilhelmina.'

Jeremy regarded her blankly, and Markingham with polite interest. 'Haven't I told you about Wilhelmina?' Caroline asked, surprised. 'But then I wouldn't have, yesterday. It's a rather odd story. She's a child of perhaps five who was left here a few days ago.'

'Left here? Who left her?' Jeremy asked, puzzled.

'A man brought her, saying only that she belonged here. The child seems to think that Lord Hartville is her father.'

Jeremy whistled. 'Pretty rum doings for a viscount. What does *he* say about it?'

'That he's not her father.' Caroline set her cup down carefully on the fragile saucer. 'But he's agreed to keep her here for the time being.'

'I see what it is.' Jeremy grinned. 'You couldn't bear to see some little moppet sent off to an orphanage, could you, my soft-hearted sister? And you totally unnerved the poor viscount and convinced him that she should stay here.'

Caroline offered a rueful smile. 'Something like that. Well, she's just a child and *we* know what orphanages are, don't we?'

Her brother had the grace to flush. 'Now, Caro, no one ever really meant for us to end up there.' He turned to Markingham with a

130

careless shrug. 'Before my aunt agreed to take us in, there was some discussion of our being put in an orphanage, what with both our parents being killed in an accident. Turned out they hadn't tuppence between them. There were debts, the house we lived in was rented, and so on and so on. I remember our nanny taking us to inspect the local orphanage. Thought she was going to leave us there, too.'

Markingham looked shocked. 'But that's absurd. Some provision must have been made for you.'

'None, I'm afraid,' Caroline admitted. 'Our parents were not especially responsible. But thank heaven Aunt Matilda chose to take us in.'

'How old were you at the time?' Markingham asked.

'Jeremy was seven and I was ten.'

'What a dreadful situation.' Markingham's gaze locked with Caroline's, his dark eyes full of compassion. 'And I dare say it wasn't easy being the 'poor relations' at your aunt's, either.'

Jeremy snorted. 'Exactly so! But enough about that. It's in the past, thank God. And for the present I have the greatest wish to take my sister for a drive to the village and back. Since the three of us can't sit on the seat, perhaps Giles could borrow one of Hartville's horses, eh?'

'I'm sure he wouldn't mind. He put me on a dear little mare called Holly, but I suppose she'd be a little tame for Mr. Markingham.'

Though Markingham protested that he would willingly accept the mare, Jeremy scoffed at such sacrifice. 'For depend upon it, his lordship has good cattle. We'll just mention to the head groom that you breed race horses, Markingham, and before we know it they'll mount you on their best just to prove how splendid their stable is.'

'Well, their best is probably with Lord Hartville,' Caroline said, but she did not dispute Jeremy's reasoning, which as usual was dead-on accurate, if just as familiarly on the self-serving side. Having had very little all his life, Jeremy had developed a charming cockiness which had served him well in getting what he wanted. Though it often made Caroline cringe at his presumption, she had long since given up trying to curb his spirits and determination. As he always said in rebuttal, 'My dear sister, if you don't ask for something, you are certainly not going to be given it!'

The head groom led a powerful chestnut gelding from the stables. 'This is our fastest,' he said. 'Never been in a real race, mind you, but his lordship has been known to place a private bet on him. Bit temperamental, he is, so have a care.'

Jeremy threw a cocky wink at his sister as he helped her into the carriage. Despite the horse's skittishness, Markingham mounted the gelding with elegant ease. They were just turning toward the lane when a young woman and a child emerged from the Hall. Both Jeremy and Markingham studied the pair, then turned inquiring eyes on Caroline.

'Yes, that's Wilhelmina, with the nursery maid. They must be on their way to the home farm for her promised treat.'

'An attractive child,' Markingham remarked.

'No wonder you didn't want her sent off to an orphanage,' Jeremy muttered. 'You must have looked very much like that when you were her age, Caro.'

'Perhaps that's it,' Caroline agreed, her gaze following the child as she skipped across the courtyard. 'But she could be Lord Hartville's child. She has eyes very like his.'

'Ah, so you're looking at the viscount's eyes, are you?' her brother teased as he gathered up the reins and urged the horses forward.

'It's a little hard to miss them when we're all dining *en famille*,' she said tartly. 'Rest assured he has no more interest in me than in a headache.'

Since Caroline was aware that Markingham could not overhear them as they started down the lane, she added, 'His lordship has spent two weeks avoiding me whenever possible.'

'I can't imagine why. You're not a bad-looking girl, when you're done up.'

Caroline laughed. 'Why, thank you, Jeremy. I do believe that was meant as a compliment.'

'Of course it was. What else would it be?' But the question was rhetorical. Jeremy had turned his attention to the horses and began pointing out their finer points. 'Would you look at those shoulders? And watch this, Caro. I can make them fall into a different gait by merely curling my whip like this.'

Markingham now rode past them and allowed his horse's stride to lengthen. As proud as Jeremy was of his driving skills, he knew very well that his friend was by far the more expert horseman. But in London Caroline hadn't seen Markingham riding at anything more than the sedate pace required by the city's congestion. Here, she saw that he was testing his mount's mettle, with every evidence of enjoyment.

Though the groom had referred to the horse as Touched, Caroline thought the name she'd seen on his stall was Touchatt. But he might very well have been Touched by some god of speed, given the pace he achieved on the dusty road. Markingham maintained his elegant seat as the gelding seemed to almost fly down the straightaway. Within minutes the horse and rider were so far ahead of the carriage that they were specks on the horizon.

'Bet you a pony he makes an offer for that horse,' Jeremy said. 'Faster than anything I've seen on his stud farm, except for maybe one or two of them.'

'Really?' Caroline was no expert on horseflesh, either in terms of body part or speed, but somehow it did not surprise her that Hartville would be a good judge of horses or that he would own an animal of particular value. She believed he would always have good judgment, and take care in selecting his belongings. Of course, he had the wherewithal to purchase whatever he wished, she reminded herself.

'By Jove, yes. I think I'd like to ride that horse!' Jeremy exclaimed. 'Maybe Giles will exchange with me in town.'

When they drew into the village, narrowly missing the tree which, according to Jeremy, really oughtn't to be where it was, they found Markingham dismounted and talking with Mrs. Biggins. The shopkeeper disappeared into her store before they had brought the carriage to a halt, but she soon returned, bearing a wrapped parcel. 'These are the shoes for the little girl, miss,' she said to Caroline. 'And one of the dresses.'

As Caroline thanked her, she could hear her brother bargaining with Mr. Markingham about who would ride and who would drive on the way back to the Hall. The thought of driving with Mr. Markingham pleased Caroline, and it reminded her of the various trinkets Mrs. Biggins had for sale inside the shop.

'I need to just step inside for a moment,' she told her brother.

Jeremy paid very little attention, but his companion smiled and shook his head. 'We'll be here waiting for you, Miss Carruthers,' he said.

Caroline had the strongest urge to purchase the rouleau of roses she'd seen the last time she was in the shop. Jeremy had seen her gowns so many times that he must surely be bored to tears with them. The rouleau would make practically a new gown of her pale yellow round dress.

Knowing they would drive into the village, she had spirited a few coins in her purse. In the dim interior of Mrs. Biggins's shop she pulled them out. Probably there were more important things that she should spend them on, but at the moment she could not restrain the impulse to have something pretty and new.

The contents of the little bin of ornaments had changed somewhat, and for a moment Caroline feared that the little rouleau was gone. She dug carefully through the various ribbons and clips and silk flowers. And there was the rouleau of yellow roses, just as she remembered it. Triumphantly she lifted it from the bin and handed it across to Mrs. Biggins. 'I'll have this, please.'

'Lovely,' Mrs. Biggins murmured. 'And the hair clip that matches? Did you see it?'

Caroline had not, but she declined to purchase it.

Mrs. Biggins continued to dig through the assorted ornaments. 'Oh, the price on the rouleau is for the both of them,' she insisted, finally unearthing a hair clip with a delicate bunch of yellow silk roses. 'It will look a treat in your hair, miss, all golden as it is.'

Though she suspected that Mrs. Biggins had never had the intention of selling both items for the price of one, Caroline was enchanted with the hair clip. 'Thank you so much, Mrs. Biggins. I shall wear it tonight.'

11

When Caroline emerged from the store, she
found that Jeremy was mounted on Touched
and Markingham waiting to hand her into the
carriage. Jeremy grinned at her and said, 'I've
made him promise that he'll let you handle
the reins, at least for a short while.'

She glanced at Markingham, who cocked
his head at her and nodded. 'If it is your
pleasure, Miss Carruthers, then you shall
have your turn at being a whip.'

'You must think me a veritable hoyden,
Mr. Markingham,' she said as she allowed
him to hand her into the carriage.

'Not at all. Jeremy assures me it will not be
your first such attempt. I did just wonder,' he
said, his voice lowered sufficiently not to
reach her brother, 'where it was you had
practiced this skill on previous occasions.
London seems a rather unnerving place to
begin one's career as a driver.'

He sprang up and seated himself beside
her, gathering the reins in his gloved hands.
Caroline knew that her own gloves would not
protect her hands as well, but they would
have to suffice. She answered, 'Jeremy drove

me to Richmond, once, and on another occasion to Hampstead Heath. Both places were far less crowded than in the center of the city.'

She was conscious of his closeness and his interest. His dark eyes seemed to linger on her lips when she spoke. Caroline felt the pulse in her throat throbbing and hoped that he could not see it. To break eye contact with him she leaned down and pushed the parcels for Wilhelmina and her own purchase under the seat. But when she raised her head again, his gaze was still on her.

With apparent effort he turned his attention to his horses, guiding them away from the row of shops and out past the poplars and onto the road toward Berwick Hall. Jeremy, impatient to test his horse's mettle, waved a hand at them and urged Touched forward. Caroline could see that he wasn't the elegant rider Markingham was, but he managed to control the horse well enough and was soon almost out of sight.

It occurred to her that she had never actually been alone with Markingham before. There was nothing inappropriate about it, of course. This was merely a drive in the country, their destination known, her chaperone brother at no real distance away. And yet Caroline felt especially alert, and perhaps a little daring. Aunt Matilda would not have approved of Jeremy leaving her alone with such a presentable young man.

The bays moved along at a good clip, and Caroline and her companion swayed with the well-sprung carriage. The spring day was slightly overcast, but no rain threatened.

Markingham smiled across at her, a lazy sort of smile. 'The wind has given your cheeks some color, Miss Carruthers. And your eyes are especially bright. A little fresh air brings out the best in you.'

'Why, thank you.' Caroline's eyes dropped to her hands. 'I'm afraid London air is not quite so bracing.'

'No, indeed. Nor is there half the opportunity there for enjoying oneself outdoors. Country life has a great deal to recommend itself.'

'Even to you?' she asked, teasing. 'I thought you were the consummate London gentleman — pistols at Mantons, sparring with Gentleman Jackson, balls and routs and gambling and your clubs on Bond Street. Jeremy vastly admires your ability to take advantage of every pleasure of the city.'

'Jeremy is young. He's still sowing his oats.'

'And you're not?' Caroline asked with a daring Aunt Matilda would certainly not have approved of.

His lips twisted ruefully. 'I believe I'm past that stage of my development. Even the most hardened *bon vivant* can find himself at a standstill. There comes a time when simply entertaining oneself doesn't seem a wholly satisfying pursuit.'

'Really? Well, I hope Jeremy will arrive at that point before he finds himself completely under the hatches.'

'Jeremy hasn't been struck by lightning yet, I fear,' Markingham said enigmatically.

Caroline could not ask him if *he* had been. But she thought he meant precisely that, and even perhaps that she was the bolt that had struck him. His eyes remained intent on her until she almost shuddered with the sense of possession he seemed to convey.

Foolish girl, she warned herself. He was much too sophisticated and wealthy to be interested in a poor, green, and *aged* woman such as herself. 'Will you let me handle the reins now?' she asked.

'Gladly.'

Caroline was surprised when he reined the horses to a complete stop. Jeremy was in the precarious habit of merely handing the reins over to her as they barrelled along. Markingham had no such intention.

'Hold your hands like this,' he instructed, showing her the angle at which she would have the most control. 'No, in a little more.' He reached over to correct the amount of turn to her left hand. 'That's right.'

His hip of necessity pressed firmly against hers as he made sure she had a good grip. When he indicated that she should start, Caroline made the clicking sound with her teeth that she had heard Jeremy use. Markingham laughed. 'Not all horses have been trained to your voice, Miss Carruthers. Give the reins a flip.'

This proved to be an awkward movement for Caroline, and the horses did not budge. Markingham put an arm around her and grasped each of her hands with one of his. 'Like this,' he said, flipping the reins with an expert movement.

The horses immediately took off, and Markingham's arm was still around Caroline. 'Now draw them in again,' he said, indicating how she was to manage that maneuver. She could feel his considerable strength as he pulled back on the smooth leather. 'You try it,' he said.

Caroline was totally disconcerted because his arm was still around her. She swallowed hard and forced herself to flip the reins vigorously. After the horses had moved some paces down the road, Markingham indicated that she was to draw them in again. Caroline did so successfully, and only then did Markingham remove his arm.

So far as she could see, their physical proximity had meant nothing to him. But she felt a heightened awareness of him, his closeness, his strength, his skill. She wondered what it would be like to be held in his arms, and she deeply regretted that she would not be able to waltz with him at her friend Miss Salston's ball.

★   ★   ★

Hartville had made good time coming cross country on Warrior. Every hill and dale of the area was familiar to him, and he had neither the need nor the inclination to stick to the main roads. Though he was only vaguely alarmed about what was happening at his estate, he did feel a particular urgency to be home.

Just as he trotted out from the woods and into a field beyond, a carriage on the road caught his attention. He was more than fifty yards from the scene, and he could not be certain, but it looked as though a man had drawn his horses to a halt and was in the process of making up to the woman beside him. A most unseemly sight, to be sure.

But what offended his lordship most was

143

that the woman, even from this distance, appeared to be Miss Carruthers. No one else he knew in the neighborhood had such long blond hair. And that stupid little hat of hers — the one she'd worn the day they drove into town — could not be mistaken. Surely it was the same offensive brown bird's nest on the woman.

He saw the carriage start forward with a jerk and then the horses were slowly reined in. And then the carriage started forward and was reined in *again*. Hartville could feel his temper rising. What the devil did the girl think she was doing, allowing some man to manhandle her that way? No wonder his mother believed Cousin Caroline had gotten into trouble. Hartville could see that she was lucky to be considered presentable at all!

When the carriage started forward for the third time, the man — Hartville would not dignify him with the label gentleman — removed his arms from around the female. But Hartville could see now that the fellow didn't have hold of the ribbons at all. For a moment he thought the horses were running off with the carriage, and was about to spur Warrior to the gallop. But the bays were doing nothing more than trotting solidly down the road, with Miss Carruthers handling the ribbons. All then became clear

144

to Hartville, but his understanding did not restore him to an amiable frame of mind.

Where the devil was the girl's brother? What did he mean by leaving her alone with some practiced rake to teach her how to drive? And then he saw a man on Touchatt, riding hell for leather toward the carriage, and he decided he didn't want to know anything more about the lot of them!

It did occur to Hartville. as he rode slowly toward the trio on the road, that perhaps it *was* Miss Carruthers's brother in the carriage, and that the other man was a companion. But the closer he got to them, the more easily he could see that the fellow on Touchatt was blond and had a cast of features similar to the young woman seated in the carriage. Indeed, the young man could have been nothing less than a relative, given his spirited teasing of Miss Carruthers's skill, which Hartville could discern as he drew within hearing distance of the group.

He had ridden parallel to them and just behind, so that they weren't aware of his presence until just before he drew quite close. Miss Carruthers was the first to see him, and he thought she looked a trifle guilty, her cheeks bright and her eyes wide.

'Why, it is Lord Hartville!' she exclaimed, drawing on the reins to bring her horses, once

145

again, to a halt. Hartville thought the bays must be heartily sick of all the stopping and starting they'd gone through at her hands.

He touched his hat to her, and nodded to the two men, bringing Warrior alongside the carriage. His Cousin Caroline said, 'We had not expected you so soon, Lord Hartville.'

'And yet here I am.'

'Yes,' she said flatly, 'here you are. Sir, may I present my brother, Jeremy Carruthers? And his friend, Mr. Markingham.'

The gentlemen eyed each other with suspicion overlaid by civility. Hartville thought Jeremy Carruthers looked young and wild, while his companion, though a strikingly handsome man, had about him an air of consummate worldliness that Hartville thought Caroline Carruthers should be able to see through. Why, for instance, would a man his age — at least a dozen years older than Jeremy Carruthers — bother with that young pup?

Well, perhaps Hartville knew the answer to that question. Markingham was no doubt interested in Caroline Carruthers. But only a very rich man could consider a woman in Miss Carruthers's situation. Hartville wondered if Markingham was *that* wealthy.

But there was Jeremy Carruthers commenting on how spectacular Touchatt

146

— whom he called Touched, of course, like the stable lads — was, and how even Markingham with his stud farm hadn't anything to surpass him, though perhaps to match him, etc., etc. Hartville realized that perhaps Mr. Markingham *was* very well breeched indeed.

'Yes, he's a fine animal,' Hartville agreed, to shut up the young pup. He was not interested in Jeremy Carruthers's opinion of Touchatt, though he did wonder if the boy's conviction was shared by a stud farm owner. 'As are these bays,' he said, turning his attention to Markingham. 'Splendid action. Have they worked together long?'

'Only for the last week or so,' Markingham admitted, 'though Rival, the one on the left, has been in my stables for two years. I picked up Trevor's Choice from Sir Ralph Cinnes at the last Tattersall's auction.'

Hartville, who knew Sir Ralph to speak with, had to admit that his judgment of horseflesh was impeccable. And it was more likely he had disposed of the horse for its lack of a perfect match than that there was anything wrong with its abilities. He had himself purchased a horse from the baronet a few years previously, and the acquisition had never failed to please him.

Miss Carruthers at this point offered the

reins to Markingham, but he smiled and said, 'No, no. This is your stretch of road, and I think you're doing very well. Why not take us all the way back to Berwick?'

Hartville thought she looked delighted by the praise. In the viscount's opinion it had been a pretty mild compliment, but the girl was obviously besotted. With an answering smile to Markingham she gave the ribbons a vigorous flip to set her horses in motion. Hartville found himself riding alongside the carriage, trying to determine whether the man was seated as close to Miss Carruthers as he appeared to be.

12

Caroline tried to keep her mind on handling the horses, and not on her proximity to Markingham, or her concern about whether Hartville would find Jeremy a bit ramshackle. It was exhilarating, feeling the power of the horses down through the leather reins. Her hands ached from pulling them in when Hartville appeared, and she knew she'd have blisters before she was finished.

But purchasing a pair of driving gloves thick and strong enough to protect her was out of the question, far too expensive for the rare occasion such as this. The one time she'd tried Jeremy's gauntlets, they had been so large it had proved impossible to work with them.

So either she endured the pain, or she didn't attempt her hand at driving. Jeremy would consider her poor-spirited if she declined an offer to learn, and Markingham . . . Well, he wouldn't think her quite as unique, would he? Not so very many women of his acquaintance, Caroline felt sure, took up such a hobby.

Sensing that they were close to their

destination, the horses seemed to gather momentum. 'Pull them in a little,' Markingham suggested. 'You have the turn into the drive to make.'

Much to the detriment of her hands, Caroline exerted her strength to check the horses' pace. What she had seen Jeremy and Markingham do with ease, she found almost beyond her ability, but gradually the bays slackened their speed to a more reasonable level. Under her companion's tutelage she was able to guide them through the stone pillars and into the carriage drive without incident. She caught the skeptical look on Lord Hartville's face as she let out a relieved sigh. Well, he had already let her know what he thought of her driving *his* cattle.

The viscount was welcomed back with enthusiasm by his stable employees. The head groom was eager to assure himself that Lord Hartville didn't mind his allowing the visitors to ride Touchatt. Hartville shrugged with forbearance, saying, 'No harm done.' Caroline thought this was less than he might have said. Didn't hospitality and graciousness require him to appear all delight, especially in the presence of his visitors?

Caroline found herself approached by Hartville even before she walked from the stable yard. 'I need to speak with you about what happened last night,' he said, slapping his gloves restlessly against his thigh. 'I hope your brother and his friend won't consider me rude if I take you away from them for a while.'

'I'm sure they won't.' Caroline glanced up at Jeremy and suggested, 'There's a conservatory off the library. Perhaps you and Mr. Markingham would like to spend some time there.'

'Please don't concern yourself about us,' Markingham interjected smoothly. 'We can stretch our legs, maybe take a walk along the stream toward the woods.'

'Yes, I'd rather be outside,' Jeremy agreed. 'You go along with Lord Hartville.'

Hartville had already turned toward the house and begun striding away from the stables. Caroline had a difficult time keeping up with his long-legged pace, so she allowed him to outdistance her. When he realized that she was well behind him, he stopped, an impatient look on his face. 'Don't dawdle, cousin. I'd like to get this matter cleared up.'

'I'm not dawdling, Lord Hartville. I'm walking as fast as I'm able with these long skirts and my short legs.'

She had gained his side by this time and frowned at him. 'You're not likely to be able to clear the matter up any more than we were, of course. But I'm glad you're here to be in charge of whatever needs to be done.'

'Why wouldn't I be able to clear it up?' he demanded, falling into step with her.

'Well, I'm sure you've been told what happened. Have you any idea who the intruder on the nursery floor was?'

'None whatsoever.' He held the side door for her and kicked the dirt from his boots before entering. 'Couldn't you tell by the footsteps on the stairs whether it was a man or a woman? Were they heavy? Light?'

'I expected it to be Meg. Nothing about the footsteps caused me to question that, but I was in Wilhelmina's room, and away from the hall. Whoever it was must have been brazen indeed to coolly lock Meg in the kitchen and come up there.'

'You don't subscribe to the idea that it was one of our people there by mistake?'

'How can I?' Caroline stopped in the center of the hall where a pale sunlight shone through the high windows. 'Why would one of your people lock Meg in the kitchen? That makes no sense.'

'The whole business makes no sense,' he growled.

Caroline had been in the process of drawing off her gloves. She stopped abruptly and said, 'Perhaps you'd like a few minutes with your mother first. Why don't I join you there in half an hour?'

Hartville looked puzzled and frustrated. 'I don't need to be alone with my mother,' he said. 'I want to get to the bottom of this matter now.'

'I'm sure Lady Hartville would appreciate the chance to welcome you home in private.' Caroline turned away from him, as though to climb the grand staircase to the first floor.

'Stay.'

Just the one word issued from his lips, but there was an authority to it that Caroline did not choose to disobey. When she paused, he took a firm hold on her elbow and turned her back toward him. Then, even more to her surprise, he held his hand out. 'Give me your gloves.'

'I beg your pardon?'

'You heard me. Give me your gloves, cousin.'

'Don't be absurd. What do you want my gloves for?'

'Merely so that I can see your hands. Now, Caroline.'

She considered laughing at him and walking away. What could he do? But his eyes, determined as they were, intimated that he would not be gainsaid. Gingerly she removed the gloves, trying hard not to wince. First one and then the other she placed in his open hand, quickly tucking her own hands in the folds of her skirt.

'Your hands, Caroline.'

With a poor grace she held them up for him to see. The area between her thumb and forefinger on her right hand had a large blister. The same area on her left was bloody from the rubbing it had taken in pulling on the reins. 'I just need to wash them off,' she grumbled. 'It's of little moment.'

'So I see.' Hartville took each hand and inspected it for further damage, before allowing it to drop. 'Mrs. Bluestone will have some basillicum powder. Let her clean and wrap the area so it doesn't become worse. My mother has old driving gauntlets that you can wear, cousin. You had only to ask.'

Caroline's chin came up. 'How was I to know that, Lord Hartville? I'll join you and Lady Hartville in her room shortly.' Stiff with dignity, she turned away from him, this time making good her escape.

★　★　★

When Hartville had heard everything his mother had to say, and then details that Caroline had filled in, he could make no sense of the previous night's disturbance.

Meg had not returned from the home farm with Wilhelmina yet, but he felt certain she would have nothing essentially different to tell him.

Gazing out the window of his mother's sitting room, he saw the nursery maid and her charge come over the crest of a hill, walking toward the main house. They were swinging hands and laughing. Around them a puppy bounced and tumbled, returning always to the child's side. Hartville beckoned Caroline forward so that she could witness the scene.

'Her night's adventure doesn't seem to have discomposed the child,' he commented.

'No. She has proved remarkably adaptable. Think what a change this must be from her previous life, yet she never complains.'

'What is there to complain about?'

Caroline, whose hands were kept tucked behind her back, frowned at his obtuseness. 'She must miss her former companions, both the children and the adults. I wouldn't like to be uprooted that way, especially if I were only five.'

Hartville turned back toward his mother. 'I've been thinking about that. There seem to me several options. Certainly we must attempt to find these people, Molly and JoJo, to learn what we can about the child. We could even offer to provide a trust to pay for their care of her.'

Both his mother and Caroline regarded him with disapproval. He shrugged. 'You just said that she must miss them, cousin. What would be so awful about returning her to them?'

It was his mother who answered. 'Richard, the child is obviously gently born. No matter how caring Molly and JoJo might be, they could not provide her with a suitable setting from which to venture into the world as a young lady.'

'I've also considered this idea that she is gently born,' he said. 'What evidence have we that it's true? That Molly and JoJo told her her father was a 'fine man'? They probably think the baker in their village is a fine man when he's dressed for church. The picture in the locket? That could be anyone. It might have nothing whatsoever to do with her.'

'But how likely is that?' Caroline protested. 'Given the setting she appears to have come from, it's more a wonder that Molly and JoJo didn't sell the locket for what it might have brought them to support her.'

Hartville raked energetic fingers through his hair. 'Very well. I will concede for the time being that she is gently born. But I'm positive that she is not my daughter, and therefore I cannot believe that she is my responsibility.'

He held a hand up to still their protests. 'I'm not saying that I won't provide for her. Heaven knows she would just be one more to add to the list,' he said with a frustrated look at his mother. 'But I can't think it is wise for her to be raised here, as though she were my daughter.'

'Perhaps not,' Lady Hartville agreed reluctantly. 'What did you have in mind?'

The viscount paced across the floor and back, ending up once again looking out the window. The nursery maid and the child were much closer now, and they had encountered Jeremy Carruthers and Giles Markingham. Hartville was struck by how much the child resembled Jeremy Carruthers, with her blond hair and blue eyes. Just as she resembled Cousin Caroline.

Was there some sort of chicanery going on here? Hartville drummed his fingers on the windowsill, his brows drawn down over narrowed eyes. There was the coincidence of Caroline Carruthers arriving just two weeks before the child, and then her brother showing up practically on the child's heels. What if Jeremy Carruthers was the child's father, and this was all an elaborate plot to provide for her?

Absurd, he cautioned himself. Caroline

Carruthers would never be party to such a hoax. Or would she? Hartville realized that he really knew nothing about the young woman, and that his mother knew very little more.

'Hartville?' his mother prompted. 'You were going to tell us what you had in mind.'

Below him Meg seemed to be prompting the child to curtsey to the gentlemen. Jeremy Carruthers was laughing and riffling Wilhelmina's hair. Markingham bowed gravely to the girl. The four stood chatting for a while before they parted in different directions.

Hartville turned back toward the room, his piercing gaze falling on Caroline. 'No, I believe I need to consider more options, more possibilities, before I voice my thinking, Mama. If you will excuse me.'

Their astonished expressions did not deter him from a speedy departure.

* * *

Caroline found Jeremy and his friend in the stables, where they were discussing the various animals with Hartville's head groom. Though the lad reckoned Touched was their prize for speed, it was Warrior whom he most admired. Jeremy was wont to be dismissive of the stallion in comparison, but Markingham had a more discerning eye.

158

'Speed isn't everything,' he was saying as Caroline approached them. 'Look at the strength of that beast. His hindquarters are magnificent. I'd like to see him jump.'

'Perhaps tomorrow, sir,' the groom said. 'Warrior has come a long way today and his lordship means for him to be rested up a bit.'

'Of course.' Markingham turned toward Caroline and smiled. 'Everything sorted out, Miss Carruthers?'

'Yes,' she said, though of course nothing was sorted out at all. Hartville had actually behaved quite erratically, to her mind. 'Won't you come in and have tea?'

'By Jove, I could use something to wet my whistle,' Jeremy declared. He moved away from the loose box and started walking with Caroline toward the wide door at the end of the stables. 'He's got some decent cattle, Caro. Have to say that for him.'

Caroline wasn't at all sure why Jeremy seemed to be indicating that he didn't find a lot good to say for Hartville. But she knew her brother frequently took instant likes and dislikes, and this seemed to indicate he'd taken a dislike to Hartville. She could not think why. Perhaps it was merely that the viscount had not appeared totally delighted to find Jeremy on his horse. Or perhaps Jeremy sensed that Hartville did not care for *him*, which Caroline very much feared was the case.

'Did you see the little mare I rode the other day — Holly?'

Jeremy grimaced. 'She is not one of his finest, my dear, though I am not surprised that you liked her. Always partial to the underdog, eh, Markingham?'

'In my experience women often are,' his friend agreed ruefully. 'I am convinced that is why you, Jeremy, are so popular with them.'

'Me? An underdog? Never!'

'On the other hand you are not *quite* what all the mamas would hope for in an alliance with their daughters, are you? But their daughters don't seem to see it that way.'

'Oh, well, if you're going to talk about society and alliances and such drivel, I shan't talk with you at all. No mamas have to worry that I shall attempt to snag their daughters. What would I do with a wife?'

Markingham shook his head in mock despair. 'What, indeed?'

Caroline thought his glance at her was one of collusion, as though they shared some secret. A peculiar warmth invaded her chest. While Markingham exhibited the air of an indulgent older brother toward Jeremy, Caroline could not help suspecting that he regarded *her* as more of an equal.

160

Inside the house Caroline led the way to the north parlor and asked Bluestone if he would bring them tea. 'Is Lord Hartville available to join us?' she asked.

'Let me see if I can find his lordship,' the butler murmured.

'Not just the most welcoming host I've ever met,' Jeremy grumbled before Bluestone was well out the door.

'He was not the one who invited you here,' Caroline reminded him, a little sharply. 'Try and see if you can behave yourself, Jeremy. I've been treated splendidly since I've been here, and I have a lot for which to be grateful to the viscount and his mother.'

'Is Lady Hartville indisposed today?' Markingham asked, his intent clearly — to Caroline's mind — to ease the tension between brother and sister.

'Only slightly. I trust she will join us to dine, as she did last evening.'

'She seems a right one,' Jeremy admitted. His gaze fell on his sister's hands, and his brows lifted. 'What happened to them?'

'Blisters, from driving. I'll use gauntlets next time.'

'Well, we're off first thing in the morning, so we won't be offering you another chance to drive this time through.' Jeremy turned to Markingham. 'What do you say we stop here on our way back to London, Giles?'

Markingham's eyes met Caroline's. He seemed to be seeking her approval, or some sign that she would wish him to come again. She could not very well say anything, but she allowed herself to smile quite warmly at him. 'If you don't think we would be overdoing our welcome, Miss Carruthers, I should like to stop by on our return.'

'Won't be for a week,' Jeremy assured her. 'Give his lordship a chance to get used to the idea. And maybe I could have a go on that gelding again. By Jove, that was a treat.'

Bluestone returned bearing a tray with teapot, cups, saucers and two plates of delicacies, which he set on the table in front of Caroline. 'His lordship is with his man of business, Miss Carruthers, and begs to be excused. He understands Mr. Carruthers and Mr. Markingham are to dine here this evening, and looks forward to the occasion with pleasure.'

Jeremy rolled his eyes heavenward, but behind Bluestone's back. Then his attention was drawn to the tea tray and he asked incredulously, 'Are those rhubarb tarts? I haven't had a rhubarb tart in years.'

'They are,' his sister said. 'And I'll wager you've never had ones as good as these are.'

'You've certainly settled in here, my girl,'

Jeremy complained as he accepted his tea from her. 'Pouring out tea when neither Lord nor Lady Hartville are around. So familiar with the cook's work that you know the precise nature of a rhubarb tart. Sounds to me as though you have no intention of coming back to London.'

'Why, of course I do!' Caroline exclaimed, coloring, and unable to ignore the shocked expression on Markingham's face. 'Heavens, Jeremy, I've only been here two weeks. That's hardly an unconscionable amount of time. Lady Hartville spoke of months when she invited me, and I would not like to give the appearance of being ungrateful for her consideration.'

Jeremy shrugged and looked about him, taking in the paneled walls and family portraits, the leaded glass windows and the rich Aubusson carpet. 'It's a deal more cozy than the flat in London,' he admitted. 'And I suppose Lady Hartville misses her husband and enjoys the companionship of a young thing like you, but I wouldn't get too set on hanging about. Hartville is bound to marry sooner or later, and you'll be a regular fifth wheel.'

Caroline almost laughed at her brother's inability to envision herself as Hartville's wife. Her eyes sparkled with humor, but she said only, 'You needn't fear for me, Jeremy. I know my place.'

Markingham gave a snort of laughter and Jeremy looked from one to the other of them, shaking his head. But he said only, 'I wouldn't mind another of those tarts, Caro.'

In offering one to Markingham, too, she noticed that he was eyeing her speculatively. It wouldn't hurt, Caroline thought, for him to wonder if he was up against a touch of competition. Sometimes a man needed that kind of realization to shake up his complaisance a bit — or even to spark an interest where perhaps none had previously existed.

But Caroline couldn't help believing that there was indeed already a spark burning in Markingham when he said, 'Your sister is, I think, destined for a very special place, Jeremy, did you but realize it.'

13

Hartville closed the ledger he had been going over with his man of business, Jeremiah Wilson. 'Do you have a list of *all* the family members whom we are currently supporting, Wilson?' he asked.

'Certainly, my lord.' Wilson reached behind him and drew forth a narrow, leather-bound volume. Its age was testified to by the worn areas on the top and corners, but its thinness belied the amount and importance of the information it contained. The man of business, a fellow of middle years and myopic eyesight, pushed his spectacles up on the bridge of his nose and opened to the first page. 'As you'll see, the records go back to your grandfather's time. When a member of the family was entered into the book, the date of application and approval was also indicated, and the annual sum to be dispensed.'

Hartville leaned across and flipped through the pages of the book. Then he started at the beginning and worked through the pages more slowly, counting as he did so. His brows rose. 'Thirty-two?' he muttered. 'We're supporting thirty-two members of the Carruthers family? How can so many members of one family be so insolvent?'

'I'm afraid I don't know the answer to that, sir.'

Heaving a sigh, Hartville went down the list of names more slowly. The original entries were made in a hand that he could identify as his grandfather's. There were only half a dozen of these. Then came the entries in his father's hand, which included almost all of the remainder. He himself, having been the viscount for only a year, had been called upon for many outlays of money, but a mere trio of these had been requests for an annual allowance.

And he had not actually entered the names in this book. Wilson had scrupulously inscribed the appropriate information and carried out the actual arrangements to dispense these funds and all the other allowances.

'Don't people ever die off and have their names removed?' grumbled Hartville.

'Rarely.' Wilson tapped one entry with a long finger. 'This fellow died and left no heirs. However, a cousin who had been taking care of him seemed to feel that she was then entitled to receive his allowance, as she was in the habit of spending it. I believe your father agreed to accommodate her.'

'My father was a good deal too compliant.' Hartville pushed the volume away, and then, on second thought, pulled it back toward him. He worked backward over the names, his finger moving slowly up each page. 'Ah,' he said finally. 'This one, Wilson. What do you know about it?'

The entry had been made in his father's hand. Wilson bent to read it, and his eyes widened. 'Why, it's the young gentleman who is here now, is it not? And, according to the entry, the allowance now covers both brother and sister, who were orphaned some years previously.'

Wilson closed his eyes and thought for a while, then nodded. 'Yes, I remember now. Your father was approached by one Matilda Carruthers, the boy's aunt, who had taken the pair in upon the death of their parents. The upkeep of the youngsters had been a small matter while they lived on the estate, but Mrs. Carruthers wished to send the boy to school. Your father granted that request, of course. And later the boy longed to move to London and set up an establishment of his own. Your father thought that not unreasonable, either.'

'Naturally.' Hartville drummed impatient fingers on the oak table where the ledgers rested. 'I can see that we've settled five hundred pounds on them each year since. Is there any way of telling if they've requested additional funds?'

'Certainly.' Wilson checked the listing under 'Carruthers, Jeremy and sister' and shook his head. 'This column would have any indication of correspondence, and it's empty. So he has not applied to you for additional funds.'

'Hmm. And I can see that the sum hasn't changed over the years. So Master Jeremy and his sister, Caroline, have been living on five hundred pounds a year. Certainly not enough to be living in London and buying the services of a wet nurse.'

'I beg your pardon?'

Hartville waved aside his question. 'A mere thought,' he muttered. 'How in the devil could two of them live in London on that amount of money?'

'It does seem possible that Matilda Carruthers could be supplementing that income, my lord.'

'Yes, I suppose that's true.' Hartville stared unseeing out the window. 'Our friend Jeremy does not strike me as being one to watch his expenditures overmuch. But his type can always get round an older female relation, can't they?'

Wilson looked puzzled. 'I'm sure I don't know sir.'

'Trust me, they can.' Hartville closed the ledger and rose. He was about to excuse himself when a thought occurred to him. 'What do you make of an intruder being in the house, Wilson?'

His companion frowned. 'It never happened in your father's day,' he said unhappily.

Hartville laughed. 'No, indeed. A most unsettling consequence of my stewardship, I daresay.'

★ ★ ★

Jeremy and Markingham left for the inn to change for dinner, and Caroline wandered into the conservatory to do some thinking. She felt restless and on edge, as though something were about to happen. And yet what was likely to occur? Not another midnight marauder, surely, with Hartville home. Jeremy could embarrass himself at dinner, of course. Comparing him with Hartville, Caroline could see that the viscount might find him too easygoing, too far from taking life seriously.

What of Markingham? Hartville had not seemed to be much impressed with the older man. Nor had his mother. Caroline found

169

this both perplexing and distressing. Surely they could see what a fine man he was, intelligent and generous. Caroline didn't expect Hartville to notice Markingham's particularly masculine attractiveness, of course. Nor for his mother to necessarily understand the kindness which prompted his taking Jeremy under his wing. How many men would have done that? Not Hartville, certainly.

Caroline sat down on the stone bench under a miniature fig tree and folded her hands in her lap. Looking at the wrappings around her palms, she shook her head with exasperation. How foolish of her not to find some real driving gloves before ever she took off with Jeremy. And how embarrassing to have Hartville call attention to her injuries. She had been quite surprised at the concern he had of a sudden exhibited. Not that she approved of his autocratic insistence on his will being done.

And that strange episode in his mother's sitting room. He had behaved as though something of exceeding importance had occurred, when all he had done was stare out the window. Caroline had felt an actual shiver run down her spine when he had turned from the window and met her gaze, though for the briefest moment, with one of absolute ice.

She had not thought him a man of such rapid swings of mood, or such devastating disregard.

Deep in her thoughts, Caroline only belatedly registered the opening of a door. When her gaze swung in that direction, she saw that whoever had been about to enter had turned away and was pulling the door closed behind him. She very much feared that it had been Hartville himself, and that, on finding her there, he had chosen not to join her. Which was perfectly fine, from Caroline's point of view. She was not that keen on spending time with the man who had treated her so cavalierly since his return.

★　★　★

Lady Hartville joined the rest of the party when they were all gathered in the Gold Drawing Room. Caroline thought she looked well now, rested and with much better color. No doubt it pleased her that Hartville was back in their midst. And Hartville was particularly attentive to her. He came forward immediately she entered the room to offer her his arm and see that she was seated in the most comfortable of the wing back chairs.

'A late entrance!' exclaimed Jeremy, his eyes alight with amusement. 'It must either be a new gown or a new piece of jewelry. Which is it, Lady Hartville?'

Hartville frowned at such raillery, but his mother laughed. 'Neither, you naughty boy. Though Hartville did bring me back this lovely new shawl.'

'Did he now?' Jeremy moved forward and drew out a quizzing glass to view the item more closely. 'Dashed fine material, but I myself would have chosen something a deal more lively for you. Red or purple, don't you know. Grays and browns are inoffensive, but they don't half do you justice.'

Caroline could see that Hartville was not taking this teasing in good part. The viscount's eyes smoldered with an obvious wish to see his guest elsewhere, but his mother was as obviously delighted with Jeremy's easy flirtatiousness.

'I should look quite ridiculous in such bright colors,' she protested. 'Your sister could wear them, certainly, but a woman of my years? Never.'

'Gold, then.' Jeremy suggested, eyeing her with cocked head. 'And royal blue. Don't you think so, Giles?'

'Not royal blue,' Markingham offered. 'Navy.'

Caroline tried to think of some way to put an end to the discussion before Hartville lost patience. His blue eyes were narrowed and his jaw set in a formidable manner. She could tell that he was inclined to give Jeremy a real setdown, but only restrained himself because of his mother's obvious pleasure. Fortunately, Bluestone arrived just then to announce dinner. Hartville assisted his mother from the chair and offered his arm.

Markingham offered his arm to Caroline, and Jeremy followed them from the room saying, 'Yes, definitely gold and navy.'

The dining parlor was, naturally, exactly as it had been the night before. The candles in the chandelier gleamed on the silver and fine china and cast shifting shadows beyond the table. Hartville's presence, however, seemed to cast a pall over the assembled group. Where the previous evening they had laughed and teased and been excessively informal and lighthearted, his presence at the head of the table was not conducive to conversation.

Caroline thought that Hartville looked stern, and she cast a warning glance at her brother, who shrugged and applied himself to his lamb cutlets. Markingham, seated beside Lady Hartville, looked totally at his ease. The two of them carried on a desultory exchange, about the difficulty of finding properly treated leather gloves in the village shops. Trust Markingham to at least have something to say for himself, Caroline thought mutinously, casting an annoyed look at the viscount.

Hartville raised his brows. 'Is there something the matter, Cousin Caroline?'

He looked abominably haughty, and worse, as though he no longer felt any of the camaraderie that had seemed to be growing between them before he went away.

'Nothing whatsoever, my lord,' she answered formally.

'Dashed fine cutlets,' Jeremy interjected. The footman moving around the table had stopped beside him with croquettes of chicken, and Jeremy helped himself to a hearty serving. 'Must have a very fine cook, from what I've seen. Those rhubarb tarts this afternoon were the best I've ever had, and I'm something of a connoisseur of rhubarb tarts.'

'Are you?' the viscount asked. 'I don't believe I've ever met anyone who considered himself a connoisseur of rhubarb tarts before.'

'I daresay you haven't,' Jeremy retorted, not in the least put out by the viscount's acerbic tone. 'Some men are connoisseurs of wine, others of . . . well, other things. But I,' he said, with a smile and a wink at Lady Hartville, 'am a connoisseur of rhubarb tarts.'

Lady Hartville laughed, delighted with him

once again. 'And how did that come about, Jeremy Carruthers?' she asked.

He shrugged, but immediately launched into a long, patently ridiculous story that involved country fairs and whimsical maidens and a wandering pig and, not to be outdone by legend, a pieman named Simon. His audience, with the lone exception of the viscount, was thoroughly enchanted by his tale.

Markingham shook his head at its conclusion. 'I think you've missed your calling, Jeremy. You could make your fortune by writing down such nonsense and having it published. I'd buy a volume, if it were illustrated with all those fantastic creatures.'

Jeremy nodded thoughtfully and turned to his sister. 'What do you say, Caro? You could do the watercolors. We'd become famous in no time, and we'd be invited everywhere, like that Byron fellow. Only I wouldn't do it in poetry. Never could stand the stuff. Just amusing tales, but a little out of the ordinary. Fairy tales, don't you know. But these would be for grownups of discriminating taste, like Lady Hartville.'

Taken with the idea, and not at all bothered by the flattery, Lady Hartville nodded enthusiastically. 'I could be your patron, Jeremy. I've always thought it would be most rewarding to support a struggling artist.'

Caroline thought she heard Hartville mutter something that sounded very much like, 'We're already supporting him,' but she could not be absolutely sure, and her attention was drawn back to his mother, who had continued to run with the idea.

'You have the tongue for it, if perhaps not the patience to actually sit down and write.' Lady Hartville turned toward Caroline. 'Do you think you could be his amanuensis, my dear?'

Caught between the excitement she could feel radiating from her brother and her hostess, and the disapproval evident in Hartville's face, Caroline pursed her lips and said, 'I'd have to think about it, ma'am.'

Markingham set down his glass and turned to her. 'I've seen some of your watercolors, Miss Carruthers. They're exquisite. Of course, drawing piemen and pigs and country fairs is a little different than drawing plants and landscapes.'

'Oh, she could do it, right enough,' Jeremy assured him. 'Caroline can draw loads of things. Some fellow once asked her to do those fashion plates for his magazine, didn't he, Caro?'

Alarmed now at where this discussion

might take them, Caroline said dismissively, 'Mr. Random was merely teasing, Jeremy.'

But Hartville's gaze had sharpened. 'Who is Mr. Random, Cousin Caroline?'

'Works for Ackermann,' Jeremy informed him. 'You know the *Repository* surely.'

'I do. 'Arts, Literature, Commerce, Manufactures, Fashions and Politics.' He wanted you to do fashion plates, cousin?' He looked pointedly at Caroline, obviously intent on having her answer for herself.

'Well, he indicated that he found my drawing interesting. You know very well that all the artwork is done by men, sir.'

'Is it? How did Mr. Random happen to see your drawing?'

'Now there is a fascinating tale,' Jeremy informed him, once again taking over the conversation. Caroline was very glad indeed that her brother was not aware that she had been providing Mr. Random with fashion plates for the past six months. Had he known, he would have been unable to refrain from divulging that knowledge. Instead, he recounted the whole in his usual whimsical style.

'It was at Madame D'Arbley's. She's the modiste half the fashionable world uses,' he explained, in case Hartville should not happen to know. 'Caro only went in because

177

she was with her friend Miss Salston. Madame D'Arbley was torn between fawning over the gentleman who was there ahead of her, and serving Caro's companion, whom she knew to be wealthy and in need of a complete wardrobe for her first season.'

'And how could she possibly have known that?' Hartville asked.

Jeremy tapped his nose and grinned. 'Some people have the insight, don't you know. Actually, Miss Salston had been there previously, hadn't she, Caro?'

'Yes.'

'So Madame is fluttering back and forth between the gentleman and the ladies, trying to divide herself equally, but finding it difficult. Her assistant has brought out two or three dresses which the gentleman is not taken with, and Miss Salston is trying to make Madame understand what it is she's looking for.'

When Jeremy mimicked Madame's busy course with flapping hands and distressed French murmurs, Lady Hartville let out a peal of laughter. 'Oh, I've seen her do it!' she exclaimed. 'You have her perfectly, Jeremy.'

'Thank you, ma'am. So, as Caroline knew what her friend was looking for, she offered to draw a sketch on Madame's pad.' He turned to Hartville to explain, 'Madame keeps a sketch pad at her elbow at all times to record her own ideas and make notes.'

Hartville, looking annoyed at being treated as though he would not understand all of this, said sharply, 'I know that Madame D'Arbley keeps a notepad.'

Markingham caught Caroline's eye and raised his brows in amusement. She was not sure that she found it amusing that Hartville knew who Madame D'Arbley was. Just why would he have had reason to frequent the shop of a famous modiste?

'Well, then,' Jeremy said with a smile at the viscount, 'you will understand that Madame does not allow anyone to draw on her pad.'

'But *I* didn't know it,' Caroline protested.

'Of course not,' he agreed. 'And Madame was so distracted by a request from the other gentleman at just that moment that she dashed off, leaving the pad behind her. All unknowing, Caro picked it up and began to sketch, while Miss Salston looked on and added details — a wreath of green silk leaves at the bottom of the skirt, a sleeve edged with white crepe — you know the sort of thing.'

Lady Hartville nodded, her expression bright with delight. Her son continued to listen attentively, though he gave no sign of agreement. And Markingham, Caroline thought, though he'd undoubtedly heard the story before, maintained an amused, and perhaps admiring, silence. Caroline tried to pay more attention to her food than to the gentlemen around her.

Jeremy had come to the climax of his story. 'Now Madame turns and sees Caro with her sketch pad. She's enraged, but she daren't show it, as she has two clients observing her closely. She grabs the sketch pad from Caro's hands, saying coldly, 'I did not give you permission to scribble in my book, miss.' But by this time the gentleman has taken note of Caro's drawing. Which is, as always, highly proficient and wonderfully detailed. She has even sketched in her friend's physiognomy with uncommon ability.'

'The other gentleman is Mr. Random, I take it,' Hartville said.

'He is. His eyes widen, he turns to Caro and explains who he is. He offers her his card, telling her that he would be enchanted to have her do fashion plates for his publisher.'

'How extraordinary!' Lady Hartville exclaimed, her cheeks pink with excitement. 'I had no idea you had such a talent, my dear. What did you tell the gentleman?'

'Naturally she thanked him for his kind offer and expressed her appreciation of his praise,' Jeremy interjected. 'But Caroline is a gentlewoman. She could no more sell her drawings than she could sing for an income.'

Caroline was very aware of Hartville's curious gaze on her. There was something in his intense stare that made her wonder if he somehow knew more about her than he had ever let on. But, no, there was no possible way in which he could have learned of her enterprise. She and Mr. Random had kept it a closely guarded secret.

Hartville leaned toward her and asked, 'You sing, cousin?'

'Oh, Lord, Hartville,' his mother sighed. 'I'd forgotten you weren't with us last evening. They sing together, Jeremy and Caroline, like angels. You will hardly credit it.'

'Oh, I'm sure I shall. Miss Carruthers seems to have unending talents.'

Attempting to look meek and accommodating, Caroline folded her hands in her lap and lowered her eyes. 'You are too kind, Lord Hartville.'

'Not at all. I believe we have already established that you are also something of an actress.'

'An actress?' Jeremy's brow wrinkled. 'Now there you're out, sir. My sister has no talent in that regard. Well, she couldn't have, could she? Caro is an open book.'

Caroline could see the disbelief in

Hartville's eyes, and the puzzled expression on Markingham's face. What a lowering thought that Hartville should actually know her better than Markingham did! Well, she *meant* to be meek and accommodating — occasionally. Fortunately, there was no need for her to make any response to Hartville's remark, since his mother had taken the notion into her head that Caroline and Jeremy should sing for them after their supper, and she turned to urge Hartville not to dawdle over the port.

'I shan't, Mama,' he assured her with a playful smile. 'But you must remember that my companions may have more of a thirst than I, and I would dislike to be a disobliging host.'

His mother snorted at his teasing. 'You have only to ask Bluestone to bring the port into the drawing room,' she reminded him as she rose.

Caroline was instantly on her feet as well. Even a few minutes away from Hartville's profound scrutiny would be welcome. This newly discovered bent of his for suspecting her of heaven-knew-what was more than a little discomposing. She followed Lady Hartville from the room without a glance at any of the men remaining there.

14

Hartville was actually not in a hurry to join the women. It seemed to him that his chances of detecting Jeremy's motives and character were greater when he had the young man away from Lady Hartville and her delighted enjoyment of the lad's company. Hartville was not jealous of Jeremy's rapid inclusion in Lady Hartville's affections. He trusted in his own mother's fondness for himself. That Carruthers was devilishly charming Hartville would have to take on faith, as he couldn't see it himself. The lad seemed far too full of himself, far too careless in his treatment of his elders, and a regular loose screw to boot.

What Hartville wasn't as sure of was whether there was guile in Jeremy. The boy had protested that his sister was an open book, and he was certainly wrong about that. But Hartville suspected that Jeremy himself was pretty much as he appeared. If he was hiding deeper and darker levels to himself, he was by far the better actor than his sister.

Markingham, on the other hand, was a complete mystery. His surface polish was exquisite, but Hartville was unable to see beneath that surface. Markingham was older, by a number of years. He had the confidence of a man who moved easily within society but was not a slave to it. His intelligence was obvious, his amiability only slightly less so. But he made no effort to divulge his thoughts or feelings over their port, although Hartville casually introduced a variety of issues into the conversation.

While Jeremy was ready to leap on any tidbit and give his uncensored opinion, Markingham sat back with a slightly reserved air, his comments always indicating his knowledge but never revealing his thoughts. If Hartville had not been very much afraid that this was how he appeared to people himself, he would have found these qualities disagreeable in Markingham.

And yet Caroline Carruthers apparently found the gentleman very much to her liking. True, he was handsome, tall and dark, with an ease of manner that might have been expected to attract a green girl. But, then, what was Cousin Caroline but a green girl, when all was said and done? Certainly she'd spent very little time in society, as far as he could decipher. Her accomplishments notwithstanding, she had very little experience of the world, cooped up in her brother's lodgings in London. No wonder the first man who came along had won her favor.

Tired of his own speculations, he put down his half-full glass and asked, 'Shall we join the ladies? I find I have a desire to hear you and your sister sing, Mr. Carruthers.'

Though he said this with a slightly mocking air, Hartville found, a quarter of an hour later, that there was nothing to be amused by in the performance of the brother and sister. He had assumed that his mother, obviously intrigued by the pair, had overstated the case for their singing. If anything, he thought as he sat back in the wing chair, she had not conveyed the extent of their expertise.

Not that they had that annoying polish of professionals. Indeed, they were completely natural and so engrossed in their singing that they hardly seemed conscious of the room around them. When Jeremy invited him to sing with Caroline, Hartville politely declined, saying, 'I'm afraid I haven't the talent you do, Mr. Carruthers. I would prefer to hear the two of you sing again.'

But it was Markingham who sang with Caroline next. Hartville did not in the least like the way the pair looked at each other, but he was pleased to hear that his guest was nowhere near as delightful a singer as Jeremy. When their duet was completed, Hartville was surprised to see Caroline smile and beckon to his mother. 'Come. I think perhaps I know a song you'll enjoy singing with me, ma'am.'

'Oh, my dear, I couldn't,' Lady Hartville protested. 'If ever I had a voice, it is years since I've used it.'

'And yet here is this piece of music which is so well worn that I cannot believe you would forget how to sing along with it,' Caroline insisted as she handed across a sheet of music for Hartville's mother to peruse.

Lady Hartville sighed and nodded. 'Mercy, you take me back, Caroline. Where did you find this?'

'In the bench, when I was searching through it this morning.' She grinned when her gaze fell on Hartville. 'And I'm certain Lord Hartville will remember it well, too, for it must have been the lullaby you sang him to sleep with when he was a babe.'

Hartville would dearly have loved to throttle her for this piece of embarrassing nonsense. When he was a babe, indeed! And yet, as her fingers wandered over the keys, teasing out that long-ago melody, he recognized it instantly and was filled with a profound sense of warmth and well-being. *Drat the girl, anyhow.*

His mother had begun to hum along with the music, and Caroline softly sang the words

186

to the lullaby. After the first verse, Lady Hartville joined in, her voice rusty with disuse at singing, but as soft and loving as it must have been twenty-five years previously. And suddenly, Jeremy muttered, 'Yes, I remember this,' and added his voice to the other two.

With an effort, Hartville kept his face perfectly immobile, but he was deeply touched by the episode, and his mother was frankly crying. For a long time after the last note drifted away, no one said anything.

And then Caroline rose from the pianoforte and moved to the games table, which was always pushed back behind the blue sofa. She shifted it into position, asked Jeremy to bring forward the chairs and skillfully palmed a deck of cards. At Hartville's surprised stare, she said, 'Your mama has expressed a desire for a hand of whist, my lord. We aren't often enough to make up a table, and this seemed the perfect opportunity.'

Hartville, who would have preferred to have her continue to sing for the remainder of the evening, promptly rose to help with the arrangements. He had forgotten what a devotee of whist his mother was, and could not remember the last time he had played with her.

'Which of us is to sit out?' he asked, since

his cousin seemed intent on managing the entire matter.

'I shall. Jeremy will partner your mama, and you and Mr. Markingham can be partners.' The idea appeared to please her. There was a decided twinkle in her eyes. 'You do play, don't you?'

'Of course.' In the ordinary course of things Hartville was accustomed to partnering his own mother, but he could see that the dowager was intrigued by the idea of having Jeremy as her partner so he did not protest. Besides, he was curious as to what kind of a player Markingham would be.

When his mother cut the cards and proceeded to deal them, Cousin Caroline drifted back to the pianoforte, where she played softly but did not sing. As might have been expected, Jeremy played with panache which Lady Hartville obviously found charming. Hartville himself was something of a cautious player, never having found the game of much interest, and therefore never bothering to learn the finer points.

Markingham was vastly more skilled. He could easily have bested any of the others with his good memory and clever moves. But that was not enough for him, especially when Jeremy and Lady Hartville continued to have a spectacular run of luck.

Jeremy could not resist baiting his friend. 'Thought you had us there, didn't you, Giles? Just goes to show that you can't always count on skill. We've had the cards, every hand, haven't we, Lady Hartville?'

'We have indeed,' she agreed, taking another trick. 'I think you're bringing me luck, young man.'

She'd never said that to him, Hartville thought with mild irritation. But then, he had never been particularly lucky at cards. Trust Jeremy Carruthers to be, though. It was all of a piece.

Since Hartville did not particularly care whether the other pair won, he was astonished to see Markingham make a play so reckless that it stood to win or lose the game. And he did it with no indication that he was doing anything out of the ordinary. Hartville played along with him, of course, and shook his head wonderingly as his elegant guest scooped up the trick and they won the rubber.

'You were saying, Jeremy?' Markingham mocked gently.

'He wouldn't have managed that if we hadn't been distracted, would he?' Jeremy asked Lady Hartville.

'Distracted by what?'

'The tea tray being brought in,' Jeremy said

promptly, though it had only just arrived, borne by Bluestone himself. 'A lovely cup of tea that quite diverted our minds from the trick.'

Hartville could see that Jeremy wasn't in the least put out by losing. He merely enjoyed the verbal sparring with his companions. The lad remained in high gig as they abandoned their places at the games table and joined Caroline around the tea table.

'Pity we're moving on tomorrow,' Jeremy said to the room at large.

Lady Hartville urged them to remain for a few more days in the area, but Markingham was insistent that they had an obligation to meet. 'Well, then I hope you will return on your way back to London,' she said.

'Oh, we shall certainly do so,' Markingham agreed, his gaze on Caroline. 'Nothing would be more delightful.'

Hartville noted that Caroline's hand shook slightly as she poured Markingham's cup of tea. The viscount frowned, and decided that he would be very glad indeed when his two guests made themselves scarce and the household at Berwick was able to get back to normal again.

★ ★ ★

When the party had made significant inroads into the tea and biscuits, Lady Hartville rose. 'Please don't let me break up the party,' she said. 'You must all stay and enjoy yourselves. But I shall fall asleep right here in my chair if I remain a moment longer.'

Jeremy was on his feet so quickly that Caroline almost laughed. In truth, it was obvious that he truly liked Hartville's mother. Of course, it did her no harm in his eyes that she just as obviously enjoyed him. He now possessed himself of her hand, lifting it to his lips and murmuring, 'Ah, dear lady, I shall count the minutes until we meet again.'

'You are too foolish,' she protested, her eyes sparkling. 'None of your nonsense, now, or Hartville will be tempted to call you out.'

Hartville did look like he wished to call someone out, Caroline thought, amused. She turned to Lady Hartville and said, 'I'll see you upstairs, ma'am.'

'No, no. You must stay and enjoy your brother's visit. I told Bluestone to send for my dresser, and she'll be waiting for me in the hall.'

But when she had left, the party broke up despite her urgings. The viscount did not second her suggestion, and Markingham explained that they needed an early start in the morning to reach their destination near

Grasmere in good time. Jeremy was accommodating as always, and moved to say his farewells to his sister.

'You might think about joining us when we return to London,' he suggested. 'Otherwise you'll miss Miss Salston's party, and that would be a great pity.'

Caroline shook her head. 'For you, perhaps. I'm content here for the time being, Jeremy. But I'll look forward to your return.'

'Bet we liven things up,' he said, with a meaningful glance in Hartville's direction. 'Some fellows are altogether too stiff rumped to find any amusement in life.'

'I don't think his lordship is one of them.'

'Really?' Jeremy looked astonished. 'Well, he did a fine job of portraying such a fellow.'

'Off with you before he hears your insults,' his sister begged, only half teasing. She rumpled his hair and gave him a hug. 'I'm so glad you came to see me.'

'Well, of course you are,' the irrepressible Jeremy stated. 'I'll be back soon.'

'Good.'

Markingham, who had been conversing desultorily with Hartville, now moved toward her with his hand extended. 'Miss Carruthers, a pleasure, as always.' His hand enveloped hers, pressed it firmly, and perhaps held on to it a little longer than was strictly necessary.

His eyes spoke volumes to her, didn't they? Something burned in their depths, communicating itself to Caroline with an almost shocking intensity. She felt a shiver run through her and found herself unable to speak. Instead, she flashed a shaken smile at him, blinking as though dazed.

'Perhaps when we return,' he said, his voice low and intense, 'you and I will have more opportunity to converse. In fact, I shall insist upon it.'

Caroline nodded. She could see that Hartville was watching them, and perhaps listening as well. 'Have a safe journey,' she managed to say.

His gaze had locked on her lips, and stayed there. Caroline felt as though she'd been kissed, and her cheeks flushed with color. Only at Jeremy's interruption, and with reluctance, did Markingham finally withdraw his gaze, a rueful twist to his lips.

'I'll take care of your brother,' he said.

'Thank you.'

And then they were gone, and she was left alone with Hartville.

15

The viscount regarded her with what Caroline took to be suspicion. 'Are you feeling well, Miss Carruthers?' he asked.

'Perfectly.'

'Your cheeks are a little flushed.'

'Are they? I wouldn't regard it.'

'And your hands? How are they?'

Caroline had almost forgotten her hands. They had hardly troubled her at all when she played the pianoforte. She held them up now, each with a little strip of gauze covering the blisters. 'They are entirely comfortable, my lord. Not giving me even a twinge of pain.'

'May I see them?'

'There's no need.'

Hartville held out his hands and said again, 'May I see them?'

Caroline reluctantly placed her hands in his. He pushed aside the gauze to check one and then the other, nodded, and released them. 'Basilicum powder does wonders sometimes,' he commented.

He was standing very close to her. Caroline could almost feel the warmth from his body, could see the depths in his eyes. He made no

194

move to put distance between them, so she backed up a step herself. 'It's late, my lord,' she said.

'Is it?'

'Well, of course it is.' Caroline felt almost annoyed with him for being so obtuse. 'Your mother has already gone to bed. Your guests have left.'

'And yet it is only half nine.'

'It feels a great deal later,' she insisted.

'Does it?'

'To me it does. I believe I will go upstairs now myself.'

'Or you could sit here with me and have another cup of tea.'

Caroline hadn't the least desire for another cup of tea. Nor did she have the least desire to spend any more time with Hartville. But for the life of her she couldn't seem to move away from him. 'Perhaps one cup,' she murmured, taking her seat again at the tea table.

The teapot didn't feel very warm to the touch, she noted, but she poured each of them a cup anyhow. Hartville added cream and sugar to his, but he did so while scarcely removing his gaze from Caroline.

'Your brother is a bit of a rogue,' he said finally.

'I suppose he is. He has a fortunate

disposition, and is accustomed to being liked.'

'Yes. It was obvious that my mama likes him very well.'

'And you don't approve of that,' she guessed.

'I think it makes me a little jealous.'

His confession struck her dumb. It was at once an apology and a bit of knowledge so personal that she could hardly credit his having uttered it. She could only blink in surprise.

'Not that you are to think my mother neglects to pay me every attention,' he assured her, a touch of whimsy in his tone.

'Your mother is exceedingly fond of you!'

'I know. And I of her.'

'Yes,' she said, feeling surprisingly touched. 'I can see that you are.'

'My father was a good man, too, but more difficult to know,' he mused. 'Kept to himself a lot, except when Mama brought him out. She thinks I am a good deal like him.'

'Does she?' Caroline felt totally confused by the direction of the conversation. Why was he telling her these things? As far as she could tell, he'd not had too much to drink, and she could not think what she had done or said to encourage his confidences. 'I believe your father died fairly recently,' she said, hoping her remark sounded like a logical response to him.

'Yes, within the year. I know it's been hard on my mother. Do you think illness can be brought on by that kind of grief?'

'I really don't know.' Caroline relaxed somewhat, believing that this had been the goal of his remarks all along — to discuss his mother's state of health. 'I believe there are occasions when a spouse has been said to have given up and died after the death of a beloved mate, but I don't at all think your mother that type of person.'

'No, I doubt she is. But I think she misses him more than she lets on, you know. Several times I've come upon her sitting in a room, or in the conservatory, just staring into space, totally unaware that anyone else is around.'

Caroline nodded. 'Yes, I've seen her do that. But one has only to speak to bring her attention back to the present.'

Hartville said thoughtfully, 'And there is her sending for you. She never had need of a companion when my father was alive.'

'She merely invited me for a visit,' Caroline reminded him. 'And then . . . decided that we might suit,' she added with a touch of embarrassment.

He regarded her with a rueful grin. 'But we knew better, didn't we?'

Her shoulders rose in a careless shrug. 'I'm

197

sure it was a temporary whim. She hasn't made any effort in that direction for some time.'

'No, she hasn't, has she?' But the grin faded, to be replaced by a frown. 'I'm afraid that's because she hasn't been feeling well. And now, with her obvious attachment to your brother . . . '

Caroline absently took a sip of cold tea, blinked in surprise, and set her cup on the table beside her chair. 'Well, Jeremy will be out of her way for a while now.' Then she said abruptly, 'Do you know what I would do if your mother's health were my responsibility?'

Hartville looked wary. 'What?'

'She doesn't at all like the local doctor and will have nothing to do with him. So, if I knew a good doctor in London, I believe I would send him a detailed history of her illness and request his opinion. It might be necessary to have him come here, but it might not.'

'I doubt my mother would be inclined to give me a detailed history of her illness,' he protested.

'Perhaps not, but Mrs. Bluestone and Lady Hartville's dresser could both probably contribute to a fairly comprehensive description of what her symptoms have been.'

Hartville shook his head in amusement.

'Do you know you're a very bright girl, cousin?'

Caroline smiled broadly. 'Oh, yes, my lord. I do know.'

'I do love a modest woman,' he muttered.

'No one asked you to love me,' she countered.

And, strangely, she found herself staring into his eyes, and he into hers, for a very long moment. It was akin to the moment when Markingham had looked so deeply into her eyes just an hour previously — but different. There was a tug-of-war going on here, a fight for acknowledgement and respect between the two of them. But Caroline could feel a level of distrust on his part, warring with something else.

And on hers? She felt suddenly confused by her own response to him, because it was not a neutral response. Her heart had sped up, her nerves tingled with awareness of him. She pressed her lips tightly together, as though they might betray her into saying or doing something rash. And Caroline was the first to drop her gaze before the intensity of his scrutiny.

'It's late,' she said, as though she hadn't previously used the same excuse.

'And so you're going to run away.'

'Run away?' Caroline uttered a patently

false laugh. 'Don't be absurd. It's been a long day, and I'm ready to bring it to a close.'

'Without checking on Wilhelmina?'

Her head snapped back toward him. 'Do you think she's in danger?'

'Probably not, but I have every intention of checking on her before I call it a day.' He regarded her with a distinct challenge in his eyes. 'I thought perhaps you would come with me.'

'Of course I will,' she retorted. 'In fact, there is no need for you to go at all. I'm quite capable of looking in on her and seeing that all is well.'

'Hmm. Still, I prefer to see for myself.'

'Very well,' she agreed stiffly. 'Did you wish to go now?'

He rose and offered her his hand. 'I would not wish to keep you from your bed any longer than necessary, cousin.'

Caroline allowed him to assist her to her feet. She could feel the nerves jump in her hand at his touch, but she felt sure he could not detect the tremors himself. What was the matter with her all of a sudden? Caroline decided she would be very glad to close the door of her bedchamber behind herself this evening, and the sooner that happened the better. She disengaged her hand and moved swiftly toward the hallway, knowing that Lord Hartville would be right behind her.

★ ★ ★

At the doorway to the attic, when Caroline paused, Hartville cocked his head at her and said, 'If you would rather not, cousin . . . '

She frowned at him. 'I merely wished to open the door quietly, and listen for a moment, before we go stomping up the stairs and frightening anyone away who shouldn't be there.'

His brows rose. 'You really think it possible that someone is there?'

'I don't know. I just keep wondering why all of this happened,' she admitted. 'Because it did happen. Meg and I weren't dreaming, you know.'

'I trust your account, cousin. What concerns me is whether the incident was a mere prank gone wrong, or something more sinister.'

Caroline felt a shiver race down her neck. 'If it wasn't a prank, what could it have been?'

Hartville shrugged and carefully opened the door. They listened for a while, but no sound reached them from the floor above. He motioned Caroline to go ahead of him and she stepped onto the first stair, saying, 'They all squeak abominably. The carpeting doesn't help in the least.'

'So I apprehend.' There was amusement in his voice as each tread protested under her weight, and then his. 'I don't suppose anyone got up here undetected.'

'No, but consider what happened last night. Meg and Wilhelmina were undoubtedly asleep when someone came up the stairs. Wilhelmina was frightened but may not have realized what awoke her, and I don't think Meg heard it. She went down to get the child some warm milk to calm her and help her sleep. Whoever was up here must have followed her down and blocked the kitchen door so she couldn't come back up. And then returned to the nursery floor when I was here. Instead of coming into the room when I called out, she — or he, I suppose — turned around and hurried off.'

They were at the head of the stairs now. 'Where is Wilhelmina sleeping?'

Caroline pointed down the hall. 'Her room's above mine. At least the nursery is. Actually, I suppose the room at the end isn't quite over mine. The thump I heard might have come from the nursery itself.'

'Let's make certain they haven't heard us and become worried,' Hartville suggested, leading the way down the corridor. At the door he tapped lightly and called softly, 'Meg? Wilhelmina? It's Miss Carruthers and Hartville checking to see that all is well tonight.'

When there was no response, he opened the door and held his candle so the light shone into the room, which was empty. No Meg. No Wilhelmina. The beds were made. There was no sign that anyone had used them that night.

'What the devil?' Hartville muttered.

He heard Caroline draw in a startled breath behind him. 'You're positive this is where they slept last night?' he demanded.

'Absolutely. Wilhelmina was in that bed,' she said, pointing across the room. 'I sat down on it to speak with her.'

'Well, she's not there now,' Hartville said, stating the obvious. 'They must have decided to sleep in one of the other rooms.'

He moved on to the nursery, next door, and they found it empty of human habitation, though it was obvious that Wilhelmina had spent time there recently. There were toys neatly stacked on a table, including a set of toy soldiers Hartville had played with as a boy. A child's chair with a book on its seat was pulled up to the hearth. Hartville gave a tsk of annoyance at the emptiness. Caroline's face showed her alarm.

'Are there other rooms here with beds?' he asked.

'I have no idea. It's your house.'

'Well, I don't hang around the nursery floor much anymore.'

Methodically they opened each of the doors off the short hall to check if the maid and her charge were bedded down elsewhere. Each of the other rooms had obviously long been given over to storage. There were chests and boxes, broken furniture and forgotten portraits. But no Meg, no Wilhelmina, and no sign of where they might have disappeared to.

16

Caroline felt her alarm growing, try as she would to control it. Hartville stood at the top of the stairs and shook his head, as though she had questioned him.

'I refuse to believe that they have come to any harm,' he said. 'Where does Gladys sleep?'

Meg's sister had worked at Berwick Hall for several years, which meant that she probably shared a chamber with another maid in the attics of the south wing of the building. Caroline did not point out again to Hartville that he should know this sort of thing better than she. Instead she led the way down the stairs and back through the main portion of the house to the south wing. Here, however, she was at a loss.

'I don't actually know where the stairs are,' she admitted, feeling slightly confused by the twists and turns they'd taken, and the blackness beyond their feeble candlelight.

'It's been years . . . ' Hartville stood for a few moments taking his bearings, then nodded and led the way down a short hall which had only one door giving onto it. He opened the door and they faced a staircase much like the one to the nursery attic.

'As I recall, this is only for the female servants. The men are in the west wing. All very proper, you see, cousin.'

Caroline did not find his hearty announcement reassuring. 'I'm fascinated that you remember exactly where it is then, cousin,' she retorted. 'Shall I go up and check?'

'If you would. I'm sure there's no danger, and it would be considered improper for me to be up there.'

She did not believe that there could possibly be danger above, either, but that hardly seemed to pacify her thudding heart. As she climbed the stairs, with her candle flame flickering wildly, Caroline had to steel herself against faintheartedness.

Not for the world would she allow Hartville to see that she was frightened, however. When she reached the door at the top of the stairs, she looked back down at him, standing in the doorway, and she smiled brightly. And then she reached for the doorknob.

Because of their early work hours, the various household staff generally settled down for the night at a reasonable hour. Only a few of the manservants maintained a presence on the living floors to cater to Hartville's whims in the late evening. The maids and kitchen help were mostly in bed before nine.

So Caroline expected all to be dark and quiet on the second floor when she opened the door. She was not relishing the thought of wandering around, tapping on doors, alarming housemaids and disturbing the sleep of innocents. But Wilhelmina and Meg had to be found or a general alarm raised to find them.

The door to the attic opened easily and Caroline stepped out into the whitewashed hall with trepidation. The first thing she noticed was a buzz of voices, excited but low-pitched. The second was that there was light coming from a room halfway down the hall, where the door stood partially open.

Caroline immediately moved toward the source of the light. She made no attempt to hide the sound of her movement, and when she reached the door, she called out in warning. 'Gladys? Are you there? It's Miss Carruthers.'

A head popped round the door almost instantly and a pale face regarded her with alarm. 'Miss? Is anything wrong?'

'Meg and Wilhelmina aren't in their room. We've come to see if they're here.'

'We?' Gladys peered out into the hall beyond her, alarmed. 'You haven't his lordship with you, now?'

'He's waiting on the floor below. He's very concerned.' Caroline herself was feeling strangely better, perhaps because Gladys had shown no surprise at her sister's disappearance. 'Are they here — Meg and Wilhelmina?'

'Yes, miss. Right here in this room.' Gladys lowered her voice. 'They come right after dinner because the wee one was that worried. Meg tried to explain, but Willy was having none of it. Said she'd rather sleep in the stables than in her bed, you see.'

Though she didn't precisely see, Caroline nodded. 'If I might speak with Meg . . . '

'Yes, miss.'

Gladys disappeared as quickly as she had appeared. In a moment her sister emerged in her stead, and stepped outside into the corridor. 'Oh, miss, I'm sorry to have worried his lordship. Who was to know that he'd come to see about Willy?'

'Oh, I quite understand. But he has taken the events of last night seriously, Meg, and wanted to assure himself that the two of you were safe.'

'And we were, miss,' Meg assured her. 'But for the life of me I couldn't make Willy see that. She just kept insisting that a man would come in her dream to harm her. She says she knows that dreams are make believe, but there was no winning her over. She wouldn't even come up to the nursery floor to get her night dress.'

Meg shook her head, perplexed. 'I didn't like to upset Lady Hartville or Mrs. Bluestone, as I'm sure Willy will be right as rain in the morning. So I just brought her here. But even here she can't settle down, Miss Carruthers.'

'Perhaps there are too many people involved in helping her,' Caroline suggested with a slight smile. The voices from inside the room continued unabated. Half the female staff must be squeezed into this one small room, Caroline supposed, with the stated purpose of helping poor Wilhelmina achieve a good night's rest.

Meg bit her lip. 'Mayhap. You know how it is, miss. Every one of them has a story about when a dream of theirs came true. All nonsense, of course. Easy to remember a dream after something havey-cavey happens. But Willy's wide-eyed at their tales. I should have sent them all about their business, should I not?'

'Never mind. We'll do it now. Are there beds enough for the two of you?'

'Oh, yes. I'll share with Gladys. We used to at home. And Willy says the pallet reminds her of where she lived before. You don't mind, miss?'

Caroline shook her head. 'But I'm a little surprised. Wilhelmina seemed to have quite accepted what happened last night. She appeared to go off to the home farm in high gig. Did something untoward happen there?'

'Not as I recall. Willy loved the animals and we planned to go there again. At dinner, though, she hardly said a word, and she ate like a sparrow. I was with her the whole time, and I saw nothing as would trouble her.'

'Well, clear out the room so she can sleep now. Say I insisted upon it. And I'll talk with her in the morning.'

'Thank you, miss.'

* * *

Hartville watched impatiently as Caroline slowly descended the stairs. 'They're there,' he guessed, seeing that she no longer had the intensely worried look on her face. 'But why aren't they on the nursery floor?'

'Meg said Wilhelmina refused to go back there to sleep, talking about a man coming to harm her in her dream.' Caroline explained what she'd learned, concluding, 'I don't suppose we can expect a five-year-old to be rational about such a matter. I'll speak with

210

her in the morning.'

'What man does she think is going to harm her?'

Caroline shook her head as she stepped down into the first-floor hallway. 'Meg didn't say. I don't imagine Wilhelmina meant you.'

'*Me?*' Incensed, Hartville glared at her. 'Well, of course she didn't mean me. Why would she think I would harm her?'

'Last night she did say she thought you didn't like her, and she asked me if you were going to send her away.'

'Caroline,' Hartville said with exaggerated patience, 'this is something you failed to mention when you were enlightening me about what happened last night. Are you certain you haven't just made it up?'

'Believe what you wish,' she snapped, turning from him and proceeding down the corridor.

'Well, it is rather odd that it's just come up now,' he insisted, catching up to her with a few long strides.

'What is so odd about it, Hartville? Did you want me to remind you that Wilhelmina is not a duty you took to gladly?'

'Wilhelmina is not my duty. She is not my child, cousin. How many times do I have to explain that to you?'

'She *could* be your child.'

'As she could be yours, or your brother's.'

Caroline spun so quickly that her candle flame came dangerously close to catching her sleeve on fire. Hartville instinctively reached out, trying to rescue her. His own candle, swinging wildly in his attempt to commandeer hers, sprayed hot candle wax down the front of Caroline's gown. She screamed and dropped her candle. Hartville tossed his own after it and grabbed hold of the spattered bodice of her gown. In one swift movement, he tore it from her body, leaving her standing there, astonished, in her underclothes. Her wrecked gown lay in disarray at her feet.

For a moment, neither of them spoke. Hartville quickly knelt down and picked up both of their candles, which had been extinguished against the carpet.

'I beg your pardon,' he managed as he rose again. 'I didn't want you to be burned by the hot wax. Are you all right?'

'Am I all right? Of course I'm not all right. Dear God, how could I be all right? You've destroyed one of the four gowns I have with me and left me naked here in the hall with you.'

'You're not naked. And of course I will replace the gown. What I meant to ask, Caroline, is whether you've been burned.' Hartville was not, of course, looking at her.

Not that it made much difference, he thought, since the hall was black as sin. Well, not sin perhaps, but rather dark. He had caught a glimpse of her white underclothing.

Caroline bent down and retrieved the wretched piece of fabric from the floor. Holding it to her chest, she said formally, 'I do not believe I've been burned. I screamed more out of surprise than out of pain. Hot wax cools very quickly, you know, and it did not touch my skin. However, I should very much like to be somewhere where you aren't, Hartville. All in all this has been a rather trying day.'

'I'll see you to your room.'

'I think I would prefer it if you did not.'

'Well, I intend to,' he said stubbornly. 'I'm not going to molest you, cousin. I just want to be sure that you get to your room safely.'

'All things considered, I believe I am more likely to make it safely to my room if you do not accompany me.'

'Do you intend to stand here arguing with me?' he demanded. 'For I warn you that I will pick you up and carry you to your room if you don't start moving in that direction.'

Indignant, Caroline stomped away from him, muttering, 'As though I were to blame for this! *You* are the one who tried to grab my candle, and *you* were the one who poured hot wax on me, and *you* were the one who ripped my dress off. To say nothing of your decision to place Wilhelmina's parentage at my feet, or those of my brother. *And* I haven't heard a word of apology for any of this.'

Hartville knew that he owed her an apology. Perhaps many apologies. But the sight of her stalking down the hall in front of him clutching her torn bodice had taken his breath and his tongue away from him. His eyes had rapidly accustomed themselves to the darkness and he could see her tidy figure marching bravely forward, hugging the ridiculous piece of cloth to her chest, when it was her back that presented itself to him.

Hartville realized that she must think, because the sleeves remained intact, that only the front of the gown had come off under his vigorous treatment. In fact the entire overskirt had landed on the floor. Only the most rudimentary piece of fabric remained across the back of her shoulders to shield them from his view. Her bottom, covered by a snug piece of white muslin, swayed enticingly away from him.

Though he knew it would be the gentlemanly course to shut his eyes to his guest's state of undress, Hartville was not feeling particularly gentlemanly at the moment. He followed Caroline at some distance, so as not

214

to upset her further, and perhaps under the pretext of behaving better than he was. But he had always had good night vision, and even from several yards back he was able to distinctly enjoy her enchanting figure.

Fortunately for both of them, they did not encounter anyone in their progress to the wing where Caroline had her sleeping chambers. Miss Carruthers did not bother to pause when she reached the door of her room. She did not bother to wish him a good night. Hartville assumed that she wished with all her might that he would *not* have a good night. Without casting back even the briefest of glances at him, she opened her door and closed it sharply behind her.

'Good night, cousin,' Hartville called after her. And before he turned away from her door he heard her moan. No doubt she had caught sight of herself in her mirror.

★   ★   ★

Caroline reminded herself, for perhaps the hundredth time, that there was no call for her to be embarrassed. She entered the breakfast parlor with her head held high. A series of misadventures, which could not for a moment be construed as having emanated from her, had served her very ill the previous night. She could take them in stride as well as any woman. Better than most, she assured herself. For she was not, and had never been, a missish girl.

So what if Hartville had witnessed her nearly naked body? It had been very dark with neither of their candles lit after he had torn her gown from her helpless body. Only an unreasonable woman could blame him for his impetuous act. After all, he had only been trying to prevent her from being burned.

But Caroline found that she must indeed be an unreasonable woman, for she wanted nothing more than to box the viscount's ears for his behavior. She would have been quite pleased to learn that he had finished his breakfast and left the house, but that was not what she discovered in the breakfast parlor.

Hartville was seated at the head of the table, his meal obviously finished, sipping from a cup of hot chocolate. The London papers were spread around him and he was perusing an article with keen interest. He glanced up as the door opened, and rose swiftly to his feet.

'Good morning, cousin,' he said politely. He wore a bland expression, but gave Caroline the impression that he was a trifle annoyed at being interrupted in his concentration on the news.

'Good morning, cousin,' Caroline responded with a tartness that could not help but disabuse the viscount of any charitable feelings on her part. 'Please don't let me disturb you.'

He regarded her warily as a footman pulled out the chair next to his for her. Caroline looked for a moment as though she would refuse to sit there. Her hesitation distorted his face in a way that told her clearly he was attempting not to smile. Oh, she would have boxed his ears all right, if she had had the courage. Instead, she pointedly ignored him as he reseated himself.

When he moved to put aside his paper, she said coolly, 'I beg you'll continue with your reading, sir. There is no need to make conversation with me.'

'To be sure,' he agreed, and settled back to consider the London weekly once again.

Caroline helped herself to the eggs and toast which a footman offered. She sipped at her tea and took dainty bites of her food, all the while staring straight ahead. Her state of nerves did not augur well for her digestion, but she refused to admit that in Hartville's presence her appetite had disappeared.

Hartville paid no attention to her at all. After a while he waved away the footmen and the two of them were alone, but still he said nothing. Caroline almost wished that Lady Hartville would appear, but it seemed unlikely, as she had been breakfasting in her room for some days now.

When she had finished her meal, what she was able to eat of it, she slid her chair back in preparation for rising. Hartville looked up and said, 'Why don't you join me for a ride this morning, Caroline?'

'No, thank you.'

'Then perhaps you'd be interested in a driving lesson.' His glance went to her hands, and he added, 'I'll procure a pair of gauntlets for you.'

'That won't be necessary. I have no desire to take so much as a minute of your time.'

Hartville shook his head sadly. 'You're angry with me.'

'Now why would I be angry with you?' she asked with deceptive sweetness. 'You have been all kindness and consideration of your poor relation. It would be most ungracious of me to feel anything but the most profound gratitude to you, would it not?'

'Ah, your tongue. I had almost forgotten how delightfully wicked it can be. Come, ride with me, Caroline, and I'll afford you every opportunity to exercise your acerbic wit.'

If she had been angry before, this mocking drove her to something akin to rage. Color flared in her cheeks. She rose and stood over him, her eyes narrowed, her hands formed into fists at her sides.

'How can you behave in this fashion? You humiliated me last night. I did absolutely nothing to provoke you. In fact, I tried in every way possible to accommodate you. But, you . . . You treated me like a . . . like a . . . a tart!'

'Good God, Caroline,' Hartville groaned, reaching out to grasp the fists that appeared ready to pummel him. 'I was only hoping to tease you out of any embarrassment you might have felt. I have the greatest respect and admiration for you, I promise you. You have no idea what you're saying.'

'I assure you, I do.' Caroline tore her fists from his hold, feeling provoked beyond endurance.

Striking out was never a solution to a problem, as she very well knew. But there was something so distressing about the way the viscount chose to deal with her that her reason was consumed by the heat of her anger. Caroline instinctively aimed her fist at his chest.

The sound of the thud so unnerved her that she fell back, alarm registering deep within.

17

Hartville remained seated at the table, a stunned expression on his face. In a low but intense voice he said, 'I see that I've royally bungled this, cousin. First, let me apologize. I meant you no harm last night. Surely you must realize that.'

Caroline could feel the tears pricking at her eyes but she refused to let them spill over. 'I know that you did not intentionally douse me with hot wax, and I know that you thought you were protecting me by stripping off my gown, but I also know that you made no effort to shield me from your view. You stood and watched me when I was . . . almost . . . when I had no . . . That shows absolutely no respect for me, my lord. None. You smirked at me, when I didn't know I was so exposed to your view.'

'No, I did not smirk at you, Caroline.' Hartville paused, apparently searching for the correct words. 'I did watch you. Not because you were an object of amusement or scorn, but because . . . well, frankly, because you're a very attractive woman.'

He held up a hand at her growl of protest.

'I know I shouldn't have watched. I knew it last night. But I seemed helpless to obey my better instincts. The whole situation was so ridiculous! And it was dark. Remember how dark it was in the hall.'

'Oh, I remember,' she retorted, her anger not at all assuaged. '*I* had no difficulty making my way to my room. Nor did I hear you stumbling along behind me. Why couldn't you have told me that I had nothing on?'

Hartville shrugged. 'My dear girl, you did have something on. And it would only have served to embarrass you if I had called attention to your . . . um . . . state. There you were, marching along so bravely with your dress clutched to your chest . . . '

'Oh, you are impossible! I don't know why I'm bothering to speak with you at all.' Caroline turned abruptly and headed for the door.

Hartville didn't know whether to attempt to stop her or not. She had every right to be angry with him, he knew. And yet, didn't her anger have more to do with her misperception of his attitude toward her than her actual embarrassment at being observed in such a distressing state?

'About Wilhelmina . . . ' he said.

As he had intended, she paused. But only

for a moment, before swinging around to glare at him. 'And you are to stop using the child as a sort of peace offering, Hartville! I don't believe you care a fig about her or what becomes of her, and your show of interest is merely a ploy to manipulate me for your own amusement.'

Always, there was a little truth to her accusations, Hartville realized. Which made it exceedingly difficult for him to refute them entirely with the vigor he wished he were able to. Not that he wished to manipulate her for his amusement, but he *did* wish to hold her attention. Unable with a simple statement to sort out the complexities of the situation, he merely asked, 'Have you spoken with her yet this morning?'

'No, I have not. But I intend to, once she is settled into the nursery.'

'Do you think she'll be willing to go there?'

'In the daylight, yes. Her fears seem to play around her dreams.'

'And why do you suppose that is?'

Caroline shrugged. 'I have not the slightest idea, sir. Perhaps it is because of her being frightened night before last, when it was dark and there was an intruder on her floor, and possibly in her room.'

'She hadn't spoken of dreaming before last night, had she?'

'Not that I'm aware of. Meg might know more.'

'I trust you'll fill me in on the situation once you've talked to them.'

Her hesitation worried him. He spoke a little more forcefully than he had intended. 'I need to know, cousin. If there is something afoot under my roof, I have every intention of discovering it. I could speak with the girl myself, of course . . . '

He knew that would arouse her protective nature. Caroline began to shake her head vigorously before he even finished speaking.

'I beg you won't do that, my lord. Wilhelmina would undoubtedly believe you were upset with her. She's too young to withstand the pressure you would bring to bear on her.'

'I would not pressure her,' he protested, though once again realizing that she was right. Despite his intentions, the five-year-old would undoubtedly be alarmed by being questioned by 'the fine man.'

'Promise me you won't interrogate her,' Caroline said.

'Very well. I won't question her if you will ride out with me after you've spoken with her.'

For a long moment Hartville thought she would refuse. Then Caroline nodded abruptly and left the room.

223

Hartville spent an hour with Wayne Davis before heading out to the stables, since he felt certain Caroline would put off joining him as long as she could. He also wondered what she was going to do about that riding habit of hers.

The spring day felt fresh if damp after an overnight rain. A watery sunshine bathed the new greenery with scarcely enough energy to highlight its determined growth. Hartville caught a glimpse of horses frolicking in the pasture as he came around the side of the ice house. He paused to watch their high spirits.

Spring was in the air, no doubt about it. Blood was rising in even the dumb animals, he thought, which apparently included himself, since he was experiencing an uncommon excitement, an unaccustomed vigor and well-being. Perhaps the same thing had happened on previous April mornings; he would have been willing to believe that. Surely nine-and-twenty years had not gone by when he hadn't felt this fire within himself, this urgency to grasp life with both hands.

Leaning on the fence rail, grinning at the playful colts, Hartville could not understand why he had spent so little time here at Berwick. The very air was intoxicating! The scent of grass and horses wafted to him, light as the breeze on which they rode. The twittering of birds, the stomp of horses' hooves, the murmur of voices from the stable, all of it seemed absolutely perfect.

And then Caroline was at his elbow. She, too, was perfection, if one overlooked the annoyance in her eyes and concentrated instead on the sweet bow of her lips, the curve of her soft cheeks, the pertness of her nose. One could hardly refrain from smiling at the scarf she had tucked down under the snug front of her riding jacket. But one must certainly avoid glancing at that ridiculous hat. Whatever had possessed her to purchase it? Hartville wondered.

'My brother gave it to me,' she said dryly, proving she could read his mind. 'Jeremy does not have exquisite taste in female clothing.'

'Then why do you wear it?'

She shrugged and turned to watch the colts. 'I suppose I keep hoping that a gust of wind will tear it from my head and dash it hopelessly into the mud.' She gave him an impish sidelong look. 'From your expression, I gather you feel similarly.'

'It's god-awful,' he agreed. 'I imagine we could arrange for its demise when we're out riding.'

She seemed to remember then that she was

put out with him and turned her head away. Hartville decided it would be best to get the matter of the child out of the way. 'Have you spoken with Wilhelmina?'

'Yes.'

'Tell me about it.'

Caroline sighed, but turned toward him again. 'She and Meg were in the nursery. It didn't seem to bother her. She'd had breakfast there and was using some old blocks to build a fortress. 'The fine man's house,' she said.'

Hartville remembered those building blocks. They had looked like the local dark Ordovician stone limewashed to prevent rainwater penetrating the cattle houses. Over the years he had built a goodly number of fortresses with them himself. 'What did she have to say about last night?'

'She couldn't explain why she had got so concerned about a man coming to harm her. I asked her,' Caroline said, her chin lifting defiantly, 'if it was you whom she thought might harm her, and she vigorously denied it.'

'I should hope so,' he muttered. 'So what man was it?'

'She couldn't say.' Caroline sounded as frustrated as he felt. 'A big man, she said, but it turns out all grown men seem big to her. When I asked her why he would want to hurt her, she shook her head. I couldn't press too hard for fear of upsetting her.'

'Which I would have done.'

'Well, you might have done. I think she's more comfortable with women than she is with men.'

'She was apparently comfortable enough with JoJo.'

'Yes, but you're not JoJo,' she pointed out. 'You would not have been able to pull more information out of her than I was, Hartville, I assure you.'

'I daresay. Very well, we'll let it go for now.' He leaned back against the fence and frowned. 'But I do have a suggestion on how to further pursue the matter.'

'And what might that be?' she asked, skeptical.

'Later, you and I might go to her and join in her game of building Berwick Hall. We could show her where the nursery falls in the building, and ask her if she has any memory of a man in that part of the house. Or if she remembers what woke her by imitating the sounds of doors opening, drawers closing, people walking in the hall. Make a game of it, so as not to frighten her.'

Caroline looked surprised. 'Hmm. It might work. She's a clever child, when all is said and done. Just so long as you don't run roughshod over her.'

'As if I would.'

His companion sniffed. 'You might, if you had a mind to. People who are accustomed to always having their own way don't learn to tread so lightly as the rest of us do.'

'Hah! So what accounts for your brother's heavy tread, cousin?'

'Jeremy does not have a heavy tread. He has learned to handle people with humor, a quality which you perhaps do not appreciate.'

Hartville grimaced. 'Not all of us find the world so vastly amusing as your brother does.'

'More's the pity.'

'I can see that I'm not going to sway you from your firmly held opinions. Come, let's have a ride. Will you be satisfied with Holly again?'

'More than satisfied,' she said.

As he turned to lead the way to the stables, he said, 'I like your scarf, Caroline, so . . . modest.'

She scowled but said nothing as she fell into step beside him.

★   ★   ★

Holly was in high spirits. This time, however, Caroline felt more comfortable in the sidesaddle than she had on their earlier

228

outing. The mare's speed was exhilarating, and Caroline trusted her surefooted stride. Hartville kept them on a route headed toward the water.

The lake beckoned blue through the trees. Caroline was surprised by the size of it, bending away beyond their sight. By the time they reached the level of the lake, however, its color had oddly changed from blue to a dull gray. Caroline pointed to it and asked, 'How does that happen? It was blue not twenty minutes ago, at least from farther away.'

Hartville shook his head in amusement. 'My dear cousin, have you not noticed that the morning has clouded over? Ullswater is merely reflecting the clouds above it.'

In truth Caroline hadn't noticed the change in the weather. She had so thoroughly enjoyed the ride that the change from sun to shadow, not infrequent in this neighborhood, had totally escaped her. Now she noticed that it was not only darker, but cooler, and she realized that already there were light drops of rain falling.

'Oh, dear. We'll never make it back to the stables before that threatening bank of clouds reaches us,' she said, pointing beyond the lake to gathering thunderheads. 'I'm not good in storms, Hartville.'

'Oh? What do you mean by 'not good'?'

Caroline turned her head away from him and patted her mare's neck. 'They frighten me,' she said, so softly he almost did not hear her.

'Well, we could make a dash for it,' he suggested just as fat drops of water began to fall in earnest, quickly dampening the path with the accompanying smell of wet soil. 'Or,' he said, changing his mind, 'we can take cover under those trees.'

Taking cover did not really appeal to Caroline. Not that she wished to get soaked to the skin as the temperature continued to drop. But under a few trees there would be almost no protection from the brunt of the storm — the rain, the wind, the thunder, and especially the lightning. Caroline was, to put not too fine a point on it, terrified of being outside in thunder and lightning.

Hartville regarded her pale face and stiffly erect carriage, and motioned to the stand of trees. 'We're going to have to take cover, Caroline. With luck the storm will pass over in twenty minutes, half an hour, but my guess is that it's going to be a rough one until it does.'

Before she could even set Holly forward, there was a crack of thunder that proceeded to rumble noisily across the valley. Caroline shuddered as a jagged flash of lightning quickly followed. 'Oh, dear,' she muttered, her hands beginning to shake.

Hartville, obviously startled by the depth of her alarm, took hold of Holly's bridle and led her under the stand of evergreens. Warrior became a little high-strung during storms, too, but Holly scarcely seemed to notice the rain or the noise as she clopped along beside them.

The evergreen boughs were an effective roof above them, the pine needles thirstily absorbing water before it could pelt down upon the riders. Hartville slipped from his saddle and tied Warrior to a tree, then turned to help Caroline down. She sat her horse rigidly and appeared to have no intention of dismounting.

'Come, Caroline,' he said firmly, holding up a hand. 'You'll feel better on the ground.'

Her eyes were huge with an exaggerated alertness. 'No. If I stay on Holly, I'll be able to gallop home on her if lightning should strike us.'

'Lightning is not going to strike us,' Hartville said patiently. 'I'd like to tie Holly near Warrior so she'll calm him. He's 'not good' in storms either.'

A rueful grin played across his face, and he cocked his head at her. 'It's a great relief to me to find that there is something you are not

231

exceptionally talented at, cousin. Here, give me your hand.'

Caroline did as he bid, though her hand was trembling uncontrollably. As she allowed him to hand her down from the mare, another roll of thunder crashed about them, closely followed by a flash of light.

Caroline found herself somehow enveloped in his arms. She could not be sure if she had moved there of her own volition, or if he had pulled her in to comfort her. In either case, she found herself totally unable to withdraw from his support.

The storm raged around the stand of trees, and a cold wind raced through it. Caroline felt it tug at her hat again and again, until finally the hat tore free from her head. Since she had no love for that ridiculous item of apparel, she made no move to save it. She could hear, and feel, Hartville's laughter at this pass. Pressed against his chest as she was, the beat of his heart, and the shaking of his body with amusement, communicated themselves to her in a startlingly immediate way.

'Oh, Caroline,' he said, shaking his head, 'your brother will be vastly disappointed to find you've lost that remarkable chapeau. I could, even now, retrieve it for you, if you were to unhand me.'

But the wind shrieked and the thunder

roared and the lightning smacked something not so far from them, and she clutched all the more fiercely at his coat.

'Ah, well,' he said, his voice a whisper into her hair, 'I trust it will serve its purpose in life by decoying the lightning from us. We shall find it tomorrow, a cinder in the path, sacrificed to the gods of stormy mornings.'

'How can you be so amused?' she demanded with trembling lips. 'It seems quite likely to me that it is the two of us they will find as cinders.'

'Well, it has been very enjoyable while it lasted,' he said philosophically.

'How can you say that? It is the most wretched storm I've ever been exposed to!'

'I wasn't referring to the storm, actually.'

Caroline fell silent. She would have pulled away from him then, if she had found it possible. But the storm continued in all its noisy, dangerous fury, and she felt shielded by his arms, protected by his body.

'People aren't hit by lightning all that often,' he offered after a while. 'And it's usually those odd fellows who stand out in some field with a scythe in their hands, daring the gods to strike them down, isn't it? I've never heard of a woman being hit by lightning, come to think of it. Have you?'

Caroline did not remember whether she

had or not, but that seemed irrelevant to her at the moment. What was relevant, and a little alarming, was the way Hartville had turned aside from her, as though he meant to let her go. His arms were still around her, true, but in a very awkward way. Instead of his broad chest, she found herself pressed up against his arm and shoulder and hip.

His voice sounded a little husky now, as though he had caught a chill. 'You know, I am exactly the opposite of you, Caroline. I find storms exhilarating. They're a natural event accompanied by their own drums and bugles and fireworks. The air is positively charged with excitement. The power, the beauty of it all!'

'There is no beauty that I can see,' she said dampingly.

'No? Look there.' He pointed out across the lake, where a bank of clouds seemed to roil on the horizon. Sheets of rain slanted across the landscape, blown by a gusty wind. A shaft of errant sunlight slid past the clouds to create a magical rainbow. 'You have to admit that's remarkable, cousin.'

Caroline thought it was the most beautiful rainbow she'd ever seen, possibly because it seemed to her that if the sun was coming out, the storm was largely past. She murmured her appreciation and, reluctantly, using a great deal of determination, pushed herself away from the sturdy viscount. 'Yes, indeed. It's a wonderful sight.'

Hartville tipped her chin up and considered her thoughtfully. 'You're going to be all right now, cousin?'

'Perfectly,' she assured him. 'The storm seems to have largely passed us by now.'

Though a distant faint rumble made her shudder slightly, Caroline stood her ground. Her companion thrust his hands back into the gloves he'd removed after dismounting and turned to check on the horses. Holly and Warrior were aligned head to tail with shoulders touching, and though Warrior tossed his head restlessly, he did not appear much disturbed by the storm.

Hartville brought Holly around, leading her out from under the dripping evergreen branches into the open air. Caroline could not see what his hurry was. They could have avoided the remaining sprinkles by staying under the trees. But she followed him out, receiving something of a shower from the branches, and allowed him to give her a leg up onto the mare.

The water dribbled down her neck, since she had no hat-brim to catch it. Her hair, released from its captivity and blown by the wind, hung in strands on her forehead and her neck. Caroline thought she must look disheveled indeed. Hartville swung into the saddle with an effortless ease that Caroline would have admired had she not been distracted by another rumble of thunder.

'It's miles from here,' he assured her, swinging Warrior around beside her. 'I've lived here all my life, and I promise you the storm has passed. We're not going to be struck by lightning today.'

There was such amusement in his voice that Caroline glared at him and tossed her head. 'Much you know,' she muttered.

Hartville cocked his head at her. 'I beg your pardon?'

'Nothing, nothing.'

Caroline clicked her tongue to urge Holly forward. She knew something had happened to her when Hartville had held her in his arms. Not going to be struck by lightning indeed, she thought with a sigh. Perhaps he wasn't going to be. Caroline feared it was too late for her.

Though it was not particularly wise to set a brisk pace for her mare on the muddy path, Caroline had a great need to be back at the Hall and alone. Holly didn't slip or stumble, but her hooves splashed up mud which spattered on Caroline's gown. Just one more difficulty to be overcome, Caroline thought with resignation.

18

The viscount had not lied about his fondness for storms, but he thought perhaps this one would have been better sat out at home. His surprise at Caroline's fear had been nothing compared with his surprise at his own response to holding her in his arms.

And he was still uncertain as to how that had come about. Surely she must have been the one to initiate such close contact between them. It would never have occurred to him to hold her that way — would it? She was, after all, an attractive young woman and something of a relative as well.

But worst of all was his traitorous body, of course. Heaven knew he had had no thoughts of an amorous nature when they started their ride — no more than he would have at any given time. Nor had he had them when she propelled herself off her horse and into his safekeeping.

Safekeeping? Hardly! At first she had just been there, shaking and in need of comfort, and he had felt a little foolish but perfectly capable of soothing her alarms.

So what had changed? Certainly there had

been the moment when he realized that he was cradling in his arms that same body with its elegant hips and shapely legs he had seen marching away from him the previous night — to say nothing of the tantalizing sway of buttocks under thin muslin.

Well, he must be a wretch indeed to have pictured her that way when the poor woman was helplessly frightened by thunder and lightning, shaking like a blancmange right against his chest. And though he had attempted to hide his ungentlemanly — but surely quite natural! — response from her, he very much suspected that something of his misbehavior had impressed itself on her mind. Hadn't she muttered something just when she had gotten on Holly?

Hartville wondered if a gently bred woman of Caroline's age would understand what had happened. How innocent was she, after all? There was that decided awareness between her and Markingham. How far would a flirtation between them have progressed? Hartville found that he did not like the idea of a flirtation between Markingham and Caroline one bit. If there was some understanding between them . . .

Well, there wasn't, or he would have been informed about it by his mother. Caroline would have had no reason not to confide in

Lady Hartville any plans she might have for the future. Except that Caroline Carruthers was a mystery in several ways, was she not?

On more than one occasion Hartville had wondered just what role she was playing here at Berwick. Perhaps it was time to find out the answers to some of his questions instead of allowing his suspicions to slip away when his guest managed to beguile him with her charms. It was time for the real Miss Carruthers to be revealed.

*   *   *

The real Miss Carruthers was in a highly emotional state, and it had nothing to do with the storm. She was confused by her feelings for Hartville, which were not at all what they should be. He had embarrassed her the previous evening; she should be extraordinarily put out with him. And he had laughed at her fear of the storm; she should be ready to have nothing more to do with such a callous fellow.

Not to mention that her heart was already given to Giles Markingham. What a feckless chit she was turning out to be.

In disgust Caroline tossed her riding gloves on her bed and was about to remove the jacket of her habit when there was a timid knock at her door.

'Who is it?' she called, surprised.

'Gladys, miss. If I might have a word with you?'

'Of course. Come in, Gladys.' Caroline watched as Meg's sister slipped through the barely opened door and stood hesitantly on the threshold of the room. 'Is there something wrong?'

'Well, not to say wrong, miss.' Gladys continued to look uncertain but determined.

To encourage the maid, Caroline beckoned her further into the room. 'Could you give me a hand with these buttons, Gladys? My fingers are so cold from my ride that they don't seem to be working properly.'

'Oh, certainly, miss.' Gladys sprang forward and immediately began unfastening the long row of buttons with capable fingers. 'That was a sudden storm, wasn't it? And you've got your habit all spattered. Why don't I take it downstairs and see to its cleaning?'

'Thank you. I'd be grateful.' As Caroline allowed Gladys to remove the jacket, she said, 'Did you want to ask me something about Wilhelmina?'

'Not so much ask, miss.' After the briefest of pauses, Gladys continued as she laid the jacket carefully on the bed, smoothing out its wrinkles. 'Yesterday, I was a little late for my supper because I took Lady Hartville a special posset cook made for her. Meg and Willy were already at table when I came. But I happened to notice them from the doorway.'

Caroline realized this would have been the point at which Wilhelmina began to behave rather oddly. She stopped attempting to unfasten her skirt so she could concentrate her full attention on what Gladys had to say. Gladys had a troubled frown, and she gave a slight shrug.

'Mayhap it were nothing, miss.'

'Please tell me what you saw.'

'Well, Meg was being pestered by that footman with the yellow hair and green eyes. He's sweet on her and tries to sit next to her and get her to pay attention to him. You're not to think I'm jealous, miss! I've taken that one's measure, you may be sure.'

'Um, yes, I'm sure you have,' Caroline said faintly, not knowing what else to say. 'And was Wilhelmina bothered by the way the footman was behaving?'

'Oh, no, miss. It was like she didn't even notice him, or anyone else at table. No, miss, the thing was, she had the strangest look on her face, all crumpled looking it was. And she had that locket of hers clutched tight in her hand.'

'Her locket?'

'Yes, miss. So tight that the chain must

have broke, 'cause it came off from around her neck and I watched her stuff it in her pocket.' Gladys had moved forward and unfastened Caroline's skirt. As Caroline stepped out of it, the maid said diffidently, 'I know it don't sound like much, miss. But if you had seen her face, well, it was that peculiar. And she didn't take her hand out of her pocket for the whole of the meal. Now that's odd, don't you think?'

'Why, yes, I suppose it is.' Caroline had no idea what to make of the story, but she trusted Gladys's instinct that there was something significant about Wilhelmina's behavior. 'I appreciate your telling me, Gladys. I'll have to think about what would make Wilhelmina so concerned about her locket.'

Gladys gathered the pieces of the riding habit over her arm and walked toward the door. 'She's a dear, is Miss Wilhelmina. I hate to see her worried.'

'Fortunately, Meg takes good care of her.'

'As you say, miss.'

Gladys slipped back out the door without another word, leaving Caroline puzzling over the small bit of news she'd brought. Was it important enough to carry the tale to Hartville? Caroline caught sight of herself in the looking glass and sighed with frustration.

If she was going to seek an interview with his lordship, she had best get her hair under some kind of control. Hartville had seen more than enough of her worst side for one day.

★   ★   ★

Hartville was pleased to see that his mother was feeling much better that morning. When he called on her at her room, he found her dressed for an excursion downstairs, something she hadn't done except to welcome their company for several days.

'You look in plump currant!' he exclaimed, finding her on the verge of leaving her room, a book in her hand. 'What have you got there?'

'A book of fables and fairy tales. I thought I'd read some of them to discuss with Miss Carruthers. This idea of having her brother become a writer has captured my imagination, I must tell you. And Miss Carruthers herself is an accomplished artist. You must have some influence in London, Richard. Could you not find them a publisher?'

'My dear Mama, they have yet to set pen to paper! This is putting the cart before the horse indeed.'

'Oh, I know it is, but I suspect Jeremy

Carruthers could use some encouragement. A charming fellow, but perhaps not the type to carry through with a scheme.'

'I fear you are all too right,' Hartville agreed, smiling fondly at his parent. 'Unlike his sister, he's a will-o-the-wisp.'

She gave him a shrewd look. 'You've discovered some of Miss Carruthers's virtues finally, have you?'

'I will grant you that Miss Carruthers has many virtues. Mama, not the least of them being that stunning voice.'

He walked with his mother down the carpeted hallway to the grand staircase, where she invariably paused for a moment to appreciate the elegance of the entry hall below with its rich wood paneling and acres of white marble. He heard her sigh as she began her descent, and wondered what memories she was indulging — or what plans.

'I wish I were not so old,' she muttered.

'Old? My word, Mama, you're not old. It's having been a little under the weather that's brought your spirits low. They would pick up quickly enough if that imp Jeremy were around, I daresay.'

Lady Hartville reached across to pat his hand. 'Don't think I value you the less for being of a more solid disposition, Hartville. If you are,' she added with a twinkle in her eyes.

'I am most decidedly of a more solid disposition than Jeremy Carruthers.'

'Yes, and I'm glad.'

They had reached the vast expanse of white marble, and Lady Hartville turned toward the winter parlor. 'Have you seen Miss Carruthers today?' she asked.

'We rode, but our ride was cut short because of the storm. Would you like me to have her come to you?'

'Oh, no. I'm glad you're spending some time with her. A remarkable girl.'

'Hardly a girl,' Hartville protested, just as Caroline stepped out of the winter parlor. He flushed with annoyance at himself. She could not have helped but overhear their last remarks at the very least.

Lady Hartville tut-tutted this faux pas, and linked her arm with Caroline's. 'You must forgive him, my dear. At times he can be remarkably obtuse.'

'So I've noticed,' Caroline agreed, throwing Hartville a look of amusement.

'I've found a book that we might study for this writing project of yours and Jeremy's. Have you time to take a look at it with me?' her hostess asked.

'Of course.'

Since he had not been invited to join them,

Hartville shrugged and headed for the estate office.

★ ★ ★

The three of them gathered for a light midday meal. Caroline was partial to the Scotch mutton broth with pearl barley and the boiled neck of mutton with suet dumplings and caper sauce. This particular combination, with a baked rice pudding to follow, was served at least once a week, and she assumed it was a favorite of either Lady Hartville's or her son's. Both seemed to be in good appetite, and Lady Hartville, at least, in a good mood.

'Ah, Hartville, we should have had you join us to discuss the fairy tales,' she commented as she sliced a bite of mutton. 'You would have been better than either Miss Carruthers or I at judging how to relate them to London society. But I daresay Jeremy will be best of all at it.'

'I feel certain he will,' Hartville agreed dryly.

Caroline returned her soup spoon to her bowl and gave him an assessing look. 'Almost all the fairy tales have a moral of some sort to convey. I feel certain Lord Hartville would be much better at that sort of thing than Jeremy.'

Lady Hartville laughed. 'Don't let him fool you, my dear. Hartville may be acting the prig these days, but his sterling character is of recent vintage, I assure you.'

'Surely not,' Caroline protested, feigning shock. Then she asked hopefully, 'You don't mean to say that in London he has been a shocking rake or a reckless gambler?'

'Shall we say he has not been as sober as a judge or as prudish as a pastor,' his mama said, not without a certain amount of pride.

'Ah.'

The viscount shook his head at this disclosure, but refused to be drawn into their discussion. Caroline thought he rather liked being described in roguish terms. But it occurred to her that indeed he must have been something less than admirable, since his mother had had no hesitation in suspecting that Wilhelmina might be his child. This sobering thought made her frown, and Hartville instantly noticed.

'What is it, cousin? Are you afraid to associate with someone whose reputation is not as pure as the driven snow?'

'No, I was thinking about Wilhelmina.' Caroline turned to Lady Hartville as she spoke. 'Has his lordship told you that the child wouldn't sleep in the nursery last night?'

'He did mention it. Rather odd, I thought.'

Caroline turned back to Hartville and explained what Gladys had told her. In the telling it seemed even less important than when the maid had offered it to her. But Hartville sat musing for some time, not in the least dismissive.

'I've always thought there was something about the locket we needed to pursue. I've let far too many things distract me.'

This with a frown directed at her, as though she had set out to deceive him! 'What was it precisely that you planned to pursue, my lord?'

'It seems to me that we could find out who the woman is. Hire an investigator to show the miniature round London and ask if anyone could identify it.'

Lady Hartville looked surprised. 'But, Hartville, there's no saying that the woman was from London, surely. She might have come from the north, or the south, or anywhere at all. She might even be a foreigner.'

'She looked English,' he insisted.

Caroline pointed out the most difficult part of his plan. 'You can't very well take the locket away from Wilhelmina to have it shown round the capital. The child is very attached to it.'

Hartville's eyes narrowed as he studied her. 'I feel certain we could manage, cousin. Or is it that you don't want the locket shown? Are you quite certain you don't know who the woman in it is?'

'Hartville!' his mother exclaimed, looking very put out with him. 'Where are your manners? Of course Miss Carruthers knows nothing of the woman. She would have told us if she had!'

Unrepentant, Hartville said, 'Do you think so? I'm not so certain. The child arrived here in such proximity to Miss Carruthers's advent that I cannot help but think the two events linked in some way.'

Shaken by his obvious sincerity, Caroline lifted her chin. 'Perhaps you would be as good as to explain how that could be possible, sir.'

Hartville gave an irritable shrug. 'I don't precisely know, but I wonder if it doesn't have something to do with your brother.'

'What could Jeremy possibly have to do with the child?' his mother asked, bewildered.

'He could be her father.'

Caroline and Lady Hartville regarded him as though he had lost his mind.

'Well, he could be. He's blond and well favored. Taken in conjunction with the portrait in the locket, there is no reason why he should not be Wilhelmina's father.'

'Except that he most certainly is not,'

Caroline retorted. 'For heaven's sake, Hartville, think for a moment! The child is perhaps five. Jeremy would have still been a boy had he . . . consorted with her mother.'

Hartville was patient. 'Nothing could be more likely. Sowing his wild oats at that age is hardly an unusual thing for a spirited lad.'

'Yes,' Caroline agreed, her tone sweet and far too reasonable. 'Naturally you would know all about such things. But how would Jeremy have found Molly and JoJo, and where, pray tell, would he have come up with the funds which have been sent them for her care over the years?'

'Your brother is a clever fellow. No doubt he could have managed. He is not, after all, totally resourceless.'

'His resources, as you call them, barely run to managing his small household.'

'It would not have cost much to satisfy Molly and JoJo.'

Lady Hartville had listened to this discussion with mounting irritation. Now she used the fork in her left hand to rap Hartville's knuckles. 'You're fair and far out if you think Jeremy Carruthers plays some role in this farradiddle you've concocted. Anyone can see that he is as guileless as a puppy. My guess is that he hasn't really discovered women — not in the way you have, Richard,' she added sternly.

Hartville had the grace to flush. 'I am not saying that he had any intention of ruining some poor girl. Probably it was a matter of youthful enthusiasm and inexperience.'

'Oh, and how do you explain his arranging for his 'daughter' to arrive here during my stay?' Caroline asked.

His expression hardened. 'That must have been calculated. Knowing you, he probably thought that you would interfere in some helpful way, as you have done, to see that she was taken care of.'

'And then he arrived here to make sure his scheme had worked?' Lady Hartville queried, her eyebrows almost reaching her scanty hairline. 'You have most decidedly formed a different impression of Miss Carruthers's brother than I did. You think him somewhat Machiavellian, I take it.'

'Not precisely. His aim, no doubt, was to see the child provided for, and being unable to do so himself, he chose me, since . . . '

Caroline and Lady Hartville frowned at his hesitation. 'Since what, Lord Hartville?' Caroline pressed.

Though it was evident he had not intended to disclose the information, Hartville's face set stubbornly. 'Since I have been his benefactor for many years.'

19

Caroline was too stunned by the revelation to say anything. His mother frowned, but asked, 'Just how did that come about, Richard?'

Hartville gave an irritable shrug. 'I don't mean that I was the one who added his name to The List,' he said, obviously expecting his mother to understand his reference. 'That was done by my father some years ago, apparently. I had Davis track down the details for me, as I was not aware that Jeremy and his sister were on it.'

Confused, Caroline looked first at Hartville and then at his mother. 'I don't understand. To what list is he referring, ma'am?'

Lady Hartville sighed. 'Well, my dear, it's a matter we don't discuss much. Suffice it to say that this family has for many years undertaken to support relatives who were not as well off financially as ourselves.'

Feeling a little sick to her stomach, Caroline switched her gaze to Hartville. 'The money Jeremy receives quarterly comes from you?'

'From the estate.' Hartville's face was unreadable. 'The money is designated for both Jeremy and yourself.'

'What you're saying is that you've been supporting me since I left my aunt's home.' The words came stiffly, each one feeling like a wooden block in her mouth.

'Caroline, it is simply an estate expense.' He leaned toward her, earnestly explaining, 'There are literally dozens of Carruthers relatives who receive a similar draft. It's a family obligation of very long standing. You and your brother, as many others, were left without provision on your parents' deaths. My father quite naturally made arrangements to rectify that omission.'

'Dozens?' Caroline stared at him. 'Surely you exaggerate.'

'No,' he said dryly. 'Being a Carruthers seems to entail being impoverished.'

His mother's lips twitched. 'Oh, I daresay it is not quite so bad as that. Perhaps the Carruthers family was born under an unlucky star, so far as providing for itself. Many of the men are charming, but they don't seem to be able to hold onto any of the fortune that comes their way for more than a short time. There was that fellow from York, you will recall, Hartville. Came into an astonishingly large inheritance.'

Her son shook his head in wonder. 'An estate worth ten thousand a year if it was worth a penny. And not a sou of it left three years later.'

'But that's impossible,' Caroline protested. 'Unless he was a gambler.'

'Oh, I imagine he was a gambler all right,' Hartville agreed. 'He undertook to establish an orphanage, pledged the estate as collateral, and — poof! — no more estate.'

'Yes, and your father had warned him to have a care what he was about,' Lady Hartville reminded him. 'The man was too trusting by half. Unscrupulous people are always willing to take advantage of those who haven't an ounce of sense.'

Caroline was not particularly interested in the poor fellow in York. Though her hostess had perhaps hoped to divert her with the tale, Caroline had locked onto the fact that, all unknowing, she had been living on the largesse of her current host for several years. It was a bitter pill to swallow, and she felt resentful that she had just learned of it. Was Jeremy aware? Had he known when he came here that it was Hartville's generosity that had sustained them since they'd left their Aunt Matilda's home?

'I'm sure we have never properly thanked you for your support, Lord Hartville,' she forced herself to say. 'Unfortunately, I was not aware that you were behind the quarterly income. You must think us ramshackle indeed.'

Hartville glared at her. 'Don't be a gudgeon! You're far too sensible a woman to act like a peagoose, Caroline. The allowance has nothing to do with . . . anything. My father established it, and I have no more than carried out his wishes.'

'Heavens, yes,' Lady Hartville agreed. 'You are not to give it another thought, my dear. I am persuaded that Hartville never meant to mention it at all — or I would be most put out with him.'

'Thank you, Mother,' the viscount said, a note of long-suffering in his voice. 'I appreciate your confidence.'

Caroline's fingers pleated the skirt of her gown, but her eyes met Lady Hartville's. 'I can see that whoever directed Wilhelmina here must have known of Lord Hartville's generosity. Not that I believe for a minute that it was Jeremy! He simply isn't capable of such duplicity.'

Lady Hartville smiled beatifically. 'Of course he isn't.'

Hartville groaned. 'Really, the two of you are besotted with that lad. Of course he's capable of duplicity. Anyone is capable of duplicity.'

His mother frowned at him. 'That is a very

cynical attitude, Richard, and not worthy of you. Jeremy may be capable of impertinence or profligacy, but there is no guile there. I would swear to it.'

Though Caroline agreed with her, she was still so disturbed by the news of Hartville's unsuspected role in their lives that she said nothing. She was aware of the viscount's gaze on her, but she found it impossible to meet his eyes. Her new knowledge seemed to turn her life upside down. And it left her with a feeling of acute discomfort.

'I wonder if you would excuse me, ma'am,' she said to Lady Hartville.

Her hostess knew better than to question her. 'Of course, my dear. Run along now. I'll keep Hartville company for the sweet course.'

Hartville opened his mouth to speak, but shut it again. Caroline nodded in his direction before hurrying from the room. Her only thought was to hide away in her bedchamber for the duration of her visit.

Maybe she could leave immediately. She could pack her small trunk with all her belongings and beg the fare to London from the good-hearted Lady Hartville, who had sent her own carriage and a maid for Caroline when she traveled to Cumberland. She could take the mail coach today, or at the latest tomorrow, and be in London in no more than a few days.

Caroline fled up the staircase as though the devil himself were chasing her. She rushed into her room and threw open the doors of her wardrobe. She pulled out the first two dresses that came to hand, tossing them on the bed.

And yet how could she leave? Lady Hartville had not been well. Caroline felt an obligation to remain with her to offer companionship and perhaps even encouragement to get a new medical opinion. What a poor-spirited chit she would prove herself if she took leave of her hostess for no better reason than that Hartville had been supporting Jeremy and herself for several years without her knowing it.

With a supreme effort, Caroline stilled her hands and forced herself to sit on the chair beside her window. She attempted to look at the situation rationally, to tell herself that there was nothing unusual about someone in Hartville's position making an allowance to various relatives whose resources were extremely limited. For all she knew, dozens, hundreds of peers did precisely the same thing.

After all, it was hardly her fault, or Jeremy's, that they had no income. Perhaps someone should have pointed out to them that it would be necessary for them to earn their keep, but even Aunt Matilda had not done that. Caroline supposed that her aunt had assumed Caroline would live with her until the old woman died, keeping her company and running her household. Jeremy, on the other hand, with his good looks and his witty conversation, could be counted on to marry well.

Granted, there had never been the suggestion that Jeremy or Caroline would inherit anything of substance from Aunt Matilda. Their aunt felt she had more than done her duty by taking the pair of them in. Her own son and his family would no doubt be her only beneficiaries.

Caroline had supported herself, after a fashion. And not that Hartville would ever realize it. Because of Jeremy's inability to live within his straitened means, Caroline had done the fashion drawings for Ackermann's, which had brought in enough money to supplement their quarterly income. Mr. Random had also indicated that he was in a position to pass along more work to Caroline, should she have the time or inclination to handle it.

Now wild schemes of setting up as a modiste, or hiring herself out to sing at public occasions, raced through her mind. Ludicrous, every one of them. What difference did it make, after all, if the money supporting them came from Berwick? Was there really much difference between that and its coming from Aunt Matilda? Both were relations, even if Hartville was a much more distant one.

Besides, wasn't it entirely likely that Caroline herself would receive an offer of marriage soon, from Giles Markingham? He was showing all the signs of a smitten man on the verge of throwing aside caution and offering for her, despite her penury. Then she would never again be obligated to Viscount Hartville. And Jeremy, who would continue to be supported by him, probably wouldn't care in the least.

A watery sunshine wavered over the landscape outside. Caroline recalled the storm, and the way she had cowered in Hartville's arms. Everything seemed totally confused and unsettled to her. Hadn't she come to Berwick with the knowledge that Markingham was attracted to her? Hadn't it been her heart's desire to bring him to the sticking point?

But now, the thought of marrying him made her edgy and uncertain.

There was a soft tap at the door. Caroline forced herself to allow the young girl who served as her dresser to come in. The maid curtseyed shyly and said, 'If you please, miss,

Lord Hartville would like you to join him in the conservatory.'

Caroline was more than tempted to beg off, pleading a sick headache. But she knew the viscount was determined to find out more from Wilhelmina and expected her to help him. With a sigh, she agreed to join him. The maid turned to go, and then asked hesitantly, 'Was there something the matter with the dresses, miss?'

'No. No, I was just deciding which I would wear to dine tonight. The blue one, I think.'

'Very good, miss.'

When she had gone, Caroline sat for a while staring unseeing into the pale afternoon. Things had changed for her in the last few days. She wasn't sure exactly how, and she felt quite certain that she didn't like the change, but it was useless to pretend that her affections now were as they had been on her arrival at Berwick.

Which was neither here nor there, she decided with a determined shake of her head. What had been could be again, if one willed it so, surely. Caroline rose and pressed out the wrinkles of her sprigged muslin gown with capable fingers. She would finish with Hartville as quickly as possible and then spend the afternoon with her hostess. It was time she gave some thought to Lady

Hartville's situation and stopped bemoaning her own troubles.

★ ★ ★

The viscount was not at all sure Caroline would appear. He knew that his disclosure at luncheon had upset her, but he was not as certain as to why. In any case, it was far too late to take back his words; he'd have to make the best of it.

He paced along the narrow aisles of the conservatory, his hands clasped behind his back. The air felt moistly warm, and the rich loamy smell should have been soothing, but Hartville could scarcely distract his mind from his thoughts of Caroline. He did bend to push an aggressive fern out of his path, only to find that this particular fern was equipped with sharp little thorns that stuck in his fingers. He was attempting to extract them when he heard footsteps behind him.

His cousin hesitated in the doorway before drawing the white ironwork door closed behind her. She looked particularly unapproachable with her hair severely pinned back and a less than welcoming expression on her face. 'You sent for me, Lord Hartville?'

Hartville sighed and gestured toward the bench. 'Yes. Thank you for coming, Caroline.

I thought we might discuss how to approach Wilhelmina now.'

Though she looked skeptical, she took the offered seat, a bench wide enough for two people. Except that she had sat down directly in the center of it and looked up at him with that old meekness he knew better than to trust. 'Have you changed your mind about building a model of Berwick with her?' she asked.

'No. Well, if you happened to think that wasn't a good idea, I would certainly consider other suggestions.'

'But I think it is a perfectly acceptable idea.'

Hartville felt like grinding his teeth. Instead, he frowned at her. 'Look, Caroline, I don't know why you're so upset with me, but there's no need to be.'

'I'm not upset with you.'

'That is patently untrue! If I've done anything to offend you, I'm sorry. I promise you I had no intention of distressing you — or making you feel uncomfortable.'

'Really, my lord, you are quite mistaken. I'm perfectly comfortable.'

Since she sat stiffly upright, Hartville could see that he was getting nowhere quickly. 'Very well, let's go visit Wilhelmina and see what we can learn.'

Caroline ignored the hand he held out to her and rose without assistance. 'It's your mother who could use a little of your help, Hartville,' she said as she headed toward the door back into the house.

'Why? What's the matter?' he asked, suddenly alarmed. 'She hasn't had an attack of some sort, has she?'

His companion gave a long-suffering sigh. 'No, of course not. But something must be done with regard to her health. Have you sent to London for a doctor?'

'I've sent off a query, but have had no reply. I'm very much afraid that I shall have to go myself to find an appropriate man and bring him back with me.' He regarded her closely as he held the ironwork door for her. 'Do you think there is some urgency about this, Caroline?'

She shrugged almost irritably. 'Well, I cannot find myself in agreement with you if you are determined to put it off forever.' She added under her breath, 'As you appear to be doing.'

'And you appear to be searching for ways to find fault with me,' he grumbled. 'Not that I don't realize there are issues enough, but I would ask your indulgence, Caroline. For now, let's concentrate on Wilhelmina. This evening we will concentrate on my mother.'

'Very well.'

Hartville had no difficulty keeping up with her rapid stride, though he knew she had rather he fall behind and leave her alone. But he stuck like a court plaster, determined to win her over, as he always — so far — had been able to do. 'So you think she's a bright child, do you?'

'Yes.'

'Why do you think so?'

'Because she's curious and learns quickly.'

'What's she curious about?'

'Oh, almost everything — the size of the house, the layout of the kitchen, the plants in the kitchen garden . . .'

Hartville looked puzzled. 'What's unusual about the layout of the kitchen?'

'Apparently, even Molly and JoJo have a more reasonable setup,' she said, her eyes showing just a flicker of amusement. 'Their fire is closer to the table and the food doesn't get cold before it's served.'

The viscount could not remember the last time he'd visited the kitchens at Berwick. He felt almost certain that his father had approved an upgrading of them before he died. 'Don't we have a modern stove?' he asked reasonably. 'I'll wager Molly and JoJo didn't even *have* a stove.'

'You do have one, but it has been tucked

264

away behind the food preparation area. Very inconvenient, according to Wilhelmina.'

'And where would our budding architect place the stove?' he demanded.

'Right where the cooking fire is, of course.'

'Sounds logical. Why didn't we?'

'Probably because Cook was suspicious of the stove and didn't believe it would truly supplant the fires. I doubt the difference shows up much at your dining table, Hartville, as they would cover the hot dishes right at the stove. But the servants' food is taken to the tables straight from the back areas, which are even farther from their dining table than from yours.'

'Demme, how would a five-year-old notice something like that?'

'I told you I thought she was bright, Hartville. It's the sort of thing she notices. I don't mean that ideas spout from her mouth fully formed. She just says things like: 'Why's the food cold, Gladys? Where do they cook it?' '

'And you think I should look into that, too?'

'My dear Hartville, I have absolutely no opinion on that subject. I am merely relaying evidence of the child's curiosity.'

'But if you were . . . responsible for the arrangement of the kitchens, you'd make some adjustments, wouldn't you?'

Caroline flashed him a quick look. Hartville kept his face uncompromisingly neutral and she said, 'Perhaps.'

'And I suppose there are other things I haven't noticed that should be taken care of around here.'

'I don't go around looking for signs of your negligence.'

'I'm pleased to hear it.'

They were climbing the stairs to the nursery floor now, and Hartville determinedly turned his thoughts to Wilhelmina. 'What we want to find out from her is whether she remembers anything from the night the intruder was here,' he said. 'And why the locket seems to have special meaning for her. And whether she can tell us anything more about the man she's afraid of.'

Caroline stopped on the steps and turned to look back at him. 'You aren't going to press her until she becomes alarmed, are you?'

'Trust me.'

'I . . . hope I can.'

20

They stopped at the schoolroom door and called attention to themselves by commenting on Wilhelmina's large construction of building blocks. 'Is it Berwick?' Hartville asked.

'Part of it,' Wilhelmina admitted.

The viscount crossed the room to crouch down beside the construction. 'Where in the building are we now?' he asked.

Wilhelmina without hesitation pointed to the right-hand wing of her building. 'Here. And this is the room where I sleep with Meg.'

'Is it noisy there?' Hartville asked.

'No. It's real quiet.'

'Well, what kinds of noises do you hear at night?'

'Nothing,' she said.

Caroline had remained in the doorway and now closed the door with a snap. 'Do you hear doors closing like that?' she asked.

The child shrugged. 'Sometimes.'

'Something that loud would wake you up, wouldn't it?' Hartville persisted.

Wilhelmina nodded. 'But nobody slams doors at night.'

'Never?'

Wilhelmina looked to Meg for guidance.

Meg, a bright young thing herself, said, 'Maybe it was a slamming door that woke you up the other night.'

'Uh-uh.'

Caroline had moved to the windows and now allowed one to slip closed with a thud. 'Maybe something like that woke you up.'

The child shook her head. 'Noooo.'

This time Caroline moved to a chest of drawers and opened and closed a drawer. 'How about something like that?' she suggested.

Wilhelmina looked uncertain. 'I don't know. Maybe.'

Hartville's head came up. 'It might have been a drawer closing that woke you the other night?'

With a quick shrug, the girl said, 'Maybe. I'm not sure.'

'Do you think it came from inside your room?' Hartville asked.

'I was scared.' Her hand went unconsciously to her locket.

Caroline seated herself on the floor beside the child and asked, 'Do you keep your locket with you all the time, Wilhelmina?'

The child nodded.

'Even at night?'

She shook her head.

'Are you afraid it will get lost?'

'Uh-huh. Or someone might take it.'

'Who do you suppose would take it?' Caroline asked casually.

'I don't know.'

Caroline smiled at her. 'No one at Berwick would take it, would they?'

Wilhelmina glanced around the assembled faces. 'No. I guess not.'

'But then how could someone take it?' Hartville pressed. He tried to appear casual as he pointed to the building blocks on the floor before him. 'It's just people at Berwick who have access to it, don't they?'

Caroline rolled her eyes heavenward. 'Access? Really, Hartville, she's five.'

Wilhelmina watched this exchange with interest. 'A bad man might take it,' she said.

'Yes, but how would he get in?' Hartville asked her, with a withering glance at Caroline.

Wilhelmina shrugged.

Suddenly, Caroline crouched down in front of the child. 'Have you seen the bad man, Wilhelmina? Here at Berwick?'

'I don't know.'

Hartville felt totally frustrated by this kind of answer. Surely the child knew whether she'd seen the bad man or not. He was about to press this point when Caroline gave him a warning look. He clasped his hands behind his back and strolled off toward the windows, pretending to an indifference he could not feel.

Behind him he heard Caroline continue her gentle dialogue with the child. 'Sometimes, we just get a feeling that something is wrong, don't we?' she asked.

Hartville turned in time to see the child nod.

'And yesterday you got the feeling that someone wanted to steal your locket, didn't you?'

The child's hand moved instantly to clutch the locket with its picture of her mother. 'Yes.'

'But you didn't know who might want to take it from you, did you?'

Wilhelmina shook her head.

'When you were in the servants' dining hall, you started to worry about it — is that right?'

'Uh-huh.'

'You weren't worried at the farm?'

'Oh, no. We had fun at the farm. The puppy came home with us.'

Caroline looked straight across the room into Hartville's eyes before saying carefully, 'I think you met someone on the way to dinner, didn't you?'

Wilhelmina frowned, but Meg nodded.

'The two gentlemen, miss. Your brother and the other. We stopped to speak briefly.'

'Did they frighten you?' Caroline asked Wilhelmina.

'He was funny, the yellow-haired one. He said I must be a magician, to teach the puppy to roll over. I didn't really do that,' she confessed. 'The puppy just does that for fun.'

'And the other man? Did he say anything?'

Wilhelmina shook her head doubtfully. 'I don't think so. Did he, Meg?'

Meg shrugged. 'Just good day, I think. He was very polite.'

Hartville had moved closer to observe the three of them. Once again, Caroline had surprised him with her willingness to put to the test her fervent belief that her brother was blameless. And yet, from Wilhelmina's answers there was no certainty that he was. Might Jeremy not have displayed his usual charm to gain the child's confidence? And later, as she sat down to her meal, might she not have had second thoughts?

Markingham, with his dark good looks, the viscount dismissed as Wilhelmina's father. From all appearances he was well-heeled enough to support a dozen illegitimate children, had he had them. There was no reason for him to send a child to Berwick.

Caroline smiled at the girl and rose. 'Well, I

don't think you have anything to worry about, Wilhelmina. There are no strangers about now. Will you feel safe in your own bed tonight?'

The child looked doubtful. Hartville could tell that she wanted to be brave, but that she was not entirely confident. 'How about if we let the puppy sleep up here with you tonight?' he suggested.

'Oh, could he?' Her eyes shone with delight. 'I would take very good care of him.'

'If it's all right with Meg, it's all right with me,' Hartville assured her.

Meg laughed. 'He's not housebroken, the little scamp. But I think we can manage.'

'Oh, thank you,' Wilhelmina breathed, smiling shyly at the viscount.

Hartville crouched down by her, for the first time truly recognizing the child's deep appeal. He had been too caught up in trying to convince everyone of his lack of paternity to be able to see Wilhelmina for the delightful girl she was. 'And I think we need a name for him as well. Perhaps you could be thinking of one?'

'Toby,' Wilhelmina said instantly.

Taken off guard, Hartville looked mystified. 'You want to name the puppy Toby?'

She nodded. 'JoJo had a dog named Toby. I miss him.'

'Toby it is then.' Hartville reached out to ruffle her hair. 'See that you teach him some manners. He can't be rolling about all day, can he?'

Wilhelmina giggled. 'I s'pose not. But he's good at it.'

'There is that.' Hartville rose and made a small formal bow to Wilhelmina and Meg. 'Ladies, we should be on our way. Miss Carruthers has a multitude of things to do, and I have delayed her far too long.'

In the hall Hartville paused to study his companion. Her face was surprisingly blank. He was used to seeing emotion there, and intelligence, and a splendid animation that turned her distinctive features into something like beauty. Now he guessed that she did not wish him to read her thoughts. She did not pause when he did, but walked past him to the head of the stairs.

'The child didn't seem to have any fear of your brother,' he commented, hoping to stimulate a response in that neutral countenance.

'No, she didn't.'

Caroline started down the stairs and Hartville was forced to follow if he wanted to pursue the conversation. 'Did you form any particular impression from what you heard?'

His companion gave no more than a silent

shake of her head. This was most unusual, Hartville thought. Caroline seemed to have an opinion about everything. 'I thought you covered the ground very well,' he said.

'Thank you.'

At the door below she did not wait for him, but opened it and stepped quickly into the hall. Hartville could see that she was disposed to hurry off and leave him behind. 'Caroline, just let me say one thing.'

Her reluctance was obvious as she paused and turned cautiously to face him. He closed the door to the upper floor, leaving the two of them alone. 'No matter what your brother might have done, I wouldn't hold it against you. You know that, don't you?'

'Really, Hartville, you are too kind. And what if I had known of Jeremy's nefarious plans all along?'

His gaze sharpened. 'I feel confident that you did not.'

Caroline regarded him steadily. 'And I feel just as confident that Jeremy has nothing to do with this business.'

'You are his sister. Your loyalty to him would naturally blind you to his weaknesses.'

'Oh, hogwash! You are the most irritating, stubborn man it has been my misfortune to encounter since I left my aunt's care, Hartville.' Caroline made a gesture of pushing him away. 'Please just leave me alone. I'm sure you will agree that we did much better when we had as little to do with each other as possible.'

'No, I don't agree with that at all.' Hartville would have pressed the point, but he could see Caroline was close to the limits of her endurance. 'Go, then. But later we must confer about my mother's health. After dinner perhaps.'

'As you wish.'

Caroline set off down the hall at a pace Hartville would have admired, if he hadn't been all too aware that her haste was intended to put him as far behind her as quickly as she could. Much more slowly, he followed down the corridor, trying to make sense of everything that had happened so far that day. And convinced there was more of the same hodgepodge of disruptions, unruly emotions and contradictions to come.

★ ★ ★

Though Caroline managed to distract herself by waiting on Lady Hartville, and reading to her from the latest novel the dowager's friend Emma Percival had sent, always in the back of her mind was the question of who it was who had frightened Wilhelmina. When her

275

benefactress fell asleep in her large and comfortable chair before the fire, Caroline spread a blanket over her legs and left to seek out her own room.

The pale sunlight had disappeared once again, and Caroline found that her room was gloomy and cold. A fire had been laid on the grate and she set to lighting it, but her hands were awkward from nervousness, and it took her quite some time to get a decent blaze going. Drawing the chair close to the hearth, she curled up in it, covering herself with a woolen shawl.

A deep, worried sigh escaped her. She told herself that it was not fear that Jeremy might have something to do with Wilhelmina's arrival. Surely she knew her brother well enough to know that he had not sired a child and then dumped that child on an unsuspecting (and incredibly generous) relation whom he did not even know. But if not Jeremy, then who?

Her heart sped up at the logical answer to that question. Wilhelmina had encountered two men in her path on the way to the servants' dining hall. And the second man had been Giles Markingham.

Of course, it was entirely possible that it was neither of the two men who had set off the child's fears, but some more general situation — such as her expedition to the farm. The farm might have reminded her of Molly and JoJo's place, and that recollection brought on the fear of being sent away again. Obviously Jeremy and Markingham had said nothing to overset the child. Meg had been right there; she would have reported any untoward comments.

So what had happened? Caroline stared blindly into the fire, her hands clutched tightly in her lap. Jeremy had teased the girl; Markingham had been offhandedly polite. What was there in that to alarm a child?

The locket would have been visible to both men, certainly. Wilhelmina wore it proudly and almost obsessively. The locket was her link to her past. So Jeremy and Giles could have, would have, seen it about the child's neck, hanging down on her dress. For she didn't tuck it under, as some women were wont to do, hiding away the source of their pleasant memories from prying eyes. Wilhelmina seemed to need to have it visible at all times, to glance at and touch at will.

If it was not a word that had sparked her fear, then it was perhaps a look. Caroline shivered and rose to stir up the fire. Crouched in front of the grate, her eyes locked on the leaping flames, she allowed her imagination to conjure up the scene. If she were a small child, looking up at two men, they would seem like giants. If one of them joked with her and made her laugh, she would be pleased with his attention. If one of them stared at her locket, his eyes perhaps staying there too long, or holding a look of recognition, or . . . what?

Caroline jabbed vigorously at the embers. Her head ached, and her eyes had begun to burn — from the smoke, perhaps. She decided to lie down on her bed and seek the oblivion and restoration of sleep. The maid would wake her in time to dress for dinner.

★ ★ ★

Caroline and the viscount scarcely exchanged a word over the meal. Though Lady Hartville dined with them, she excused herself shortly after the three of them retired to the drawing room. Since nothing but stiff, polite conversation had graced the lips of either of her young companions, it was no wonder poor Lady Hartville was determined to escape the two of them. They'd become dead bores.

'You won't mind entertaining Hartville, will you, my dear?' the older woman queried with slightly raised brows.

'Certainly not,' Caroline replied.

Hartville bowed over his mother's hand

278

and bussed her cheek. 'Sleep well, Mama. I should like nothing better than to see you restored to full health.'

'I trust I shall be,' she said as she moved toward the drawing room door. But there she paused and turned to ask, 'The child, Wilhelmina, is she thriving?'

A quick exchange of glances between Caroline and Hartville seemed to leave both of them speechless. Finally, Caroline said, 'The intrusion has left her a trifle nervous, ma'am, but she seems to be faring well. Hartville has allowed her to have the puppy with her in the nursery.'

'You have?' Lady Hartville asked, surprised. 'Why, Hartville, I do believe you're mellowing in your advanced years.' She dimpled delightfully and beamed on the two of them. 'Perhaps you would sing a duet for me while I make my way upstairs.'

Caroline rose instantly and moved toward the pianoforte. 'It would be my pleasure, if Lord Hartville is agreeable.'

'I haven't Jeremy's voice,' he said, apologetic. 'But if Caroline will make allowances . . . '

Caroline's fingers ran easily over the keys as she nodded. Very much against her inclination, those fingers seemed to have chosen a romantic ballad. If her head had been ruling this decision, it would have picked out some solemn hymn. Hartville regarded her questioningly, but she ignored him and began to hum.

With the door standing wide, Lady Hartville began her slow climb up the stairs. Caroline raised her voice in song. The viscount soon joined in, surprising Caroline with the richness of his baritone.

At first the two kept their gazes far apart, as though avoiding the intimacy of singing together. After studying the angels and harps in the molding overhead, Caroline allowed herself a glance at the viscount, who apparently found his concentration improved by the carpet pattern. When, inadvertently, their gazes met, a shock of discovery passed between them. Their eyes remained locked on one another.

Stronger now, their voices blended in a harmony that soared well beyond the drawing room. Lady Hartville could not have failed to hear it on the floor above. Perhaps it could be heard even on the nursery floor, where Wilhelmina played with her puppy. Their song seemed to fill the entire building.

The music enveloped Caroline. That was not an unusual experience for her. She had played and sung for most of her life. It was part of her closeness with her brother, part of the intimacy she had felt with Markingham. But nothing had prepared her for quite what she experienced now.

Hartville's voice was inside her. It invaded and filled her with a luminous pleasure, one she had not experienced before. Unlike Jeremy's, his voice was not a perfect match for hers. Unlike Markingham's, his voice did not skirt and flirt with her own. Hartville's was inside her. It meshed with her flesh, it aroused her senses — she could taste it, and feel it, and smell it as well as hear it. Impossible, of course. But so it was.

Caroline was reluctant to bring the song to its conclusion. She allowed the last notes to hang in the air, fading softly into nothingness. She attempted to withdraw her gaze from Hartville's, but she could not. His eyes remained fixed on hers, his face a study in fascination. She tried to say something banal such as 'Your voice is better than you think, sir,' but she was unable to open her mouth.

For long minutes they remained thus, and then he slid onto the pianoforte bench beside her and captured her hands. 'There is some magic in your voice,' he said.

She shook her head. The magic, the mystery, was in his. Or had he felt the way she had when they sang? The color rose higher in her cheeks, which were already flushed with agitation. He drew her hands upward and kissed them, one at a time. But he did not let go of them, instead holding them against his chest as though to feel the beat of his heart.

'I've never heard anyone sing like you,' he said. 'It was wonderful last night and I was astonished. But just now . . . ' He shook his head, unable to explain how he had felt. 'The music, your voice, the experience was more like . . . Well, not quite like anything I've ever felt before.'

'Thank you,' Caroline whispered. Did you thank someone for invading you that way? Heavens, he couldn't know how she had felt about his voice — unless he had felt something similar.

Impossible.

She searched his face for his true emotions. And what she saw there was awe. Well, people were often overcome by their encounters with artistic beauty.

Very aware that the drawing room door was open, Caroline gently withdrew her hands from the viscount's grip. Another minute that way, and she would fall into his arms, she told herself sternly. And astonish the poor fellow. She turned to gather up the music that she'd set on the pianoforte.

'I'm sure your mother will have enjoyed

that,' she said lightly.

'Not as much as I did.'

'And yet you were reluctant to sing,' she teased him.

'More fool I,' he muttered. 'Tell me something, Caroline. Does every man who sings with you fall in love with you?'

21

'Don't be ridiculous,' Caroline said, feeling as if he'd dashed cold water in her face. 'My experience certainly is that men enjoy hearing themselves in a duet. They admire the strength of their voices against the lighter, gentler voices of their companions.'

'Now you're miffed at me again,' he said, obviously annoyed with himself. 'It was a foolish question, sparked by my observation of Mr. Markingham's attentions to you.'

Caroline thought perhaps she should just pull her hair out and be done with it. 'Go away, Hartville,' she muttered.

He rose from the bench, and moved a short distance from her, raking his fingers through his hair. 'I don't actually have a reputation for being so cowhanded, Caroline. You unnerve me.'

'I don't see why I should. I'm merely one of your numerous unacknowledged dependents.'

He scowled. 'Will you forget about that? It doesn't matter.'

'It matters to me.'

'Well, it shouldn't.'

They glared at each other for a long moment, then Hartville sighed. 'Let's at least not be at each other's throats,' he suggested. 'And certainly not with the door open.'

Caroline watched as he crossed to close the door into the hall. He stood for a moment leaning back against it, surveying her. Then he shrugged and came toward her, waving her to one of the matching overstuffed chairs. 'Let's discuss my mother.'

Not sure whether she was relieved or disappointed that their odd interlude was over, Caroline seated herself and smoothed down her skirts. Hartville stood behind the other chair for a minute, almost visibly pulling his thoughts together.

'I've spoken with Mama's dresser and with Mrs. Bluestone, as you suggested, and learned what they could tell me about her illness. I've sent a more detailed message to my solicitor in London asking him to inquire about a competent medical man who would come out here to assess Mama's condition. I've even sounded her out on the possibility of seeing the local fellow, but she's adamant about that. Tell me, Caroline, what you think my next step should be?'

She was gratified that he had acted so promptly on her advice — and relieved. Lady Hartville was decidedly in need of a professional opinion on her condition. 'Do you think your solicitor will be able to find someone, Lord Hartville?'

He regarded her quizzingly. 'Do you think you could call me Richard?'

'I . . . I suppose so.'

'Good. I hope you will.'

'Yes, well, it seems to me . . . Richard, that you had best go to London yourself and choose a man to come. You know your mother's symptoms now, and the duration and intensity of her spells. You're more likely to find the proper person if you describe the problem to him yourself.'

He drummed the fingers of his right hand on the top of the chair, considering. 'I don't like to be away for the time it would take to accomplish that.'

'Your mother seems to be feeling stronger each day now. It's probably the best time to go.'

Though he did not look convinced, he nodded. 'Very well. If she feels better tomorrow, I'll leave the following day. I'm sure you're perfectly capable of seeing to things in my absence, if you would be so good.'

'Certainly.' Caroline rose then and offered a tentative smile. 'I very much wish us to be friends, Hart . . . Richard. We both want what is best for your mother, and for Wilhelmina. I'll try harder to not be so prickly about dealing with you.'

She thought his face darkened momentarily, but the shadow was soon gone. 'Ah, a truce,' he said, moving quickly to her side. He possessed himself of one of her hands, lifted it to his lips — and speedily released it. 'Very generous of you, cousin. I shall do my part as well.'

'Thank you.' Caroline backed away from him, careful not to brush against his side. 'I'll say good night, then. It's been a long and tiring day.'

'Yes, indeed. Good night, Caroline.'

★   ★   ★

When she was gone Hartville possessed himself of the chair she had vacated and crossed one leg over the other. He hated the thought of going off to London just now, but he was certainly willing to do it if it would aid his mother's recovery. Staying at Berwick was only likely to prove more confusing with regard to his new and unruly attachment to Caroline Carruthers.

Hartville very much suspected that he had fallen in love with her. He had clung for some time to the possibility that it was merely a

287

physical desire he felt for her. And certainly he felt that. But this wish to be in her presence, to fence with her, to challenge her and revel in her sharp intelligence — that had nothing to do with the pleasures of the body.

How ironic! After all the available and appropriate chits he had met in London, none of whom had so much as brushed against his heart, he had to fall in love with his cousin Caroline.

Which was unfortunate, since she was obviously already in love with Giles Markingham.

★　★　★

Caroline refused to think about Hartville and what had happened when they had sung together. After all, what did it matter? As Jeremy could have told her, the viscount was not likely to consider her a match for himself, even if his mother apparently did.

Caroline would have to start thinking about returning to London. But, since Hartville would be gone for some time, Caroline's departure did not need to be precipitous. In the meantime she could be a companion to her hostess, a friendly face to Wilhelmina, and the one who lifted any household duties from Lady Hartville's shoulders.

If she slept poorly that night, it was not to be wondered. If she awoke in the morning with a dull headache, it was at least excuse enough to have a tray sent to her room. No need to join the viscount in the breakfast parlor, or accept his invitation to ride which was brought by the maid.

In fact, it seemed the perfect excuse to stay in her room for the majority of the day. With a certain feeling of guilt, Caroline had a fire lit in her room to brighten the grayness of the day and take away the chill. She curled up in a chair and sipped tea that the maid had brought hot. She unearthed two novels from amidst the periodicals and treatises on the shelves in the guest room across the hall and returned to lose herself in the more interesting of the two.

Indulging herself seemed a not unworthy occupation for such a cheerless day. Twice she surreptitiously abandoned her room, praying that she would not encounter Hartville. She listened at Lady Hartville's door to make certain there were no conversing voices before she entered to spend an hour with her hostess.

And later, she joined Wilhelmina and Meg in the nursery for an hour of play and talk. Caroline could not help but study the child's face closely, looking for some feature that she could recognize. But resemblances were illusory. Perhaps an older child would have had more distinctive elements in her countenance. Having seen the miniature of Wilhelmina's mother, Caroline could only see the child as a five-year-old daughter of the mysterious woman.

So the day dwindled away, and Caroline sent word that she continued indisposed and would not dine with Hartville that evening. The hours stretched in front of her a bit drearily, but they could be gotten through so long as Hartville intended to be off in the morning and leave her in possession of her peace of mind.

At eight there was a scratch at her door, and the maid brought in a note from the viscount.

My dear Caroline, I shall be off in the morning, since my mother appears decidedly better. I trust that your indisposition will be of short duration, as I would appreciate your special attention to my mother while I am away. My hope is to bring back a physician who can be of some assistance to her.

Your obedient servant,
Hartville

Caroline set the note aside, as it did not seem to require an answer. Fine, he would be leaving as planned. She would be able to come out of her self-imposed exile the following day. And life would go on at Berwick much as it had before . . . well, before Hartville had spent so much time in her company. *Thank heaven.*

★　★　★

On the third day of Hartville's absence, Caroline had begun to feel decidedly edgy. Lady Hartville was once again experiencing difficulties with her health and had taken to her bed. Mrs. Bluestone and the dowager's dresser conferred together and approached Caroline with their determination that my lady needed to be seen by a doctor.

'But she won't see the local fellow,' Mrs. Bluestone admitted.

'Lord Hartville has gone to find a man in London who will come down to examine her,' Caroline explained. 'I have no idea how long he'll be, but he can't possibly be back in less than a sennight.'

Lady Hartville's dresser, Griffin, sighed, her face a picture of concern. 'This attack is worse than the last, miss. Well, you've seen her. She's in pain and naught we can do for her.'

Caroline had indeed seen Lady Hartville. That good woman's color was poor, she could hold down no food, and she felt wretched. 'Is there no one else nearby who could treat her?' she asked.

Both women shook their heads. 'Nary a soul,' Mrs. Bluestone said.

'I'll send a note to my brother,' Caroline decided. 'Perhaps his hosts can recommend someone in their neighborhood. Jeremy could bring him here faster than the viscount could get back with a man from London.'

'But you'll write to his lordship, won't you, miss?' the dresser asked.

'Certainly. Mr. Wilson will give me his direction.'

The notes were soon dispatched with riders from the estate. Caroline attempted to help with nursing Lady Hartville, but her efforts were thwarted by the dresser's insistence on doing almost everything herself. So Caroline read to the dowager several times a day, usually for less than an hour owing to Lady Hartville's discomfort. The rest of her time she divided between household duties and visits to Wilhelmina and walks in the vicinity of the house.

It was while she was walking past the shrubbery west of the main buildings one morning that she was startled by the appearance of Giles Markingham. 'Mr. Markingham!' she exclaimed as she came round the corner of the path. 'I had no idea you were here. Is Jeremy with you?'

Markingham strode forward and clasped her hands. 'Not far behind, Miss Carruthers.' He lifted her hands to his lips and kissed them, as though it were something he had done every day of his life.

Caroline regarded him with astonishment. But her mind was distracted by the possibility of Jeremy having brought a doctor. 'Does he have someone with him — someone who can help Lady Hartville?'

'He should have. I chose to be his emissary,' Markingham explained, a decidedly fervent light in his eyes. 'He had to wait for the doctor to conclude a difficult confinement before bringing him. I thought you would wish to know as soon as possible that they will be here shortly.'

'Oh, yes,' she agreed, withdrawing her hands from his and clasping them tightly together at her waist. 'Tell me about the doctor. Does he come highly recommended?'

Markingham regarded her with amusement. 'Most assuredly. They could not say enough good things about him at Brocklehurst Hall. Apparently he has practiced in the neighborhood for half a dozen years, and acquired a reputation for both knowledgeability and practicality. I wonder the man doesn't move to London and reap his just reward there.'

'Thank heaven he hasn't.' Caroline frowned. 'I don't suppose you have any idea how long they'll be? Lady Hartville is in need of his assistance as soon as possible.'

'Is there some concern for her life?' Markingham asked, surprised.

'I honestly cannot say. She does appear to be failing, but apparently she has rallied before. Oh, I wish Hartville were here.'

'Really? He didn't seem particularly effective to me,' her companion allowed with something of a sniff. 'Forever scowling at Jeremy, and not so very amiable to me or even to you, from all appearances.'

Caroline wished to leap to Hartville's defense, but forced herself to say instead, 'But Lady Hartville is his mother. He should be here to comfort her, especially if there is some danger of her dying.'

'I daresay the case is not so desperate,' Markingham said soothingly. 'You're contemplating the worst possible outcome, and you've gotten yourself in a bother. What you need, my dear Miss Carruthers, is something to take your mind off the problem.'

There was a caressing quality to his voice

that reminded Caroline of his promise to spend time alone with her when he returned. How long ago that seemed! His dark good looks were less attractive to her now. His eyes, which spoke of expectation, were not the eyes she wanted looking upon her with desire. Yet she had encouraged him, hadn't she? She had thought herself in love with this man.

When she didn't speak, Markingham smiled winningly. 'Come, my dear Caroline. Walk with me. It will do you good to get away from the distress at Berwick for a few minutes.'

'But Lady Hartville might send a maid out after me . . . '

'There are more than enough capable people in that great house to see to her every need.'

'Yes, but . . . '

He raised a quelling eyebrow. 'Trust me to know what is best for you, my dear one. You would allow yourself to be run ragged, I imagine, but I will not allow it.'

Caroline would have given Hartville a piece of her mind for spouting such drivel, but she was suddenly curious to see what Markingham intended. 'You won't?'

'No, indeed.' He tucked her hand under his arm and began to lead her down the path away from the house. Wind tugged at her skirts, and at the tendrils of hair around her face. Markingham allowed an admiring gaze to travel down from her face to her feet. 'Even under such distressing conditions you are a rare beauty, my sweet Caroline.'

Her blush came readily enough, and she turned her head away.

'Too many men choose to ignore a mature woman,' he said conversationally. 'They look to the new crop of girls each year for their brides. Girls of seventeen, eighteen. What do such children know? Nothing. They're hardly out of the schoolroom.'

'But men want a bride who is impressionable, I believe,' Caroline suggested. 'A kind of *tabula rasa*.'

He laughed. 'Of course you would know that term. Do you see what I mean? A mature woman understands the situation. She doesn't fret or pine for her youth. Instead she relishes the maturity she has gained with the passage of time.'

Unsure where this was leading, Caroline glanced up at him. His dark eyes were challenging, his lips curved into a sensuous smile. 'What is it that you find so acceptable about mature women?' she asked.

'Ah, the mature woman is less constrained than the schoolgirl. She has long since adapted her expectations to the realities of the world around her. She doesn't play games like a child; she chooses to be an adult in an adult world.'

They had come to the stand of trees that marked the beginning of the home wood. Markingham paused and turned to Caroline. 'You know that you weren't meant to dwindle into someone's maiden aunt. You have the intelligence to realize that the rules made for those new-minted girls no longer apply to you at four-and-twenty. You are aware of your physical self, of the womanly nature of your body. You understand that your body harbors desires which only a mature man can satisfy.'

This is plain speaking, Caroline thought, regarding him uncertainly. 'But — '

Markingham put a finger to her lips to stop her speaking. 'Hush, my sweet. Let me finish. You know that your beauty won't last forever, that a time will come, very soon, when no man will desire you. You are too clever to contemplate spending your life as someone's companion, and too knowledgeable of the world to think that a titled man would ask for your hand in marriage.'

'I am not of that level of society,' she murmured, her eyes cast down in a pose Hartville would have warily recognized.

'But, Caroline,' Markingham said, tipping her face up with his finger, 'as a mature woman you can choose life with a man on your own terms. You can have a house of your own, a small place in the country, where you will be mistress. No longer a drain on your brother's meager resources, or cluttering up his bachelor existence in town. A place where you can play your music just when you wish. And, instead of growing old and dried out as so many spinsters do, you can share your bed with a man who would appreciate your body, who would teach it the kind of passion that few English wives ever come to know.'

'Passion?'

'Oh, yes.' His eyes had become focused with desire. He had very speaking eyes, as Caroline knew. 'You have no idea, Caroline, what a man's touch can do to a woman, the fire he can ignite in her.'

Caroline backed away from him, and he shook his head and laughed.

'Sometimes, at first, even a mature woman is afraid. She is not accustomed to thinking of the physical pleasure a man can give her. At most she dreams of his kisses. You've thought of my kissing you, haven't you, Caroline?'

'Yes,' she admitted.

'Yes, I know you have. But a kiss, the touching of lips, is only the beginning. For I would show you that there are other kisses, much more exciting kisses than you can ever imagine, my love. Kisses that would make your body ache and swell and yearn for more, for the driving of my passion. No insipid marriage would ever provide you with the likes of that.'

'You don't wish to marry me?'

His expression turned rueful. 'Ah, Caroline, marriage spoils everything. It's a ruse, no more. It dims the passion between two people. It's stultifying. You're too intelligent to think that at your age you will find a love match that will offer you the kind of passion I'm describing. And I think you're too passionate a woman to settle for anything less.'

'Jeremy would never agree to such an arrangement.'

Markingham shrugged. 'Jeremy will move on with his life soon enough. He's too fond of enjoying himself to stay tied to your apron strings. And he owes me a great deal of money. I think he'll be willing to accept our arrangement if I settle a cottage and a small allowance on you and agree to dismiss his debt. Don't be indignant, my sweet. Jeremy is given to thinking only of himself, and he'll come to see how convenient our arrangement is in time.'

'I'm afraid you have misjudged both *my* sentiments and *my* standards, Mr. Markingham,' Caroline remarked, her tone caustic.

'Your offer of an illicit liaison is offensive to me.'

He cocked a knowing eyebrow at her. 'Come, come, Caroline. Don't be so missish. What, after all, is the use of kowtowing to social mores? All that will get you is a penurious spinsterhood, and believe me, you won't enjoy that.'

'You think it preferable to be an abandoned woman with a few children clinging to her skirts?' Caroline asked.

His eyes narrowed. 'No one is going to abandon you, Caroline. I've just said I would settle a cottage and an allowance on you. As to children . . . ' Markingham shrugged. 'I will teach you how to avoid that hazard.'

Caroline's eyes flashed. 'I do not consider children a hazard, Mr. Markingham.'

'They are to the kind of arrangement I'm offering, my dear. When I come to call on you, I want your undivided attention.' He smiled meaningfully. 'We'll have more enjoyable things to do than entertain a flock of chicks.'

'Don't you want a son to carry on your name?'

'Not particularly. What happens to my name after I'm gone is of no interest to me.'

'I'm sorry to hear that' Caroline sighed and stared down at her clasped hands. 'I had completely misjudged you, Mr. Markingham. Your kindness to Jeremy fooled me into thinking that you were a generous, honorable man. Your attentions to myself were, as you obviously intended them to be, both flattering and exciting.'

He laughed. 'My dear girl, if I had not allowed my eyes to dwell on your sweet curves, and hinted with my smiles at my longing to touch them, you would not have become aware of your body. And yes, I wanted you to be aware of your body.'

'I'm sure I have no idea what you're talking about,' Caroline protested, willing the flush of embarrassment not to invade her neck.

'No? Oh, I think you do.' He surveyed her with complacent amusement. 'I think you have stood before your looking glass, unclothed, and wondered what it would be like to be with me, to have me touch you.'

He stepped forward and reached to encircle her waist, but Caroline slid out of his hands. 'I don't want you to touch me,' she insisted, backing away from him.

Markingham shook his head with ill-concealed humor. 'Caroline, Caroline. You're a practical woman. There is every advantage to you in my proposal — and to your brother as well. Why do you hesitate? Hm? Do you think you'll get a better offer?'

22

The question hung in the air between them. His tone was taunting, and his sharp eyes must have detected the faint trace of hope Caroline attempted to hide deep inside herself. He laughed.

'You think the viscount will offer for you? Think again, my dear. Why would a man so situated take on a woman of your years and poverty? He scarcely tolerates your brother, and puts up with you as his mother's companion because of her illness. I'm surprised you'd delude yourself with such daydreams.'

Caroline shook her head, unable to bring either a denial or a defense to her lips. In truth, she was shocked by Markingham's suggestion, as well as insulted. It had never occurred to her that a gentleman would suggest such a course to a lady. Though she knew men did establish liaisons with females, she had always regarded those women who would accept such an arrangement with sadness. Did they have so little regard for themselves, or so little money, that they could live such a life with equanimity?

Markingham had watched her face as these

thoughts raced through her mind. 'And if you had hoped he would offer you an arrangement such as I am, I assure you he is too much the proper English gentleman to consider a liaison with a woman of your social class.' Markingham's smile became wolfish. 'Fortunately, I don't recognize such fine distinctions. Why have a mistress who would ape her betters when you can have one of her betters for yourself?'

Her patience at an end, Caroline tried to slap the derisory smirk from his face. He caught her hand and pulled her close to him, holding her there. 'Now don't take offense, my dear Caroline. I'm well aware of your social status. It's part of your appeal. As are your remarkable voice and your sharp mind — qualities which, I have noticed, didn't get you anywhere in London's social world.'

She struggled to release herself from his grip, but he held tight, his eyes blazing down at her. 'Why let a world like that dictate to you whether you are of value?' he demanded. 'I would value you more than some paltry English squire who expected you to produce five children in six years, and manage his home, and entertain his boring neighbors, and maintain insipid country standards. With me you would have freedom you can't imagine now.'

'Let go of me,' Caroline said coldly.

He sighed and released her hands. 'You surprise me. I had thought you would be intelligent enough to see where your best opportunity lay. And your brother's. I doubt you would wish to see him in a debtor's prison.'

'Don't think to coerce me with threats about Jeremy,' she retorted, scorn lacing her voice. 'If he is in debt to you, it's his lookout.'

'Oh?' His lips twisted wryly. 'And where would you go when the bailiffs came to the door, my sweet? Home to Aunt Matilda? Now there's an appetizing prospect.'

True, Caroline could scarcely go back there. And there was no saying whether Lady Hartville would indefinitely require her services. Certainly she couldn't ask Hartville to bail Jeremy out of debt. Still, she lifted her chin and met Markingham's eyes steadily. 'I would manage,' she said.

He nodded. 'Yes, you would manage. That's one of the things I admire about you, Caroline. But why just manage? Why become some demanding woman's companion or a governess to recalcitrant children when you could live a life of pleasure?'

Caroline's face remained stony but he continued his blandishments. 'You've never traveled, have you? And you won't, I promise you, if you insist on leading a virtuous English life. But with me, you could discover Paris and Rome. With me,' he said, his voice dropping to a silky caress, 'you would discover a sensuous life that women of your class never even know exists. They think it duty to submit to their husbands. Fah! What a waste of natural gifts.'

His eyes lingered on each generous curve of her body, and Caroline found that she could not turn away from his inspection. As in the past, his gaze made her aware of her body, of its unacknowledged possibilities.

'And you have superior natural gifts.' Sounding almost bemused, he shook his head wonderingly. 'What kind of dolts are they in your precious world that they can't see what's beneath your modest gowns? Hell, they don't deserve you. But I do, Caroline, because I can fulfill that promise. I can give you more pleasure than you've ever imagined.'

'Please, don't say any more.' Caroline put up a hand to indicate the gravity of her command. 'You are insulting me, Mr. Markingham. If you believe that your offer is flattering, you deceive yourself. If you believe that there is any circumstance under which I would become your mistress, you are wildly mistaken. If you have fostered Jeremy's indebtedness to you to further your purpose,

305

I fear your plan is destined to fail.'

It was not anger or disappointment that flared in his eyes, however. It was amusement. 'You haven't the courage to follow your heart, my sweet? Perhaps I could convince you without all these cumbersome words. I would need but an hour alone with you, I think.'

Caroline moved swiftly beyond his reach. 'Don't you dare touch me, Sir! One step in my direction and I shall scream. We are not so far that the stable lads wouldn't hear and come quickly to my rescue.'

Markingham shook his head with exaggerated tolerance. 'My dear girl, I have no intention of forcing myself upon you. God knows I've never had the need to resort to such measures. I think what you need is a little time to consider my suggestion, and to face the realities of your situation. But I do hope you won't take a great deal of time, as I have in mind to be off for my estate soon and I would prefer to take you with me than have to send for you later.'

'There is nothing to consider, Mr. Markingham.'

He bowed as though in acceptance of her pronouncement, but Caroline was very much aware that he was not. Realizing that there was no sense in saying anything further to him, she turned on her heels and marched away toward the house. He did not follow her. As she turned the corner into the kitchen garden, she noted surreptitiously that he remained by the woods where she had left him.

Honestly! The man was a serpent, trying to tempt her like that snake in the Garden of Eden! Caroline fumed as she let herself in the side door of the house. Imagine his thinking that she would consider for one minute, for one second, becoming his mistress. She was a properly brought up Englishwoman indeed, and he was perfectly well aware of it. What made him think that he could succeed in such an offer?

A tiny corner of her mind — a very small and disquieting corner — wondered if he might have succeeded if she had not lost her heart to the viscount. For it was surely Markingham who had made her aware of the physical longings her body spoke of when she was alone in her bed at night. With no more than his gaze clinging to her body he had made her feel voluptuous, and needy.

If he was right and Hartville had no intention of marrying her, she would indeed dwindle into an old maid, wouldn't she? Never to know those pleasures he spoke of so knowledgeably and enticingly. Caroline suspected that there was a wanton streak in her that, under certain circumstances, might have led to her downfall with Markingham.

And suddenly everything became clear to her.

Standing in the dimly lit corridor leading to the back of the house, she felt as though enlightenment beamed on her. Of course, Markingham. He was Wilhelmina's father. He had seduced a woman such as herself, a gently born woman, who had produced the blond, blue-eyed child. And died in child bed, no doubt. Caroline shivered at the vivid image in her mind, certain that it must be close to the truth.

So Markingham had farmed the child out to nurse, and provided funds over the first few years. Perhaps, sentimentally, had even sent the mother's locket with the newborn baby, since he had no intention of ever acknowledging the child himself.

But what had possessed him to direct JoJo here to Hartville's estate?

Expediency.

Killing two birds with one stone.

A perverse sense of humor.

Probably all of those things. Wilhelmina had doubtless been raised somewhere in the vicinity of Markingham's estate, and he preferred that she not remain there. Especially if he was intending to install Caroline at some cottage in the general neighborhood. What better place to dispose of the child than where soft-hearted Caroline would insist that she be taken care of? Perhaps Markingham had even known, if Jeremy did, that Hartville was the provider of her brother's quarterly allowance.

But what a reckless, dishonorable thing to do! Caroline felt a little sick to her stomach that she had thought herself smitten with Markingham back in London. And all he had ever wanted was to make her his mistress.

A lowering thought indeed.

Caroline picked up her skirts and headed up the stairs to Lady Hartville.

23

Hartville had not made it to London. The right front wheel of his carriage had splintered soon after he gained the Great North Road. Assured by the innkeeper that a smith could repair it within twenty-four hours, Hartville had agreed to stay at the inn overnight.

What had seemed a simple enough task had turned into a monumental project when it was discovered that the axle, too, had been seriously damaged. Torn between waiting another day, and hiring a chaise to take him the rest of the way, Hartville eventually overcame his frustration and impatience, deciding that having his own carriage was worth a second day's delay.

Consequently he was overtaken by his own Berwick messenger about his mother's renewed illness. Alarmed, and convinced by the urgency of Caroline's letter (which contained not a hint of any personal greeting), Hartville determined to return home immediately. He left the carriage for the stable lad to bring back once it was again in working order, and hired a decent hack from the landlord to carry him for the first leg of his journey back.

That he was returning without a physician in tow distressed him, as he held little hope that Jeremy Carruthers would be able to find one in Grasmere. Even before learning of his mother's deterioration, Hartville had had all too many hours to consider the gravity of her illness. He could not fault Caroline for thinking that he had made so far no effort on his mother's behalf, since he had indeed failed to provide her with the proper medical attention. Hartville supposed that he had allowed himself to be lulled into complaisance by Lady Hartville's apparent improvement.

And he had definitely allowed himself to be distracted by everything that was going on at Berwick. Since he could do little for his mother during his trip to London, he had attempted to consider the various players at the Hall and what their true roles were. Away from the situation, and from the strong pull of his attraction to Caroline, he had attempted to assess the events and partici-pants with a critical, if not cynical, eye.

However, he did not have to be within Caroline's immediate sphere to feel the strength of her allure for him. Try as he might, he could not dislodge the conviction that Caroline was precisely the woman she

311

had presented herself to be on each occasion when the two of them had been alone together. Her penchant for outspoken conversation made it unlikely she would be able to hide a deeply duplicitous soul. Certainly she did not hesitate to offer the sharp side of her tongue when provoked — or even when merely disgruntled.

Hartville had to smile in remembrance of some of her more cutting declarations. And count her forthright tongue as a virtue. Heaven knew he'd seen enough young ladies in polite society who would not for one moment have thought of speaking to him in such a fashion. He could scarcely imagine living with one of them. Where would the challenge be?

But there was more to Caroline than a wayward tongue. There was her intelligence, and her kind heart, and her astonishing voice. And, as if that weren't enough, there was that charming form of hers which enticed him more than he cared to admit, even to himself.

Enough of this, he told himself firmly as he mounted a fresh horse on his journey home. Light was already fading from the evening sky, and it would be hours before he reached Berwick Hall. It was time to face up to Caroline's interest in Giles Markingham. And for a woman like his Cousin Caroline, the rank of a viscount would not weigh against an attachment of the heart. She was not a mercenary wench, a type Hartville had encountered more than once in his reveling days in London, both in and out of polite society. If it was Markingham she wanted, it was Markingham she would have.

Hadn't there been a few signs, though, that indeed she had come to regard himself with favor? Hartville could not forget that night when they had sung together . . . And in the stand of trees during the storm . . . Surely there was some reason for hope.

His horse, unfamiliar with the road, stumbled in the growing darkness and Hartville was forced to pay more attention to guiding the poor beast over rough road. He could not contemplate what dire straits his mother might be in, nor his own failure to find a doctor to aid her. His fears for her survival were strong, and very nearly pushed all else from his mind.

★　★　★

Caroline liked the doctor immediately. He was a young man, not so very much older than she. He looked rather tired from his journey, but he shook her hand with an energy and optimism that she couldn't fail to respond to.

Jeremy grinned with pride at bringing this prize to her and Lady Hartville. 'He's just delivered a woman of twins, Caro! Imagine. And I very nearly took part in it myself because the midwife assisting him was in need of another pair of hands.' He laughed, looking down at his own large hands, recently stripped of their driving gloves. 'Thank heaven the woman's sister arrived in time to offer the necessary assistance.'

Francis Knowland set his black bag on the floor of the entry hall and gazed about him. 'I haven't been here in years,' he said. 'But I knew Richard Hartville when we were at school together. I was sorry to hear that his father had died. Is Richard not here, then?'

'We've sent for him,' Caroline explained. 'He had left for London to find a medical man to see to his mother. Can I offer you some refreshment?'

'Thank you, no. I'd prefer to see Lady Hartville first.'

Relieved, Caroline turned to lead him up the stairs to the dowager's bedchamber. Jeremy made to follow them, and she shook her head. 'I don't think you should come, Jeremy. Lady Hartville will find it difficult enough to admit the doctor. She's become quite adamant about the local man,' she explained to Francis Knowland. 'She won't have him in the house.'

Mr. Knowland nodded his understanding. 'I'll remind her that she's met me in the past, and reassure her with my medical degree.'

Hoping that would be enough, Caroline hastened up the stairs and down the corridor to Lady Hartville's room. Her knock was answered by Griffin, who regarded the doctor with skeptical eyes. 'I suppose you should come in,' she said at length.

The doctor held back while Caroline explained his presence to her hostess. At Lady Hartville's protest, Mr. Knowland stepped forward with an engaging smile. 'It's been a long time,' he remarked, gazing down at her where she lay, feverish and a little jaundiced, on her bed. 'But I remember how you used to scold Richard and me for stealing all the ripe strawberries in the succession houses.'

'Francis Knowland!' she exclaimed. 'Oh, I recall the occasion vividly. Richard had brought you home from school with him, and he took you to raid the strawberries because you insisted you had never had one. Now tell me, was that true?'

'Yes, my lady. And it turned out that I was a little allergic to them. I broke out in a tremendous rash, but it was worth it.'

Her face softened and she reached a hand out to him. 'How nice to see you again. And so you're a doctor now?'

He clasped her hand warmly. 'I am, and a very good one, though I say so myself. I took my degree in Edinburgh, then apprenticed in London, and have settled here for the last few years.'

'You should have let Richard know,' she scolded. 'He would have loved becoming reacquainted with you.'

'Perhaps I should have, but I didn't wish to impose,' Knowland countered easily. 'Now, ma'am, if you will be so good as to give me permission, I will examine you and see what I can do to help.'

To Caroline's relief, Lady Hartville submitted with no protest whatsoever. Caroline and Griffin were consigned to the dressing room from which they could hear the gentle murmur of Knowland's deep voice and the dowager's softer replies. The consultation continued for a considerable time, during which the two waiting women paced the smallish space and smiled nervously at each other from time to time. When at last Mr. Knowland called for them to return, he was cautiously encouraging.

'Lady Hartville appears to be suffering from gallstones. I have several herbal treatments which will likely prove of benefit to her — dandelion root, celery seed and licorice root. If those don't help dissolve the stone and cleanse the system, we'll add wild yam root and cayenne. But I think these should be effective.'

He dug in his bag amongst the packets and jars, coming up with several of each. 'You'd best take them with tea, my lady,' he said, his eyes twinkling, 'as they don't all taste as delightful as strawberries.'

*　*　*

When Caroline emerged from Lady Hartville's suite, she felt considerably better about her hostess's prospects for recovered health. She had not been willing to admit to herself how desperate she felt the case might be with the dowager. And the thought that she had sent Hartville off, even if it had been to find a doctor, positively blue deviled her. What if he should have been away when his mother expired?

As it was late in the evening by now, Caroline arranged for the doctor to be given a meal and a room to retire to. She herself went in search of Jeremy, only to find him with Markingham in the drawing room. Jeremy was far too eager to hear how Lady Hartville went on to notice Caroline's displeasure at Markingham's presence.

'Mr. Knowland believes he can help Lady Hartville,' she said. 'Apparently it is gallstones that cause this type of distress, and some of his herbs are noted for dissolving them and strengthening the system.'

'I knew he could do it! I tell you I have the utmost faith in this fellow, Caro. Bless me if I don't. And he's no country dolt like so many of them. He went to school in Edinburgh, and apparently there's no finer education to be had than there, not even in London.'

'You did well to find him,' Caroline said. And then, including Markingham rather coolly in her look, asked, 'Have you eaten?'

'We have. The butler said we should tell you there is pigeon pie set out on the sideboard in the dining room, along with bread and butter, for you to help yourself, and that they'll bring you anything you wish. Fine lot of servants Hartville has.'

'Yes, indeed,' Caroline agreed, knowing that in the past she would have shared an amused glance with Markingham at this naïve comment. Now she wished Markingham as far away as possible.

'We thought it best to spend the night,' Jeremy remarked, sitting back in the comfortable chair he'd claimed and cradling a glass of Hartville's brandy in his hands. 'Seeing as how Knowland will be here and you a single woman and all.'

'Your concern for my reputation overwhelms me,' Caroline retorted. 'There is surely no need, with a houseful of servants.'

'Well, it's already arranged,' Jeremy informed her smugly. 'The housekeeper thought it entirely proper.'

Markingham spoke for the first time. 'Why don't I keep you company in the dining room, Miss Carruthers?'

'No, thank you,' Caroline said, a little more sharply than she'd intended. 'I plan only to choose some food and have it taken up to my room. It has been a long, exhausting day and I am inclined to retire now.'

'Pity,' Jeremy said. 'With Hartville away, we three could have had quite a jolly time together.'

Caroline wasn't up to the task of informing her younger brother of his best friend's dishonorable offer to her. Perhaps in the morning she would have a little more energy, but for now she merely said good night to the two men and left the room. She was almost too tired to choose a plate of food, but decided it would be better not to further irritate her overburdened nerves by starving herself.

It was while she was helping herself to a portion of the pigeon pie that it occurred to her what having Markingham in the house for the night meant. She could have wept with frustration. Sometimes Jeremy did the most distressing things without understanding the trouble he caused! Now she would have to make certain that Wilhelmina and Meg weren't on the nursery floor for the night, and the only thing she wanted to do was nibble a few bites of food and lay her head on her pillow.

Because if Markingham was Wilhelmina's father, then it seemed entirely possible to her that it was Markingham who had been in the house the night Meg was locked in the kitchen. Jeremy and Markingham had spent that night at the inn, but Caroline now suspected it was Markingham who had gained access to the house because he was intent on getting hold of the locket. Why he wanted the locket, she could only guess. Perhaps the miniature of Wilhelmina's mother meant more to him than he'd realized when he sent it off with the baby.

But how had he gotten into the house?

Standing at the sideboard in the dining room, she remembered that she and Lady Hartville had left the two men alone that night to enjoy their brandy. Caroline turned to face the wall of windows covered at this hour with the heavy rose-colored draperies. It would have been easy enough for Markingham to lag a few paces behind Jeremy in leaving the room, stroll over to the windows and leave one just slightly ajar for himself. Oh, he had the cool nerve for that, she was sure. If Jeremy had happened to notice and question him, Markingham would merely have commented that he needed 'a breath of fresh air,' no doubt.

A footman arrived with a tray to carry the items Caroline had chosen. Reluctantly she left the dining room, thinking there was something more she should do there. She allowed the footman to follow her up the stairs and down the corridor to her room, taking the tray with thanks so that he could push open the door for her.

There was enough light in the room for her to make her way to the little writing desk in the corner. She set the tray down and debated whether to eat then, or go immediately to the nursery floor. Best to get Meg and Wilhelmina moved before they settled in for the night, she decided. With a sigh, she turned her back on her food and hurried to accomplish her mission.

There were candles already lit in the sconces on the nursery floor. Caroline found

Meg and Wilhelmina sitting on the child's bed, reciting rhymes together from a book. Though it would probably have been perfectly all right to send the two of them to share Gladys's room in the servants' quarters, Caroline knew she'd feel better if she had Wilhelmina with her. So she improvised a story for the child.

'I thought Wilhelmina could spend the night with me. I've had my dinner brought up on a tray, and there's a plate of biscuits I think she'd especially like,' she said. 'And Meg can take the opportunity to be with her sister for the night.'

Meg looked both surprised and doubtful, but she merely nodded and said, 'As you wish, miss.'

Since Wilhelmina was already dressed for bed in her nightgown, with a shawl to keep her warm, Caroline had only to see that she slipped something on her feet. Meg had fixed the child's locket, and Caroline made sure the locket was about Wilhelmina's neck. Then she took the small hand in hers and smiled down at the curious face. 'I think you might enjoy looking at my jewelry again, too.'

'Oh, yes, Miss Carruthers,' Wilhelmina agreed. 'May I bring the dog?'

Caroline looked skeptically at the puppy, sighed, and finally nodded. Then she turned to the nursery maid and said, 'Good night, Meg. Perhaps you would come for Wilhelmina in the morning about eight?'

Meg dipped a curtsey. 'Certainly, miss.'

As they made their way down the stairs, Wilhelmina asked hopefully, 'Will we have hot chocolate with our biscuits?'

Not wishing to disappoint the child, nor feeling it necessary to disturb any of the servants at the late hour, Caroline said, 'If you will come with me, we can make some in the kitchen and take it up to my room.'

In an effort to stay away from the withdrawing room in which she'd left her brother and Markingham, Caroline chose to use the back stairs down to the kitchen. As it happened, however, the corridor into which this deposited them was also the corridor which led to the billiard room. It was not a particularly well-lit stretch of hallway, there being but one sconce at each end. Nonetheless, Caroline saw quite clearly that they were about to come face-to-face with her brother and his companion on their way to play a game of billiards.

'Caro!' Jeremy exclaimed. 'What are you doing here?'

A number of things then happened at once:

Wilhelmina grabbed the locket around her neck.

Markingham swore.

The doctor, coming out of the kitchen with a canister of hot water, stopped so abruptly that he spilled it down his pantaloons and onto his boots.

Wilhelmina's puppy, encouraged by all the commotion, began barking excitedly.

And Hartville arrived.

24

The viscount had chosen to come in the rear door in order to cause as little fuss as possible. His astonishment at seeing the assorted group and hearing the commotion turned instantly into concern. 'My mother. Has something happened to her?'

Mr. Knowland, trying vainly to ignore both his soaking leg and the puppy intent on charging the water canister, managed to say, 'No, no, Richard. She's already looking better. Gallstones, you know. And the draft I've given her has put her to sleep, so don't go rushing in there and waking her up.'

'What the devil?' Hartville peered through the gloom in an attempt to decipher who all these people were. 'Knowland? Is that you? What in the name of heaven are you doing here?'

'I brought him,' Jeremy said proudly. 'He's a doctor and he's taking care of Lady Hartville as well as any London practitioner could.'

'Better,' Mr. Knowland said, with a grin, reaching out a hand to clasp Hartville's. 'It's been a number of years, Richard.'

'Francis! Good Lord! I had no idea you were back in the area.'

'Yes, your mother has already scolded me about that.'

Hartville's brows drew down and he said urgently, 'You must tell me the truth, Francis. Is she going to be all right?'

'These things aren't certainties, Richard. But I believe she will be. She's responding well to the medications I've given her.'

Hartville's relief was short lived, because at that moment he heard Wilhelmina saying in a piping voice, 'That's the bad man.'

The child was clutching her locket with one hand and pointing a finger in the direction of Jeremy Carruthers and Giles Markingham.

'Yes,' Caroline agreed, bending down to put her arm around the girl's shoulders. 'But don't be alarmed; he won't hurt you or try to take your locket, sweetheart.'

Hartville ached for Caroline, having to recognize that her brother was a villain. He would have gone to her, except that he then heard her say, 'Perhaps you would care to give us the name of Wilhelmina's mother, Mr. Markingham.'

Hartville's gaze flew to Markingham's face. Though there was no trace of guilt, the man's eyes conveyed a hint of reckless bravado.

'I don't think I would, Miss Carruthers. But, as I'll be leaving now, this is likely to be your last opportunity to come with me.'

'Giles?' Jeremy said uncertainly. 'What are you suggesting?'

Markingham bent a sardonic eye on him. 'Exactly what you think I am, Jeremy. I have made your sister a generous offer, which she has not as yet accepted.'

'Nor will I,' Caroline said.

Jeremy stared at his friend. 'But that's disgusting. Caro would never do such a thing. I would never allow her to.'

'Wouldn't you?' Markingham's eyes became hard. 'Oh, I think in return for the forgiveness of your debts to me you might be brought in line, my friend.'

Jeremy looked ready to plant him a facer, but it was Hartville who stepped between the two men. 'I won't call you out, because you are obviously not an honorable man,' he said. 'But I expect you to be out of my house within the hour and never set foot here again. As to Jeremy's debts to you, I daresay they will be more than equaled by the expense of our raising your child. I would not, if I were you, make any attempt to collect them.'

Markingham said nothing. He made a mocking bow to Hartville and, with one last, regretful look at Caroline, turned and left the

327

hall. Wilhelmina had been watching this exchange with enormous eyes. In the silence that followed Markingham's departure she looked up at Caroline and asked, 'Was that my father?'

With obvious reluctance, Caroline nodded. 'But he isn't someone who could take care of you, my dear. Come, let's get your hot chocolate.'

'Now wait!' Jeremy protested. He still looked dazed by the turn of events.

'My, what an interesting household you run,' Mr. Knowland congratulated Hartville. 'I regret that I'm bone tired, because I would dearly love to stay and hear what all this is about. Good night, old man, Miss Carruthers, Mr. Carruthers.' With a smile at Wilhelmina, he turned and made his way up the stairs.

Hartville didn't know where to begin. Mostly he wanted to send Jeremy and Wilhelmina off so that he could be alone with Caroline. *That cad Markingham!* A generous offer indeed. How could Markingham have thought someone of Caroline's stamp would consider such a position for one moment?

That determined young woman had not waited for anyone to pepper her with questions but had pushed open the door to the kitchen and urged Wilhelmina in after her. Jeremy followed, bleating about his lack of understanding, his deception at Markingham's hands, his inability to believe that it was all true, etc., etc. Hartville wished he would simply go away.

Caroline put a saucepan on the burner above the banked fire and went to ladle out a cupful of milk for the child. When that was warming, she began a search for the chocolate, rummaging through the canisters on the shelves nearby. Hartville found that he remembered from a long-ago childhood where the chocolate was kept. He pulled the latch on the cupboard, reached down the tin and silently passed it to Caroline. She did not meet his gaze.

Jeremy was chaotically working his way through a list of his 'friend's' offenses. 'And I swear he deliberately made up to me right from the beginning because of you,' he was saying when Hartville paid attention to him again. 'Right from the start he was determined to make you his mis — ' With a glance at Wilhelmina, he stopped. 'Well, you know what I mean.'

'Mmmm,' Caroline said as she stirred the hot milk and chocolate together.

'I've never been so deceived in anyone,' Jeremy continued, aggrieved. 'How did you know about — ?'

'Hartville believed you were the villain of the piece,' Caroline remarked as she poured the hot chocolate into a cup.

'Me?' Jeremy turned to Hartville with a frown. 'Whatever could you be thinking?'

Caroline added, 'And since I knew it couldn't be you, then it probably had to be Markingham.'

The name came off her tongue with a certain hesitation, Hartville thought. Was she pained by the whole experience? Had she hoped for an offer of marriage from Markingham and been crushed by one of an entirely different nature?

Jeremy was suddenly contemplating Wilhelmina with interest. 'She's certainly blond enough to be a child of mine, ain't she? Not a bit of Markingham's darkness. Though if you look closely at her, you can see something of his cast of feature, I fancy.' He pointed to Wilhelmina's locket. 'Would you let me see that?'

Wilhelmina looked first at Caroline, then at Hartville, and finally back at Jeremy. Slowly, uncertain even though each of the adults had smiled encouragement, she lifted the locket over her head and allowed Jeremy to take it from her. He snapped open the clasp and exclaimed, 'Well, I'll be dam — Beg your pardon.' He held the locket closer to the candle and nodded. 'It's Margaret. No doubt about it.'

Caroline turned a questioning face to him. 'Margaret?'

'Margaret Multon. You remember her. No, wait a minute. I suppose you never met her. It was when I was at school. Her brother was a great friend of mine.' Jeremy suddenly held very still, his eyes searching Caroline's face. 'This is Wilhelmina's mother?'

'Yes, we believe so.'

'And she's dead?'

Caroline nodded.

Jeremy stood for some time looking at the miniature. Then he sighed and handed it back to Wilhelmina. 'Willy,' he said, using the nickname he had never been told, 'I know your uncle and your grandparents. They don't know your mother is dead. They think she ran off with someone to the Continent.'

There was a bitterness in Jeremy's eyes that Hartville had never seen there before. A part of the viscount felt sorry for Jeremy, while his more practical side insisted that it was time Jeremy grew up and learned that the world was not just a playground for himself. But he was moved when Jeremy crouched down in front of Wilhelmina and said, 'Your mother was wonderful. So bright, and warm, and kind. We were just scruffy schoolboys when I visited Three Oaks, but she always managed to get us out of trouble.'

He looked up at Caroline. 'Her family was frantic when she disappeared, leaving only a note to say that they mustn't try to find her. I suppose she was increasing. I suppose Markingham set her up in a cottage somewhere until the child came.'

He sighed. 'Almost six years she's been gone. And not a day when they didn't think of her, I know, because Multon has spoken of it.'

He rose to his full height and faced Hartville. 'I'd like to be the one to tell them, Hartville. You know, break the bad news — and the good.' He glanced down at Wilhelmina and rested his hand on her head. 'They'll want to raise Willy, of course. They're good people. The circumstances aren't going to put them off. If you'll keep her here until I can bring Multon back with me . . . '

'Of course.' Hartville extended his hand to shake Jeremy's, firmly. 'I'd appreciate that, Jeremy. Take my mother's carriage. I didn't return with mine.'

'Thank you. I'll get an early start in the morning,' Jeremy turned to his sister. 'I'm sorry, Caro. I always thought he wanted to marry you.'

'Yes, I did, too.' Caroline kissed his cheek. 'Godspeed.'

Hartville watched Jeremy leave the kitchen, all too aware that he was still not alone with Caroline. Who did not seem willing to look at him, in any case.

'Wilhelmina and I are going to take her hot chocolate up to my room now, Lord Hartville,' Caroline informed him.

'It would be safe for her to go to the nursery floor again,' he reminded her.

'Yes, but I've promised her this treat.' Caroline picked up the cup and headed for the door, then paused to turn and ask, 'Have you eaten?'

'No, but I'll find something. Don't trouble yourself.'

'There's pigeon pie. I'm sure you'll find it in the larder.'

Hartville had moved to block her retreat. He dropped his voice so that Wilhelmina couldn't hear. 'I need to speak with you, Caroline. Would you join me in my study when the child has fallen asleep?'

'Wouldn't tomorrow do as well?' she asked.

'I'd prefer not.'

'Very well. But it may be a while.'

'As long as necessary. I'll be waiting.'

* * *

Caroline was almost disappointed at how quickly the child fell asleep after drinking her hot chocolate and eating two biscuits. There was still a morsel of pigeon pie left on Caroline's own plate, but she no longer had any appetite. On the other hand, she was not at all sure she was prepared for a meeting with Hartville. But since she had promised, she made her way there after she had tucked Wilhelmina into her bed.

The door to the study was slightly ajar, and Caroline stopped to tap on the frame. Hartville motioned for her to come in as he rose from his chair behind the huge mahogany desk. From the corner of the room he drew up a spindle-back chair, placing it face-to-face with his. 'Thank you for coming, Caroline. Please, have a seat.'

Even as she seated herself, Caroline began to speak. 'I really must apologize for all the disorder I've brought on your household, Lord Hartville. I never — '

'Richard,' he said.

Caroline stared at him blankly for a moment, then nodded. 'Of course, Richard. What I meant to say was that I never intended for all this to happen. I had no idea of any of it when I came here. I didn't even expect Jeremy to show up here, let alone Markingham. And I certainly didn't know that poor little Wilhelmina was his daughter. And — '

'Caroline.' Hartville held up a hand to slow her burgeoning explanations. 'I realize that you had no knowledge of any of this before you arrived. And in fact you were quite correct in insisting on your brother's lack of involvement.'

'Yes, but he is rather immature and careless, as you've intimated to me. This evening has come as a lesson to him, don't you think?'

Hartville nodded. 'If we can keep him out of the clutches of men like Markingham, I think he'll do just fine.' His countenance darkened. 'And that is a matter which I hesitate to bring up, Caroline, though I must — Markingham.'

'I'm sure he is long gone by now.' Caroline attempted a smile that went somewhat awry. 'You were very decided in your treatment of him.'

'How could I be otherwise?' Hartville reached across to his desk and withdrew a letter from the stack of papers that had accumulated during his absence. 'This explains why he couldn't ask you to marry him,' he said, extending it to her.

'What is it?'

'A letter from my man of business in

London.' Hartville kept his eyes locked on hers as he said, 'I had written him to request information about Markingham.'

'But why?'

'You appeared to favor him with your attentions. I wished to make certain that he was an appropriate claimant for your hand.'

Caroline's brows drew together. 'But . . . but what concern of yours was it?'

Hartville pursed his lips. 'No matter what I say at this juncture, you're going to be annoyed with me, aren't you? Well, so be it. Your brother did not appear to me to be a great judge of character, and he is apparently the only one who is looking out for your welfare. So I took it upon myself to investigate Markingham's situation.' He gestured toward the letter. 'Read it, please. That whole second page. Aloud, if you will.'

Caroline was feeling the same fury she'd felt when she'd learned that Hartville was her brother's benefactor, and therefore her own. It took her a moment to gain enough control of her emotions to glance down at the page. When she began to read, her voice reflected the depth of her surprise and distress.

As to Giles Markingham, I have been able to ascertain the following: He is thirty-two years of age, was born in Southampton the second son of a marine goods merchant, and currently resides near Epsom. He was married ten years ago, to the daughter and sole heir of an ailing squire in that region. There is no issue from the marriage. Those facts are established without doubt. Further information is less assured, but still of a reasonable quality which I myself would trust. You may do so at your discretion.

The local residents believe that Markingham sent his wife away to live in the North because she did not approve of his plans to raise horses on the estate after her father's death. Though no one has seen her in many years, she is in correspondence with an old friend in the neighborhood and therefore known to be alive and well.

Caroline looked up to find Hartville closely watching her. 'He's married, and has been all this time. Even Jeremy cannot have known.'

Hartville sighed. 'I'm sorry, Caroline. Obviously it was Markingham's intent to dupe your brother as well as yourself.'

'Well, he most certainly succeeded!' Caroline felt too agitated to sit still and rose to pace about the room. 'So the whole time he must have intended to seduce me and make me his mistress. I can hardly credit it.'

'I'm sorry.'

Caroline frowned at him. 'Oh, stop telling me you're sorry and just say what you think: that I've been a fool and a ninnyhammer! That I have no better understanding of character than my brother does! That you will be vastly relieved to see the back of both of us so you can resume your accustomed life once more!'

He regarded her with amusement. 'That isn't at all what I think, Caroline. What I am sorry for is that Markingham has wounded your heart. I would not have had that happen for the world.'

His tone had turned serious, and she paused in her pacing. 'Well, I appreciate your concern, Hartville, but there is no need for it. Though it is true I was fascinated by Mr. Markingham in London, I cannot say that he held up well on closer inspection here in the country.' And that, she thought, is a circumspect way of putting my emotional state since I've been here.

'I am to understand that your affections are not engaged by Mr. Markingham?' he asked, a hopeful note creeping into his question.

'That is correct.'

'I see.' Hartville rose and went to stand by her. 'Have I any reason to hope that your affections have been engaged elsewhere here in the country?'

Caroline was not able to meet his challenging gaze. 'That is possible,' she admitted, clenching her hands together in front of her chest.

Hartville possessed himself of her hands and waited until she looked up into his eyes. 'My dear Caroline, I have realized for some little time now that my own affections are engaged. I cannot see you without wishing to hold you, nor hear your voice without feeling that it has become a part of me. In fact, I cannot bear to think that we might not have met at all save for my mother's inviting you to come and visit. And I cannot believe my own stupidity in not recognizing at once your superior merits.'

'Ah, yes,' she reminded him. 'You thought me a milk and water miss, a biddable girl. So why is it that you weren't more attached to such a one than you are to me, with my troublesome opinions and decided habits?'

'Who's to say?' he teased, smiling warmly down at her. 'I only know that I could not bear to think of you marrying Markingham, or going back home to London and leaving me here without you. So put me out of my misery and tell me that your attachment is strong enough to allow you to marry me, Caroline.'

'Oh, is that what you wish?' she asked,

cocking her head at him. 'You aren't about to offer me a position such as Mr. Markingham thought appropriate?'

'The man is a cad.' He indicated the letter lying on the desk. 'Finish reading what my agent has written, Caroline, if you will.'

My informant tells me that about a month ago Mrs. Markingham discreetly appeared in the neighborhood inquiring about a child. Apparently word had reached her that her husband had fathered an illegitimate child, who was being raised by a farm family in the area. The importance of this circumstance to her was great, because her father, in a codicil to his will, had rearranged the disposition of his property.

My informant, an intimate of the old gentleman, said that Mrs. Markingham's father had begun to suspect Markingham's motives in marrying his daughter. He had heard rumors that Markingham had had a succession of mistresses in keeping in their own neighborhood. Shortly before the old man's death, he learned that the current woman was expecting a child. He was furious at Markingham's deception and left his entire property in trust to his daughter, with the proviso that should Markingham father a child out of wedlock, the property was never to be within his control.

Since a husband has the right to do what he wishes with his wife's property, Markingham has been in control of the estate. My informant said that the gossip five years ago was that mother and child had died in childbed. If it were true, however, that the child had survived and Mrs. Markingham could prove it to the satisfaction of the trustees (who are disposed to her interest), Markingham would lose everything, because in that circumstance the trust is directed to ensure only the welfare of his wife.

'Wilhelmina,' Caroline breathed. 'Markingham had to get her out of the neighborhood quickly. But why to you?'

Hartville shrugged. 'Who knows? He wanted the child as far away from Epsom as he could possibly get her. He wanted to deposit her where there was a chance she would be taken for someone else's child.' He regarded her ruefully. '*Some* people around here were willing to believe I was her father.'

'But he didn't know you,' she protested, with a slight flush.

'But he may very well have known who I was, and that I was Jeremy's benefactor. Your brother is not so sensitive in these matters as you are, my dear. And just when he had to decide what to do with the child, you were summoned here by my mother. What could have been better for his purposes?'

'What if you had rejected the child?'

Hartville's face hardened. 'I'm not perfectly sure he would have cared if she'd ended up in an orphanage, Caroline, so long as it wasn't anywhere near Epsom. But he's a gambler. I noticed it when I was partnering him at cards. The risks themselves excite him. It would amuse him to land the child on me while you were here. And then to come and view the results of his plot, as he did.'

'Perhaps he counted on my insisting on your taking special care of Wilhelmina. He did know that I was an orphan. He may have thought I would champion such a child.'

'Perhaps.' Hartville frowned. 'When I think of what he dared suggest to you, a woman of your gentle upbringing . . . '

Caroline's eyes fell before the ire in his. She bit her lip and confessed, 'I think it was because he knew he had . . . made me aware of . . . of . . . '

'Of your warmer feelings,' he finished for her, attempting to maintain the proprieties. She was, after all, an innocent where such things were concerned. Hartville was surprised when she drew back from him, shaking her head.

'Richard, Markingham was quite wrong in thinking that my strong will and my relative independence were characteristics that would permit me to consider his proposition. But he was not wrong about my . . . my nature, in that other regard, I fear.'

'I'm afraid I don't understand.'

Caroline was at a loss to find the proper terms to explain in a way that would not shock or disgust him. 'He said that proper English marriages were . . . were bloodless things. That English women considered their . . . intimate relations with their husbands to be a duty. What he recognized in me, I fear, was a certain . . . um . . . wantonness that would distress a 'proper' husband.'

'How thoughtful of him to enlighten you,' Hartville said dryly. He held out a hand to her. 'Come, let me show you an example of my own temperament with regard to these matters.'

An instant excitement flowed through Caroline as she took his hand and allowed him to pull her close against his body. His lips descended to hers, capturing her with delight. His kiss was long and thorough, leaving her breathless and wanting more, much more. Her eyes, dazed and blinking, caught the look in his, and she nodded.

'Yes, that's how I feel,' she whispered. 'Is that so very improper?'

Hartville laughed. 'Like everything about you, my love, it is unique and wonderful. And I am tempted to carry you a little farther down this road, but I shall not do so until you assure me that it is your intention to marry me sometime very soon.'

'Is that the proper English gentleman in you?' she asked.

'Yes,' he grumbled, 'it is. But I am enough of an improper English gentleman to resort to the necessary measures to elicit your acceptance, I assure you. For instance, if I were to hold you just so . . . '

Caroline's eyes widened at his touch and the new sensations that arose from it. 'That's remarkable,' she murmured. Hartville removed his hand, much to her disappointment. He raised his brows.

'Oh, very well,' she agreed. 'I shall marry you, sometime very soon.'

'Excellent.'

'And, Richard,' she added, just to be perfectly honest with him. 'I think I have known that I loved you since that night when we sang together. Your voice filled me then in such a way . . . Well, I have no words to describe it.'

'Yes, it was an extraordinary experience.' He smiled and drew her into his embrace. 'I think, my dear Caroline, that a special license would be a prudent decision.'

'If you say so,' she said meekly.

He regarded her with amused skepticism for no more than a moment before bending to kiss her thoroughly.

THE END

We do hope that you have enjoyed reading this large print book.

Did you know that all of our titles are available for purchase?

We publish a wide range of high quality large print books including:
**Romances, Mysteries, Classics
General Fiction
Non Fiction and Westerns**

Special interest titles available in large print are:
**The Little Oxford Dictionary
Music Book
Song Book
Hymn Book
Service Book**

Also available from us courtesy of Oxford University Press:
**Young Readers' Dictionary
(large print edition)
Young Readers' Thesaurus
(large print edition)**

For further information or a free brochure, please contact us at:
**Ulverscroft Large Print Books Ltd.,
The Green, Bradgate Road, Anstey,
Leicester, LE7 7FU, England.
Tel:** (00 44) **0116 236 4325
Fax:** (00 44) **0116 234 0205**